Secrets in Cypress Bayou

Secrets in
Cypress Bayou

A Louisiana Romance

Susan Sands

TULE
PUBLISHING

Dear Reader,

This second book in the Louisiana Bayou Series is almost as special to me as the first. This was my second book as a baby writer with so much to learn about the craft and the industry. It gathered dust for years after I published my first Alabama book, but I never forgot about Carly and her giant crush on Tanner. I'm hoping you will love it as much as I do.

This series is a love letter to my college town, Natchitoches, Louisiana, AKA Cypress Bayou. Steel Magnolias was filmed there during my senior year of college. The town is older than New Orleans, and the history of the area is evident in the gorgeous old homes and the giant oaks that grace the city. The "bayou" is really Cane River Lake formed by a braid channel from the Red River. The beauty of using this town as a setting is that it's a real place, and one I encourage you to visit.

I'd like to thank everyone who's had a hand in helping this novel come to light. My editor, Sinclair Sawhney, fought for this series by championing my vision for the characters and story. Thanks to Meghan Farrell, Jane Porter, Nikki Babri, and Cyndi Parent for being such an awesome publishing team.

Thanks to Christy Hayes, who's been there with me during all the writing years. Thanks also to my mom, Linda Noel, who always reads my books first, and who supports me in everything I do. A shout out to George Weinstein for his friendship and for always listening when I need his ear.

As always, I give thanks for my kids: Kevin, Cameron, and Reagan, and my husband, Doug. Y'all are the ones that make all the hard work worthwhile.

Best,
Susan Sands

CHAPTER ONE

Carly

"CARLY, HERE'S A crucifix to hang over your door. I've got plenty more at home, but your grandmother doesn't have one for your room." Momma shoved the small artifact of Jesus dying an agonizing death at me.

I took it, and when I looked down at it, Jesus and I made eye contact. *Poor Jesus.* Momma was *so* Catholic. She loved her crucifixes and her rosary. And going to mass *every* day. My sister, Leah, and I had realized early on that Momma's religion was her crutch and her weapon, for pretty much everything. I still hoped I wasn't going to hell for my somewhat small transgressions as I'd been told I was as a child.

We lived in Louisiana, and there was a lot of Jesus everywhere. Both Catholics and Protestants. The Catholics were quiet prayers and the Protestants, according to Momma, were competitive out-loud prayers. Having known many of both, I could confirm that was somewhat true. The out-loud praying was an accomplished skill honed by Protestants from childhood. Most Catholics were secretly impressed by it.

"Is that everything, baby?" Daddy pulled me from my dogmatic musings. I was thankful for my daddy, who still tempered Momma's intensity at every turn.

1

"I think so. The van is empty and the storage room is full. And I've already brought everything over to Nana's house that I need for now."

I'd moved home to Cypress Bayou of my own free will. Hard to believe, but there was a pull to this town I couldn't explain, besides my weird family and my two best friends—Jo and Sue—though we hadn't spoken in a while. I'd been away for the better part of eight years. Now that I was done with law school, it was time to find gainful employment.

I'd put some feelers out with a few folks in Baton Rouge and New Orleans about job opportunities because I hadn't quite reconciled living in Cypress Bayou forever, so I wanted to keep my options open for anything too good to pass up. Both cities were a half a day's drive away, so even if I moved south, I'd still be somewhat close to home. Part of me didn't want to settle for good enough, because it was likely that anything I found here wouldn't be for the length of a career.

I planned to live with my maternal grandmother, Nana, for now, who was way cooler than Momma, her daughter. Nana owned a historical home right outside of town called Plaisance House. It was built back in the late 1700s and had some significance during and after the Civil War. It had burned during the war but was rebuilt in the Greek Revival style. So, yeah, really cool house.

My sister, Leah, was breaking ground on a house down the bayou with her new husband, Jake. They were sloppy in love, but it was okay because they'd worked hard to finally find their way back to each other after several years of being apart.

I was happy for them but couldn't see finding what they

had for myself anytime soon. I'd not experienced a great romance in my life. An epic crush, yes. And as a young girl it had felt like love. But I'd had nothing since that had been requited and could qualify for a deep relationship. Most of my friends had fallen in love at some point throughout our teens. Aching, crushing love. I'd had boyfriends, sure, but nobody who had brought me to my knees. It was all around me, but I didn't truly understand that kind of passion and pain, or joy either, I guess.

I'd mostly been competitive with guys throughout college in pre-law and law school. And when I'd been in a dating situation and done better on a test or ranked higher in the class, those guys lost interest. They'd shown their fragile egos when it came to being beaten by a girl they were dating. I'd decided then that it wasn't worth getting involved with a man who was so easily put off by my success. I don't think my lack of boyfriends had anything to do with my looks because I noticed that men were attracted to me—initially anyway.

The problem was finding a strong man who was my equal and had no problem with my...ambition and perfectionist tendencies. Right now, dating wasn't at the top of my list though. That made life a lot easier. That's what I told myself anyway.

I knew my family would be thrilled to have me home while I figured out what to do next. I was pretty good being independent, but with a family like mine, it was easier to come on home and accept the well-meaning advice, delicious meals, and let them bless my heart as often as they felt the need.

In the meantime, did Cypress Bayou really need another lawyer? They were neck-high in them it seemed, so I had my work cut out for me in my employment search.

As I climbed in my car and waved at my parents, who'd been kind enough to help me move my things, I received a text. I didn't recognize the number.

Hey Carly. I heard you were back in town and looking for work. Let's meet and talk. This is Tanner in case you wondered.

I stared at the text. With punctuation. And my stomach did some funny flips.

Tanner Carmichael. He'd been my secret crush. My childhood addiction. I'd been in braces with zits when he'd dated the homecoming queen. But my one-sided love for him had been fierce and true, or so I'd believed at the time. He was my older sister's boyfriend's older brother. So, when I said earlier that I'd never been in love, Tanner was the exception.

My current age of twenty-six and his current age of thirty-two didn't seem as insurmountable now as it had back then. But my twelve to his eighteen had been an ocean of impossibility over a decade ago for normal people. Not that we were normal, because of our family connection. But now, he was my sister's brother-in-law. We were family-ish.

I responded: *Hi Tanner. Thanks for reaching out. I'd love to meet.* I was cool but interested. No signs of a hormonal crush there.

Tanner was a local attorney. He really could help me. The dots waved at me as I waited.

Him: *I get out of court at five today. How about a beer and oysters at Mother's at 5:30?* Mother's Oyster Bar was a dive right on Front Street. Nothing fancy, but the beers were cold and the seafood fresh. It was a local favorite.

Me: *I'll see you there*

The sixteen-year-old me would've *JUST DIED*. But hey, I was a grown woman now. I'd been around. I'd even been around Tanner without making an idiot of myself countless times. Because his brother and my sister were married to each other, and it was required.

My girlfriends Jo and Sue would have so much to say about Tanner's texting me. But I hadn't yet let them know I was back home to stay. Jo was a paramedic in town. She was a lesbian and currently not in a relationship. She'd gone through some extremely rough times during our high school years and beyond. Her sexuality was never in question, but living here in Cypress Bayou, well, that made it hard for her. Her parents made it hard too. Jo was such a deeply nice person and hadn't deserved the small-minded responses that had hurt her so badly.

I could empathize to some degree, but I'd never know what going through that was like as a teen and young woman. I'd been different too, but in a more socially acceptable sense for this small town.

Sue and I stuck by her, but we'd gone our separate ways after graduation. Sue had been boy crazy since middle school. She'd been in desperate love more times than any of us could count. Sue always had a boyfriend, and when she didn't, she was abjectly miserable. Right now, Sue was engaged for the third time. I hadn't met the latest fiancé, but I'm certain I would soon.

We were all still in loose contact, but it wasn't the same

as before we'd gone to college. I hoped to remedy that once I got settled. We'd all shared so much growing up. I looked forward to reconnecting.

For now, I would go home and shower, put on something cute, and make Tanner wish he'd noticed me when I was a preteen. No. Ick. That wasn't right. But what really wasn't right was that on the occasions when we'd seen one another over the past several years, he continued to treat me like I was a preteen in a training bra. Like I was still that braces-wearing little sister of Leah's who tagged along and drooled after him. Though I'm not even sure he knew I had.

It was like I was invisible as a woman to him, specifically.

Tanner

"ARE WE BORING you, Mr. Carmichael?" Judge Keller's booming baritone reverberated around the courtroom.

Tanner *had* yawned. "No, Your Honor. I'm just trying to figure out how my client could have been in two places at once. We have time-stamped video showing the perpetrator committing the crime at the same moment my client was filling up with gas six miles away at the Shop-a-Lott out on Highway Six West. You know, the one that sells meat pies and boudin? I can't imagine why the prosecutor saw fit to pursue this case. Can you?"

"Objection, Your Honor! I'm not aware of a time conflict." The prosecutor's face got as red as a burnt tomato while he tried to figure out where he'd gone wrong.

Judge Keller narrowed his eyes at Tanner. "Is this legitimate?"

"It's in the record, so I'll leave it to the esteemed prosecutor to sort out his error. Might want to check your dates." Tanner couldn't have written a movie script any better.

"We are adjourned for the afternoon until you sort this mess out. We'll convene at ten in the morning, and you'd better hope you've not wasted the court's time, Mr. Grabert." The gavel came down extra hard and loud.

Judge Keller and Tanner *weren't* friends. The judge and his dad, Carson, *were*, on the other hand. Those two had been childhood cohorts, and even roommates back in law school. In fact, almost nobody here in Cypress Bayou could recuse themselves because of a previous relationship with one judge or another because everybody knew or was related to nearly everyone else in some way or another.

Tanner avoided going by the office on his way to the oyster house from the courtroom. Avoiding his father was something he did with near precision. Tanner had virtually overlaid Carson's schedule onto his calendar. That way, Tanner could make certain they were almost never in the same place at the same time. Unless Carson intentionally sabotaged Tanner and forced a meeting.

Having a father whom one despised was difficult at best. It wasn't that Carson was simply ornery or unpleasant. No, Carson was a narcissist. A true narcissist. The word was overused in the world today, in Tanner's opinion, detracting from how truly damaging those who were the real deal could be. As a father to both his brother Jake and him, Carson had been dreadful.

On the exterior, and to the world, Carson had possibly appeared a decent parent. They'd had a nice house, their mother had driven a nice car, they'd all had nice clothes. But there was a savagery of spirit beneath Carson's exterior that haunted their family. A nastiness. One misstep as kids and they'd been treated like worthless garbage by their own father.

Their mother, Judy Carmichael, had been a saint. She'd carefully maneuvered marriage to a man who could, at any moment, turn on her and her boys with a terrifying coldness. She'd pushed back when needed, but it was a learned response they now understood. She'd figured out the ways to handle Carson that manipulated his ego and his need to be seen by others as blameless and right.

Their mom had passed away just over six years ago from cancer. Carson had considered her cancer a weakness. Tanner and Jake, as adults, avoided their father as much as possible. But Tanner, unfortunately, was tied to him by profession, and trying like hell to get untied. He still worked at Carson's law firm, per their financial agreement, because Carson had paid for Tanner's education to keep him from accruing a mountain of student debt. Tanner's deal with the devil hadn't been worth it, he'd realized after the fact.

At the time, Tanner had accepted Carson's help because he'd needed it, and he was young enough to believe that maybe his father was doing it because that's what successful fathers did for their sons. But it was never about helping Tanner; it was about holding him hostage once he'd gotten out of law school.

But not much longer. That was one reason he was meeting with young Carly today.

Mother's Oyster House was a fixture along the bayou. Several high-top tables sat outside, hugging the building, as the sidewalk was narrow. The air was warm and humid as summer rolled into the area. A May evening outdoors was not to be missed if one had the opportunity.

The doors of the small dive were flung open, allowing the smells and music to meet him as he arrived. "Hi there, Tanner. Would you like to sit outside? Party of two? Is Jake joining you?"

"Hi, Becky. Yes, there's two of us. Jake won't be with me tonight though."

"Some lucky girl?"

The hostess, Becky, and he had gone through school together. And nobody around here had any intention of minding their business. Tanner laughed. "Just a friend, Becky."

Tanner ordered an Abita and stared out over the water across the brick street. Cypress Bayou, the town, was a unique and special place. Maybe that's why he was willing to fight his father to stay here.

"Hey there, Tanner." Carly slipped her purse over the ladder-back wooden barstool and hiked herself up onto it. "Pretty evening."

Carly had grown up nicely. He'd known her since she was a little girl in pigtails. He nodded and saluted her with his beer. "Beer?"

"You bet. Today was official moving day and I've had it up to here with my mother." She motioned over her head.

Becky approached when she saw Carly. "Oh, hey there,

Carly. I got excited for a minute when Tanner said he was meeting someone. You want a beer?" Tanner had been a bachelor in this town for so long that the locals were rooting for him to find someone.

"It's only me, Becky. Nobody exciting. And yes, I'll take an Abita." She nodded toward Tanner's beer.

"Y'all want me to get some oysters going? Got some in from the Gulf this morning. Special today is two dozen for twenty bucks."

"Is that what smells so heavenly?" Carly closed her eyes and inhaled.

"Yes. We broil them like they do at Drago's in New Orleans, with the Romano cheese, garlic, and butter."

Tanner laughed. "We'll take two dozen. And some bread."

"I'm starving. Thank you." She grinned at him, and Tanner was taken aback at how lovely she was. When had she become this gorgeous woman?

Carly stared out at the water and took a deep breath, then closed her eyes. The same exact thing Tanner'd done once he'd sat down.

"It's so peaceful here."

Becky plopped down Carly's beer, pulling her out of what appeared to be a moment of satisfaction.

Carly knocked her longneck against Tanner's and took a long draw. He had to appreciate a woman who enjoyed a good beer.

"So, what's up? I was a little surprised to get your text." Carly's gaze was curious, and her eyes, well, they were clear, cat-eyed hazel, just like her sister Leah's.

"Let me start by saying this stays between us until I make the move. I mean, Jake and Leah know, of course." He told his brother and sister-in-law things he wouldn't dream of sharing with anyone else.

"Sure. I won't say a word to anyone." She made a crisscross pattern over her heart, which made him smile unexpectedly.

He leaned in. "I'm working on separating from my father's law firm, but he has no idea yet."

Carly's eyebrows went up. "Wow. That's huge. Tell me more."

Tanner's desire to part ways from Carson was something he'd spoken about freely in past conversations with Carly present, since it wasn't uncommon for her to be with Leah while Tanner was with Jake. So Carly likely already knew this was something he'd wanted for a while.

"I've purchased a building on Second Street from a friend who's recently moved his business to Shreveport. He's already transferred the title but held off on filing it with the city, and we've made a mostly cash purchase, but he's willing to self-finance the rest. It's the only way I could do it without Carson sabotaging the sale."

Carly frowned. "Sabotaging? In what way?"

"The usual stuff I could see him doing. Building code violations, licensing delays, which he could still make happen, if I'm not careful who I work with at city hall."

Carly frowned. "I know your dad can be an ass, but why would he go to such lengths to keep you at his office if you don't want to stay?"

The oysters arrived then, and they dipped the French

bread in garlic butter and added hot sauce to the mix.

"Pride, mostly. He has some weird idea that keeping me as his associate within the practice demonstrates to everyone in town my loyalty to him. Going out on my own will infuriate him. In his mind, I might as well hang a banner from the bridge across the bayou that says I've defected."

"He's not somebody I'd want to piss off—that's for sure." Carly's family had had some experience with Carson's bad side quite recently. "So, I'm happy for you, but I have to ask how this affects me?"

"I need an associate. Well, at first, it would be more like an assistant. But there would be legal work involved. And court cases. And if all goes well, opportunity for advancement."

"Can you pay me?" Carly had just completed an internship, so he could see where she might want to clarify this not-so-tiny detail.

Tanner shifted on his stool. "Yes. Not well at first, but the sooner we win the first case, the better the odds of your pay increasing quickly."

She narrowed her eyes at him. "What if I bring in my own cases?"

Tanner was impressed by her business savvy. Being such a young attorney, it surprised him how she looked him in the eye with a steady stare as if she were negotiating a contract. "Your cases would be your cases minus a small percentage. We can work it out in a contract if you're interested."

She grinned at him. "Let me think about it and get back to you. I'm not sure what my long-term plans are."

"We could go into it with no strings, meaning you take

the job and work with me until you figure out what you want to do. I need someone to help me with all the minutiae of setting the practice up, so think about it, okay?"

CHAPTER TWO

Carly

"H E'S OFFERED ME a job."

"Tanner offered you a job? But there's no business yet." My sister, Leah, and I, sat watching the sun set over the water in the two matching Adirondack chairs on the dock that stretched out over the bayou where Leah was about to build a house with her new husband, Jake. They'd only been married a few months, but Jake and Tanner's mom's family had owned this land for decades. The dock was all that was left from his grandaddy's house, the original homeplace that had burned down several years back. Well, that and Tanner's Airstream camper, where he lived temporarily amidst the trees and along the water's edge. It was a running joke within the family—his camping life.

We were sharing a beer and discussing recent events. It was the most relaxing, private place in town for us to catch up. Cypress Bayou had eyes and ears. No matter where we went, somebody seemed interested in what was happening in our lives.

"Yes. And no, Tanner doesn't have his new business set up yet, but he's tiptoeing into something. I'm sure you've heard."

Leah nodded. "Yes, we've heard about it. And we're very concerned about what will happen when Carson finds out."

"What can Carson do besides throw a few curveballs to delay things opening and running smoothly?" I honestly didn't like Carson either so what was the big deal? But I could see the concern in my sister's gaze.

"The depths of Carson's need to control those boys is way beyond what we can understand. And the lengths he might go to, well, nobody knows how far that might be. I hate to see you get tied up with that."

"It's a start-up, which means lists and tasks to accomplish. We all know I'd be good at getting things organized."

"Yes, you would be a big help to Tanner if you can avoid Carson."

"We've got a controlling mother and we've managed to work around her." Controlling was a nice word for it. As little girls, the two of them had learned to avoid their momma on a bad day and be careful around her on a good one. Now they were less concerned with her extreme personality, but being raised in that environment had bonded them.

"Yes, but Momma is like the Disney Mary Poppins compared to Carson on a good day. I don't think you understand how dark some of his politics go. I guess you wouldn't since you were so young when you left town, and your exposure to the family isn't as close as mine has been. I've been hearing about Carson's low-down dirty tricks since Jake and I started dating in middle school."

Something shifted in my stomach. "Like what?"

"I've heard he keeps nearly everyone in line here in Cypress Bayou. The mayor, the judges, the city council members, you name it. It's rumored he's got a file that contains every possible speck of dirt he might use against them all."

I still wasn't buying the depths of it. "Even if that's true, surely not everyone is dirty."

"Maybe not, but someone within every family has something to hide. To bring shame or embarrassment. Or, to keep them from getting elected the next term."

I thought about that for a moment. "That's nasty. But unless someone can prove actual blackmail or extortion, it's not a real crime."

"I would think it'd be enough to convince you. But I have a feeling that's the PG-rated version of his darkness. I'm not sure how bad it gets, and I don't think that even Jake or Tanner knows."

I rolled this around for a second or two. "Maybe that's why Tanner wants so badly to extricate himself from Carson and his business." This made sense. Even if getting away from a narcissistic ass of a father was plenty enough reason. A dirty political narcissist was way worse.

"Okay. I get it. He wants to have a good reputation away from Carson's business dealings. I can't blame him for that."

"Just be careful if you decide to work with him. Tanner's a great guy—the best. But his doing this could cause him some real trouble."

"I appreciate your looking out for me. Unfortunately, my job opportunities are limited here since the town is so saturated with lawyers. Plus, if I decide to go to work for him, we'd call it a 'for now' job since he mostly needs someone to help get him set up in the business."

"You'll figure out something whether it's with Tanner or not, I'm sure," Leah said. "Are you okay for money? I'm assuming Nana gave you control of your trust when you turned twenty-five?" We hadn't talked about my trust before. I knew she'd gotten hers while she'd been living in Paris.

I nodded. "She did. I'd worry a lot more if I didn't have that." Nana came from money on her mother's side, which is how she continued to hold Plaisance House. Nobody discussed exactly how much money, and Nana wasn't someone anyone would look at and think of as wealthy—besides the house. Everybody in town knew that kind of historic real estate didn't come without a high price tag and enormous upkeep costs.

So, having the nest egg from Nana allowed me to come home to Cypress Bayou and live among my family without the immediate worry of feeding myself. Plus, living at Nana's provided a place to lay my head—for now at least—and get settled until I found my own place, should I decide to stay in Cypress Bayou permanently. And Nana didn't question my comings and goings like Momma would've, so it worked for both of us. *And* I'd missed my grandmother.

"So have you heard anything from Allison lately?" Leah asked, changing the subject.

"No, but I think she's okay. I stalked her Facebook a week or so ago and she'd posted that she'd put her momma's house on the market in Naperville." Allison was our newly discovered half-sister we'd found out about only a few months ago. She was still recovering from blood cancer, which was *how* we'd found out about her. I was a little wary about the whole situation. I mean, I wanted to get to know her but maybe that felt a little threatening to mine and Leah's close relationship, if I were being completely honest.

"I would think she'd stay in closer contact, wouldn't you?" Leah had been the one who donated the bone marrow that saved Allison's life, so Leah took it a little more personally when we didn't hear from Allison regularly. Plus, Leah wore her heart on her sleeve more than me and she had no concerns about welcoming a stranger to our family, though a sister by blood. Still, Allison *was* a stranger.

"I'm not sure about anything where Allison is concerned. I mean, we really don't know much about her life before she found us." Allison had stayed here in Cypress Bayou for a couple months after she'd been released from the hospital until her doctors had given her the okay to travel back to Illinois, where she'd lived before. For someone who'd been searching for her birth family, Allison was tight-lipped about her past.

"Do you think she needs help with the house?" Leah was frowning behind her sunglasses. I could almost read her thoughts because I knew her so well. I couldn't imagine having another sister who was as close with us as Leah and I were with one another.

"I don't know, but aren't you going to be up to your eyeballs with the gallery in New Orleans?" Leah was getting a new art gallery up and running soon. It would be a huge amount of work.

"Well, sure, but maybe she needs help but won't ask for it. It wouldn't be the first time *somebody* in this family showed herself to be stubborn." Leah cut her eyes at me.

"You can't mean me?" I was independent by nature, and

yes, I could be stubborn, but it came from being one of my mother's daughters. I could credit Momma for making me strong if nothing else.

"If the shoe fits and all that." Leah stared at her phone and raised her eyebrows. I hated it when she did that.

"I'm gonna ignore the obvious here and tell you to reach out to Allison if you want and let her know we're thinking about her." What I wanted to say to my sister is that she was the stubborn one after having lived for years in Paris, before *finally* admitting to Jake that she'd been wrong and moving home to stay.

Leah continued with the Allison thread. "I hope Allison's communicating with Momma some and keeping her informed about her health now that she's gone back to her hometown."

I took the last sip of my beer. "That's between the two of them. They've got a lot of stuff to work out, you know? She's the one Momma gave up for adoption, so it's not for us to get in the middle of their relationship." I couldn't imagine how that must be for Allison. Seeing Leah and me, Momma's other two daughters; the ones she'd kept. And while we weren't the picture-perfect family, we'd been safe, loved, and protected. We knew very little about the parents who'd raised her.

Leah added, "I'm glad Nana is working out a trust for Allison. That's something at least." We all felt bad for Allison. Not that Momma had been a real gem as a mother, but we did have a solid family unit, all told.

My phone lit up then with a text. It was from Tanner. *Can you meet me at this address in a few minutes?* I got a little tingle when I saw his name on my phone. How many times had I written our names intertwined with hearts in my diary as a tween? That crush stuff still had its residuals, I had to admit.

He'd sent an address on Second Street. Was it *the* building?

"Who is it?" Leah realized I'd stop indulging her worry about Allison for the moment.

"It's Tanner. He wants me to meet him at a building on Second Street."

"Wow. He's moving quickly."

I answered: Sure. I'm finishing up a beer with Leah at the dock.

Him: Can you drive?

Me: I've only had one, so I'm okay. See you soon.

Him: Great. Park behind the building and come in the back door.

"I'll let you know how it goes." I stood and adjusted my sunglasses and pulled my hair from its clip, allowing it to fall free. I was dressed in a white T-shirt and denim cutoffs and flip-flops. Fortunately, my shorts weren't the shorter ones I sometimes wore when hanging out on the dock. More of a boyfriend cut, so mostly comfortable and casual. But still not what I might have chosen for a meeting with a potential employer.

"Okay. Please do. And don't forget to stop by the loft and have a look at our house plans in the next day or two." Leah and Jake lived in an awesome loft apartment on Front Street where Jake had lived since undergrad.

I nodded. "It's on my list."

I wasn't used to having this much free time. Law school

and clerking had me running crazy the past few years, so I was kind of digging sitting on the dock, hanging with my sister. Since she'd been living in Paris for the past several years, having her back home and taking the time to be together was a treat, even if she was a pain sometimes.

Tanner

TANNER PARKED BEHIND the building and made sure no one was around before unlocking the back door. He was so close to having everything in place.

Maybe that was paranoid thinking on his part, but knowing his father as well as he did, it wasn't a stretch. Cypress Bayou was small. Small and generational. The families who lived here stayed here, for the most part. Even if kids left for college, they often came back to settle here. It was so easy to do. There were enough professional jobs for the college graduates and industries for those who decided to study a trade.

New turnover mostly happened with students and college faculty at the local university.

Tanner heard a knock at the back door a few minutes after he'd gotten inside and turned on a few lights.

He unlocked the door and allowed Carly to precede him toward the front of the downstairs. "Hey there. Thanks for meeting me."

Carly, who was unexpectedly dressed in a well-fitting, plain white T-shirt and denim shorts, seemed unaware of her…impact. He caught a whiff of sunscreen as she passed.

"This has a lot of potential." She moved slowly down the hallway, peering into each room as she went.

Tanner focused then. "Yes, my buddy Jason was a Realtor, so it won't take much changing to fit our needs."

She turned, and her eyebrows rose a little at that. "Why did he leave and go to Shreveport?"

"Said he was offered a better opportunity in the company's corporate headquarters there. But he'd wisely bought the building when it became available early on, not long after he'd set up the franchise office. Being in the real estate business, he'd gotten a great deal on the property at the right time."

"Hoping he passed that deal on to you." She raised her brows fully.

Tanner had been thrilled to learn of the property firsthand and surprised things had gone so smoothly thus far. "Let's just say, we came to an agreement that suited us both pretty quickly."

Carly nodded and continued to look around. "Can we go upstairs?"

Nearly all the downtown buildings in Cypress Bayou had a second story with either living space or more office space. This one had been built out as both. There was a loft apartment with a tiny kitchen, bathroom, and a personal office. It was comfortable with large windows and high ceilings. Of course, like all the buildings in town, it was old. But Jason had updated the plumbing and the electric to code. Realtors were good about thinking ahead like that.

Jason had left all the furniture, which entailed a leather

sofa, an upholstered oversized chair and ottoman with nail head trim, wall art, and some other odds and ends.

"This is fantastic, Tanner. What a find." She turned, grinning, and he nearly had to step back. Her smile had some serious wattage. "Something wrong?"

He shook his head. "Nope."

"I can see the bayou from here. Cool." She turned. "So, what's the plan?"

Every time he spoke about it, it gave Tanner a little heartburn. "I'm going to tell Carson tomorrow that I'm leaving the practice. I've got a few friends at city hall, and I've managed to keep my licensing quiet. I think I'm far enough along in the process that he can't keep it from happening."

"What about your clients?"

Tanner would miss his clients. Most of them anyway, but unless they found him individually, they were lost to him. Even though there wasn't a noncompete to deal with, he figured there would be less drama without fighting with Carson over existing clients. "I've got some court cases already on the books, so, we'll have to see. Honestly, I just want to walk away."

"Do you have to break a contract to do that?" Carly perched on the back of the sofa, dangling a tanned, bare leg.

Tanner shook his head. "I refused to sign one when I joined the firm. I've put in five years with Carson's practice, which should be sufficient."

Carly nodded. "Do you feel you owe Carson anything, monetarily?"

Tanner laughed but it lacked any humor. "I won a big

liability case against a crooked foreign steel company that alone more than covered it. So, I owe him nothing. I've been trying to figure out over the last couple years how to make my exit with the least amount of fuss."

"So I assume you've finessed your finances toward that end?" He got an inkling from her sharp questioning of him as to how she might perform in court. She'd put him in the hot seat, but not more than he would have done in the same situation.

"I've paid mostly cash for this building." This was a difficult subject. And he was offering Carly a job as his associate—to start. Who knew where they might end up in the future? Partners?

She must've picked up on his discomfort. "I wasn't trying to be nosy. Sorry if I'm being too forward." Carly made a cringy face. She looked like she wanted to take back her words.

"No, I'm sorry if I sounded defensive. I make a percentage off the cases I win, which is most of my income. And a salary, which isn't much. It's pretty cut and dried."

Carly nodded. "Well, now you've got a place to hang your shingle. Here's hoping the people will come."

"Are you willing to take a chance on this with me?" Tanner held out his hand to Carly.

She shook it and grinned at him. "Why not? I'm always up for a challenge."

CHAPTER THREE

Carly

AS I FINISHED unpacking my things at Nana's house, I planned. Planned how to help Tanner set up the office. How to grow his client base. How to manage the business with as little conflict as possible within such a small community.

There was a knock on my door. "Hey, darlin', I've got some chicken and dumplings ready if you want to take a break and eat something."

Nana made *the best* chicken and dumplings. "I'll be down in five minutes, after I empty this suitcase."

As I descended the grand staircase, I ran my hand down the railing, where I knew every nick and scratch in the wood. The one I'd dusted a hundred times during my childhood. We pitched in on Sundays helping Nana clean. It was our family day. Nana always cooked and we helped maintain the house. Daddy did the outdoor mowing and gardening. It was a family home. As in it would stay in the family.

We'd played here from my earliest memories and gone tearing in and out with no thought to its historic grandeur. It was simply Nana's house. I was able to appreciate it now. The smell of beeswax, the occasional creaking board or stair, the heavy crown molding. The gorgeous chandeliers. Our history in the place. One day, I planned to go up into the attic and look through some of the old photos and things.

The smell of a well-cooked pot of dumplings hit me as I got closer to the kitchen. Nana's kitchen had a tall, swinging door and a wall of windows where the round breakfast table that comfortably sat eight resided. The room had been renovated in the past decade to include an enormous six-burner gas range with a griddle and a built-in refrigerator. A charming hub of the home with blue accents, it's where we all gathered most of the time.

"Your sister and Karen will be here shortly."

"Oh, I didn't realize they were coming." I sat at the long counter-height bar where I could visit with Nana as she set up the food for serving. "Can I help with something?"

"I'm already done with it, but you can tell me what's happening with Tanner and your new job opportunity." Nana knew about Tanner's defection only because she'd been present a time or two when it had been discussed around her dinner table.

I wanted to tell her everything, but at this point there were so many unknowns, and I didn't want to break Tanner's trust. "He showed me the new office space. And we shook on my working with him." Nana was aware of the situation between Carson and Tanner. She and Carson had a long and contemptuous history because of Momma and how he'd bullied her to keep quiet about her pregnancy with Allison years ago.

"When do you start working together officially?" Nana asked as she started to pick up the large, bubbling pot.

"Here, let me do that." I hopped up from my seat to carry the huge Dutch oven filled with hot food from the stove and placed it on the iron trivet set out for serving. Nana was perfectly capable, I knew, but so was I.

"We haven't set a date yet. I'm guessing it'll be sometime next week. He's working on getting all the permits finalized through city hall." These were details that didn't disclose too much personal information.

"Fingers crossed things go smoothly. I realize there are concerns with his daddy causing some trouble." Nana cast a worried frown at me.

"I do wonder how a man gets so powerful that so many people are worried about crossing him," I mused.

"I guess if you can't be liked, be feared." Nana's wisdom was legend.

"Doesn't he care that everyone hates and fears him?"

"No, he doesn't. Being liked is less important than everyone showing him unearned respect."

"Is he—violent?" *That* mattered to me.

Nana paused in tossing the salad. "Nobody has ever said that out loud, but really, who knows? I don't want you to be anywhere nearby if he was ever tested."

"Don't worry. I have no intention of getting close to the man."

Nana pulled the corn bread from the oven and placed it on the stovetop. "If Carson wants to insert himself, he will, so be aware."

The heavy front door slammed, and we heard female voices. I quickly whispered to Nana. "I'd rather not discuss this around Momma since Tanner is keeping it under wraps except with the family. And Momma hates Carson."

Nana nodded and smiled a greeting to my sister and mother as they entered the kitchen. She was like a vault. Information went in and didn't come out without permission. I trusted the older woman above all people in my life.

"That smells amazing." Leah plopped down on the barstool beside me.

Momma entered a little more sedately, a trifle bowl filled with something mint green in her grasp. "I've brought a Jell-O salad for dessert."

I tried not to groan. Momma had a thing about Jell-O salad. I did too, but it wasn't a good thing. I liked green Jell-O, marshmallows, cream cheese, pineapple, cherries, Cool Whip, and 7UP. Just not all mixed up together. I knew how to make one too. We all did. It was a Southern staple. I didn't think a funeral could be had without one.

"Sounds good, Momma." I pretended to stick my finger down my throat and gag when Momma turned her back and placed the green goo into the fridge. I could tell Nana tried not to laugh. Leah punched me in the arm. She loved Momma's Jell-O salad.

"Dinner's all ready now. We'll serve from the bar and bring it to the table."

Once we were all happily eating, Momma made an announcement. "Your father has moved back into our bedroom."

We all turned to look her way in response.

Leah choked and I slapped her hard on the back. "*Ow*."

I grinned. "You're welcome. I didn't want you to die." She narrowed her eyes at me.

"So, darling, this is good news, yes?" Nana replied first.

Momma blushed, lowering her eyes. "He's finally forgiven me for not telling him about Allison."

"I think he understands the position you were in. After all, a town like Cypress Bayou has a long memory." We'd all been willing to give Momma the benefit of the doubt for keeping such a huge secret from us all these years, but the consequence of her decisions thirty-five years ago had left their mark. According to Nana, the entire experience had changed Momma.

And Daddy had held a bit of a grudge since he'd found out. They'd lived together still, but we weren't quite sure if things were ever going to be the same between them.

"He was letting you stew is all." Leah and I both knew this to be true, but Leah felt compelled to say it out loud.

"I guess I don't blame him, but it's good to get things back to normal. I just thought I would share with y'all." Momma seemed a little giddy.

"Well, we're happy for you and Daddy, Momma." I weighed in because it was expected. And it was better for us all when Momma was happy with Daddy—especially for Daddy.

"I spoke to Allison today. She still sounds so weak. Shouldn't she be better by now?" Momma shifted the subject. "I'm getting worried about her. She doesn't communicate with us enough."

Leah had expressed the same concerns about that, but I didn't want this subject to get out of hand. "Maybe she isn't comfortable enough with us yet."

"She came looking for *us*, didn't she?" Leah reminded the

group.

I tried to balance things with a positive spin. "Let's give her some time and space. She did put her mother's house on the market in Illinois, so hopefully she's still planning to move here once all her business is done there."

"I think she's got a boyfriend." Momma said this as if it was a scandalous thing. It wasn't, but it might explain some things.

"Maybe that's why she isn't in a hurry to get back here." I tried out this logic on the group.

"We can invite her back for a visit. Maybe for Christmas Festival?" Nana suggested. Christmas Festival was a sight to behold here in Cypress Bayou. Folks came from neighboring states to see the lights and participate in the festivities. Food, music, and the gorgeous lights. So many lights.

"That's too far away." Momma frowned. "I know! I'll get Bob to agree to renew our vows and invite her home for that. She'll have to come." As usual, Momma was diabolical.

"Momma, are you seriously cooking up a scheme to renew your wedding vows with Daddy just to get Allison to come back for a visit?" I had to jump in here.

Momma's eyes lit up. "Don't you see? It's a perfect way for Bob and me to refresh our marriage and to bring Allison officially into the family. We can do it here at Mother's house." Momma locked on to Nana like a predator on prey. "What do you think, Mother?"

Nana, always a good sport, answered with her usual balance. "Darlin', I'm fine with you using the house for renewing your vows with Bob. But make sure you're doing it for the right reasons. And of course, we'd love to lay eyes on

Allison again to make sure she's all right."

"I can't wait to get home and tell Bob."

"Do you think he's going to be thrilled about a vow-renewal ceremony?" I asked because I knew my daddy, and I couldn't think of anything he would want to do less. *Making a public spectacle*, he'd call it.

"Of course—he'll do whatever I want." Momma made a dismissive motion with her hand, much the same as she'd dismissed Daddy's opinion throughout their marriage, which is partly why he'd taken his sweet time in moving back into the bedroom. Plus, Momma snored like a freight train. Diabolical.

By the time Leah and Momma had gone and I'd helped Nana clean the kitchen, it was after nine o'clock.

"So, what do you really think about Momma and Daddy renewing their vows?" I asked Nana as she turned off the lights and we moved into the sunroom off the kitchen. We each had a glass of wine.

Nana smiled slightly. "I think there's nothing anybody can say to change your momma's mind once she's made it up. She's a strong-willed woman."

"I hope Daddy's willing to go along. If not, he won't be back in the bedroom for long."

"Isn't that the truth?" Nana raised her brows and took a sip of wine. "How's your day looking tomorrow?"

"I need to get in touch with Sue and Jo. The sooner the better."

Nana smiled. "I've missed those girls. Give them my best."

Tanner

THE CHARGES WERE dismissed by noon, as Tanner predicted. The prosecution had no case. He met Jake for lunch at The Pub on Washington Street for a quick pep talk. Today was the day he planned to tell Carson about his desertion. Tomorrow, he wouldn't be back in the office. If there was anything to wrap up, he could do it from his new location. At least that was the plan.

They were working their way through The Wookie, a specialty plate of homemade fries, topped with beef brisket and melted cheese. Of course they'd agreed to add jalapeños. "I hope you've got everything covered, man." Jake's appetite wasn't limited by his concern.

"I've been working on this for months. I've done everything I can think of at this point to prepare." Tanner had also quietly gone through old files in the office when no one was looking. He'd found some very interesting things that bore further investigating once he had some freedom to do so.

"I don't put anything past the old man to try and stop you." That went without saying, of course, but Jake said it anyway.

"I don't either, so legally, I should be okay." Tanner kept on with the legal mantra that if he did everything by the book, all would be okay. In fact, it should.

Jake put to words Tanner's concerns. "It's not legally

that I'm concerned about."

"I had the building checked out extensively before I bought it. There were no termites, no unmitigated water damage, no cranky plumbing or electrical issues, and the roof was replaced within the past ten years." Tanner had made certain the building would pass inspection to prevent any delays in opening the practice.

The three-quarters-eaten plate sat between them, a testament to the seriousness of the situation. "Do you want me to be there when you tell him?" Jake's offer was a kind but serious one.

Tanner shook his head. "He'll take it as a sign of weakness, but I appreciate your offer." Though it would be reassuring to have Jake there.

"I'm here for you, and so is Leah. What did Carly say about coming to work for you?"

"She's agreed to come aboard. We're going to work out contract details on how to handle clients and cases. I can't pay her much to begin, which should give her incentive to bring in her own work. I'm relieved not to do it alone."

Jake nodded. "She's smart and capable, and I've never met anyone with more incentive. You could do a lot worse than Carly."

Tanner nodded. "I know. And she understands what I'm dealing with on the Carson front. Somebody else wouldn't really get it like Carly does." Tanner felt in his bones that Carly was the right person to help him get this office up and running.

"Keep in mind that you're dealing with family though, okay? She seems super tough on the outside, but she has a sensitive side that's hidden from the world too. Just a heads-up."

Tanner hadn't seen that side of Carly, certainly not the grown-up Carly. "That's probably good to know. I haven't had any kind of personal conversation with her that hasn't involved the office yet."

"You can be pretty fierce, you know?" his brother reminded him.

"Got it." Tanner knew how to treat peers and assistants. Maybe he sent emails or texts without a lot of niceties, but people appreciated directness in this business. Didn't they? It wasn't something he'd given much thought to. Tanner wasn't a rude person, but he did work hard and expected those around him to pull their weight.

They'd gone back to eating and the plate was now empty. "Looks like we're done here." Jake wiped his mouth with a napkin and took a big swig of water.

"Looks like it."

They paid the check and stepped out into the sunlight. "I'll let you know when it's done."

"Good luck. You've got this."

Tanner took a breath of resolve as he headed toward his truck. His lunch sat heavy in his stomach. He was excited to move forward to the next phase in life. One that didn't have him dreading work every day. It would be hard for a while financially, he knew, but it was beyond time.

Once he'd gotten back inside the truck, Tanner glanced over at the file folder. There were dollar amounts he'd produced while at the firm that far exceeded the costs for Tanner's education. Tanner knew this because he'd found the file marked, *Tanner's Education*, in Carson's personal filing cabinet.

Having a father who kept to-the-penny, hard-copy records in unlocked files made it easier to get information. Carson had such an ego, he believed everyone was so afraid of him, they wouldn't dare go into his files. Of course, nobody would dare besides Tanner.

Yes, it had been sneaky, but not illegal. When members of the same law firm worked together within an office with common clients, it was expected that there was a sharing of information throughout the workspace. There was no law against Tanner going into an unlocked filing cabinet and attaining information while working there.

It wasn't like Tanner had broken into a password-protected personal computer. Carson was old-school and had an ego the size of the Gulf of Mexico. And *that* would likely be his undoing at some point.

CHAPTER FOUR

Tanner's phone vibrated in his pocket. It was a text from Carly.

Good luck. Let me know how it goes.

Thanks. He should be here any minute.

She sent a thumb-up emoji.

He replied with one.

Tanner sat, waiting. Imogene, their managerial assistant, as she preferred to be called, had welcomed him with a smile. Tanner felt bad leaving her here with Carson and his temper. The woman had stuck it out through some serious conflict between Tanner and Carson. And today would likely be no exception.

The front door to the office slammed hard, signaling Carson's arrival, the intensity of which didn't bode well. Door-slamming was a harbinger of Carson's mood for the day. Clearly something hadn't gone well. Imogene had likely cringed at the loudness of it from her post as receptionist. She wouldn't have let Carson see it of course, as Imogene was a hundred percent professional.

Carson's expression resembled a thundercloud as he entered his personal office to find Tanner seated in a chair across the desk from his own. "What the hell are you doing here?"

"Nice to see you too." Tanner forced himself to smile like he hadn't a care in the world.

"I don't have time for *this*." Carson waved his hand as if swatting at a fly.

"Sure you do. Check your schedule. I'm on it."

Carson removed his dark suit jacket and hung it carefully on the coat-tree in the corner. He wore expensive clothing and shoes from expensive stores. Only the finest.

As Carson sat down, he frowned even harder—if that was possible—at Tanner. "What are you doing in my office?"

"I've come to share my good news. I'm opening my own practice." Before Carson could respond, Tanner produced the folder and shoved a stapled document toward him.

Carson narrowed his eyes at Tanner. "Is this a joke?"

"No, it's not. I've more than compensated you for my educational expenses and it's time I went out on my own."

Carson was very quiet as he read Tanner's proposal, which was two concise pages of legal jargon describing their parting of ways. So, more statement than proposal. Since Tanner hadn't signed a contract initially, there were no terms of employment to break.

Carson tossed the pages aside. "This is utter bullshit. You'll leave when I say it's time."

Tanner was prepared for his reaction. "No. I'm leaving today. I've already cleared out my desk and bought a building in town. They're hanging the sign as we speak."

"What? Where?" Carson glared at him. "I won't allow it. You owe everything to me."

"I've paid my dues. There's no noncompete, nothing legal that says I can't practice here in Cypress Bayou." Tanner remained calm and looked his father directly in the eye.

Carson's face was quickly reddening to an unbecoming shade of crimson. He stood and slammed his fist on the desk, causing the only photo to tip off the edge and shatter the glass. It was a photo of Carson with Tanner and Jake's mom, Judy. Carson hardly spared a glance for the photo. "You'd better rethink your actions, son. Once you leave here, there's no going back."

"I'm leaving, and I perceive what you've said as a threat. And I'm assuming Imogene has heard every word you've spit at me since our conversation started. So, if you plan to cause trouble for me, keep that in mind."

Tanner turned and walked out, leaving Carson to seethe alone.

"I'll ruin you!" Carson called to his back.

"Imogene? Did you hear that?" Tanner called toward the woman who was clearly listening to every word. The question was rhetorical, of course.

Tanner grabbed the last small box from his desk across the hall from Carson. Then, as he got to the reception area, he realized that Imogene had gathered her purse and a few personal items as well. "I'm coming with you, if it's all right."

Tanner was completely taken aback by her pronouncement. "B-but, I can't pay your salary yet, Imogene."

She patted his hand in a motherly way. "That's all right. I'll be fine for a while. I won't stay here one more day." She sniffed in a disapproving way. "You're the only thing that makes this office a place that's worth staying at." She cast her eyes back down the hallway. "I heard every word he said to you."

Tanner grinned at the woman. "Well, let's get going then. I can't think of anyone I'd rather have on my team."

When they got outside, Tanner breathed a huge sigh. "I'm glad that's over."

"I've been wondering when you planned to finally quit that horrible man, even though he is your daddy." Imogene said this as if everybody knew something he didn't. But Tanner did know.

"Why did you work for him if you were unhappy?" Tanner asked Imogene.

"Carson helped my Hank with an unfortunate situation a couple years back, a few months after I went to work at his front desk. It was an intoxicated driving charge that never went to court. Hank would've lost his job if it'd come out. Carson held it over our heads that if I ever quit my job, he'd make sure everybody knew about Hank's—incident. But Hank retired a week ago, and now since you're leaving, I've got no reason to put up with any more abuse."

"Imogene, I wish you'd come to me. I wouldn't have let Carson do that to you and Hank. It's illegal. That's what Carson does to people, and I can make it stop when it's called to my attention. He wields power to make folks do what he wants or needs. Do you want to file a suit against him?"

Imogene shook her head. "Lordy, no. I'm deathly afraid of the consequences of crossing him. But at least now I can leave his employ without worry of Hank's losing his job."

"I'm so sorry that happened, but if you change your

mind, we can do it."

"I can't believe I'm free. Your leaving was the reason I needed to finally break out of there. I've got eyes and ears. I've seen and heard things, believe you me."

"One of these days, Imogene, I might need to ask about some of those things."

Imogene nodded. "Point the way to my new adventure. I'm not ready to retire yet."

Carly

I TEXTED JO and Sue in a group text. *Hi there. I'm back in town and just took a job. I'll fill you in on the details ASAP. Let's get together!*

I waited about thirty seconds before Sue answered: *OMG! I can't believe you're back here in the Bayou. How did I not hear about this until now?*

In about thirty more seconds Jo replied: *I heard. I was waiting to see how long it would take before you contacted us…*

I sighed. She was right. I'd put contacting them on the back burner during the transition. I'd thought about sending a text or calling so many times, but I hadn't. Probably because I'd been such an absent friend over the past few years.

I responded: *It took longer than it should, but I've missed you both and want to see you! How about tonight? Let's grab a beer and some oysters at Mother's* ☺

Sue replied: *I'm in* ☺

Jo's response was less enthusiastic: *I can't be there until a little after 7:00 when my shift ends*

I responded: *Great! See y'all around 7:00*

I breathed a sigh of relief now that we had a plan, even though I could feel Jo's reluctance. I knew she would take a little time to warm back up. Distance and time were tough to overcome. Jo was slow to trust after what she'd endured during her childhood. Unfortunately, I hadn't taken the time out of my very busy life to compensate during law school. I should have tried harder and bore guilt for it.

I would make it up to them both. I would.

I shifted my thoughts to what Tanner was facing now. He was likely meeting with Carson at this moment, which caused me to stand up and pace the floor. I was wearing a path back and forth across Nana's sunroom when I got the text from Tanner.

It's done. Can you meet us at the new office?

Us? I replied: *Yes. How did it go?*

Tanner answered: *He took it about like I expected. Imogene quit and is with me*

Well, that was unexpected. Imogene was a nice lady, but I wondered what we were going to do with her. I figured that would be up to Tanner.

"Nana, I'm headed out," I called in the general upstairs direction.

Nana appeared at the top of the staircase. "All right, darling. I haven't decided on dinner yet. Let me know if you'll be eating out."

"Looks like I'm meeting up with Jo and Sue, but I'll stop by here after work to change first, since that won't be until around seven." We were learning to live together as roommates. Nana liked to know if I'd be there for dinner.

"Be safe."

I'd made some notes today while I'd waited between my pacing. Lists of things to do. I was excited to get started on this adventure with Tanner. But I had résumés out to a couple big, influential firms, and part of me was waiting to hear about a possible interview. But still, I was working *with Tanner*. I still couldn't believe it. Every day. Most of the time, I didn't equate him with my godlike crush. But occasionally when I saw him, my heart sped up, and my face flushed. I only hoped I could behave in a professional way without my random lapses coming to his attention.

That would be humiliating. I wondered if he knew about my crush. I'd tried to hide it, but the diary I'd kept didn't lie. Leah had found it one time and had seen all the ways I'd written Tanner's name intertwined with mine. And all those *hearts*. My face flamed as I drove to the office. Leah never mentioned it again beyond my screaming and crying for her to give the book back to me. Her eyes had gone wide, and she'd grinned at me. She'd said, "Don't you think Tanner's a little old for you?"

I was hoping she'd forgotten that incident completely or dismissed it as a young girl's momentary infatuation. It had felt so real for a very long time. But he'd gone off to college and then law school. I'd grown up and dated boys, and then gone off to college and dated more boys. But I'd never completely forgotten the intensity of that crush.

My best friends had known of my deepest secret, but they'd never tell anyone. It was something I was one hundred percent certain of. Of course I'd known their secrets too, so there was that.

As I pulled into the rear parking area, I saw Tanner's big truck and a smaller bright blue car, which I assumed was Imogene's. Cute car.

I knocked on the locked door.

Tanner let me in. There was a tightness in his jaw.

"You okay?" I asked as he locked the door behind me.

"I will be."

"That bad?"

We'd walked toward the front of the building where Imogene was dusting off the reception desk. She looked up and answered before Tanner had the chance. "I heard every word. Carson's an asshole."

That unexpected description, while so accurate, made us both snort with laughter. "Hi, Imogene. It's nice to see you again." I'd met her on several occasions as a resident in town, though I couldn't say exactly where and when.

"Yes, it's lovely to see you again, Carly." She turned to Tanner. "I'd like to get some cleaning supplies and do a good wipe-down of everything. Looks like it's been deep cleaned, but there's dust."

Tanner nodded. "Yes, I had the place cleaned a couple weeks ago, but not since. I think there are some products under the sink in the kitchen upstairs if you want to check there first." He pointed toward the stairs.

Imogene nodded and she was off.

"Did Carson throw any legal stuff at you?" I wanted to help if I could.

"No. There's nothing he can do. He didn't even bother to bluff. Just said I could leave only when he said I could.

Can you believe it?"

I shrugged. "He's a child, it sounds like."

"An old angry one."

"Let's see what we can do to get this place ready for business. I've got some ideas about marketing the practice to start." I pulled my iPad from the tote I'd slung on my shoulder. "I made notes. I hope you don't mind."

Tanner's shoulders seemed to relax a little. "I'm glad I hired you."

We sat down at the newly wiped conference table to discuss our business relationship, contracts, and first steps. The contract would be loose and open-ended should I get a fantastic opportunity elsewhere, as we'd agreed.

"You'll need a website as quickly as we can get one going. That way, when someone looks you up for representation, they can find you. I don't know what you can do to get your name off the old firm's site, but at least the option will come up to click on your new firm's website."

Tanner

A WEBSITE. TANNER honestly hadn't gotten that far yet. "Can you find a good company for that?"

Carly nodded. "That will take a little time to get up and running, but we can get your social media done right away. Instagram, Facebook, and the rest. Those go live without delay. I'll need some professional and casual photos."

Social media wasn't his forte. Of course, Carly was

younger and likely more informed about such things. "These are things that aren't in my wheelhouse."

Carly smiled at him as if he were an infant. "Don't worry, they *are* in my wheelhouse. We had classes in school on the smart marketing of your practice."

"That's new and sounds useful in today's world. But keep in mind, this is Cypress Bayou, and we're still about a decade behind the times with the older crowd."

"Ah, but the younger crowd needs legal representation too. We can cover a more diverse population by grabbing their attention with smart marketing."

He grinned at her, feeling a little bit of the earlier stress slide off his soul. "Did I say how glad I am that I hired you?" Tanner was becoming more and more impressed with Carly by the minute. "I've been working with a dinosaur for so long that I've missed out on the new tech."

"Let me guess, y'all still used paper filing cabinets for your client files. And a paper appointment book?"

Imogene was passing by in the hallway and popped her head in at that moment. "Yes! I tried to speak with Carson about purchasing productivity software, but he wouldn't hear of it. We had email, obviously, but no intraoffice software. The office I worked in several years ago had it and wow, did it make the office more efficient. We could make appointments, keep client files, send reminders by email or text, and all our court dates were in the database. That tech stuff is amazing." Imogene had only been with Carson for a couple years, but she'd worked as an administrative assistant her entire career.

"Sounds expensive." Tanner sighed loudly.

Carly tapped her stylus on the iPad. "It's an investment in your business. You don't want to be a dinosaur from the start."

"No, and it sounds like this will make running a business a lot easier in the long haul." How could he not have thought about all this? He was a smart lawyer, but he'd been so hyper focused on his cases and getting out from under Carson's thumb, he'd not done research into all the minutiae of the latest office equipment.

"You have what's most important: a law degree, a place to practice, and a solid reputation. And now, so do I. We can do whatever kind of law we feel comfortable with, can't we? Unless there's something you want to avoid in your practice. During my internship, I worked with a lot of women in tough circumstances and gone after parents who didn't pay child support. So, maybe I can help diversify the practice with some areas where you don't normally work."

Tanner leaned back in his chair as if thinking about that. "I don't want to appear as an opportunist. No television commercials about how we can get the public paid big money over a tiny mishap that doesn't do real harm. I don't like the idea of sticking it to small businesses when somebody randomly trips on the curb outside."

"Optics are important for sure. But obviously people bring suits over that kind of thing all the time. Would you not take a case if you believed you could win?"

"No. I wouldn't take a case if I thought the person bringing the lawsuit was a scammer. Winning is easy. But my reputation is important to me."

Carly nodded. "So is mine. Sounds like we agree on the

ethics side of things."

"I do my share of wrongful death, personal injury, and family law. And I take on some pro bono work as well."

"I decided in law school that I will always take a certain percentage of pro bono. It's the way we give back to our community." Carly was firm in her conviction.

We both turned at a jingling sound. "I found these in the supply closet. Is it okay if I attach them to the front door?" Imogene stood just inside the threshold of the room holding a set of bells in her hand. "All the best places in town have them."

"I guess it's a good way to know if someone is entering the office when no one's at the front desk." Tanner couldn't argue with the idea of bells.

"What about security cameras?" Carly suggested. "It's on my list."

"I've already purchased a wireless system. It's in my truck. We can get it up and running in the next day or two. I've read the instructions and it sounds simple enough to install." Maybe he hadn't thought of social media, but security was high on his list.

"So the bells are a yes?" Imogene jingled them again to get their attention.

Tanner nodded his confirmation on the bells. "Yes. Let me know if you need any help."

As they ticked through Carly's rather extensive list of must-haves for the practice, some items he'd thought of and some he hadn't, he again was struck by how much attention to detail and time she'd taken to make certain nothing important was missed. Some of it was going to cost him a substantial amount of money, but all her ideas were worthy of consideration.

"What about parking?" Carly pointed to another bullet point highlighted on her list.

"Parking?"

"Yes. What's our situation with the parking lot? Do we share with any other businesses? Is it a private lot or public parking? Do we need to designate spots for the business?"

"Jason said he'd never had to designate any spots because there's a printing business next door that does delivery only, and on the other side is a caterer. The employees park out back, along with the catering vans, but we have several spaces so I'm assuming there won't be a problem if we schedule appointments one at a time. Plus, there are metered parking spaces out front on the street for anyone."

"You might want to check with your contact at city hall to make certain they don't require any parking lot insurance or maintenance fees."

"Wow, you really have thought of everything, haven't you?"

Carly shrugged. "I'm a bit OCD when it comes to details. I start at the bottom and work through problems with a fine-tooth comb. I've tried to do the same with this. Parking, physical building, IT, workflow, marketing—you get it."

"I'm starting to. Your skills likely make you invaluable when it comes to clients and their cases. No details left unaccounted for, right?"

"That's my goal. I'm big on spreadsheets and white-boards."

"I'm big on pens and paper."

They both laughed, but not for long as the newly installed bells on the front door jingled, alerting all that someone had entered.

Tanner tensed. "I thought the door was locked."

"Maybe Imogene unlocked it to clean the glass or something."

"Imogene?" Tanner called her name as he stood and then moved toward the front office.

But it wasn't Imogene he found.

CHAPTER FIVE

Carly

"HI, IS THIS where I can find Tanner Carmichael?"
A woman, probably around Tanner's age, stood in the foyer of the office. "I'm Tanner. How can I help you?"

"I saw the sign out front. I tried to look you up online, but I got a different address. When I went there, a cranky older man yelled at me that you didn't work there anymore. H-he said a few other things, but I'd rather not repeat them. I'm glad I drove around a bit and stumbled on your office." She smiled a little but seemed nervous. The downtown was small, so there wasn't much area to cover when looking at signs out front.

Good thing Tanner had gotten that sign put up today.

"I'm sorry you got yelled at. That man is my father, and he's not happy that I'm in my own office now." Tanner extended a hand in greeting. "It's nice to meet you—"

"I'm Lisa. Lisa Henry. I hope you can help me with something."

"Okay. We're just getting things set up in the office, but I don't see why we can't sit down in the conference room and discuss what brought you in. Please have a seat here in the waiting room for a minute while we get things ready in the conference room."

"I'll bring in some coffee." Imogene always seemed to be within hearing. And I wasn't sure where the coffee came from, but it was a nice touch to have on hand.

I introduced myself then. "Hi, Lisa. I'm Carly Bertrand, Tanner's associate. We'll be right with you."

"Hi, Carly, it's nice to meet you." Lisa sat in one of the chairs I'd indicated.

I made eye contact with Tanner that he should follow me down the hallway. He did. When we got inside the conference room, I shut the door.

Tanner spoke first. "Sorry I didn't introduce you. I'm not used to having a partner." He appeared slightly embarrassed.

I waved that off. "Did you want to see her alone first?" I hope I hadn't been too bold.

Tanner shook his head. "Let's see what she's here for first. I like the idea of having you in the initial meeting to help assess things. It lends a professional air. And since there *are* two of us, it makes more sense to meet with new clients together."

"Sounds good. I didn't mean to overstep out there."

"I'll let you know if I want things done a certain way. So far, your suggestions have been very helpful. Having both of us in the room might also make her feel more comfortable."

Imogene knocked briefly, then entered carrying a full tray of coffee, creamer, sweeteners, and cups. "Shall I show her in?"

"Thanks, Imogene. Yes, we're all set." Tanner opened his laptop.

I was ready with my iPad and Tanner had his pen and yellow notepad, which made me smile a little. It was a small snapshot of our differences. I also used a yellow legal pad for jotting down notes, but mostly I did things electronically.

Lisa wore slim black pants with a black and white print blouse and silver jewelry. Her look was understated but expensive. She didn't carry herself with a pretentious air, but a natural kind of implied grace.

"Please have a seat." Tanner stood and motioned to a chair at the head of the table. We were seated on either side.

"Thanks. I sought you out, specifically because your Google reviews are excellent." Once she was seated, Lisa pulled out a file from her oversized tote purse. I recognized the brand and knew that it, too, was expensive. "I'm looking for my mother."

Tanner frowned, as if he didn't quite understand. "I'm not sure how I can help with a missing person case."

Of course, I was fascinated. Because mysteries were fascinating.

Lisa sighed. "There's more to it than that. My mother grew up here in Cypress Bayou, but she left at eighteen and went to New Orleans for college at the University of New Orleans. She became pregnant at some point while studying there and gave birth to me." Lisa took a second to slide the document toward Tanner. "I never knew my mother because she gave me up for adoption shortly after my birth. She didn't list a father on my birth certificate. Or my adoption records."

"How can we help with your search?" My interest was piqued then. This reminded me of my new sister and her search for family.

Lisa slid over a couple other documents that appeared to be a photocopy of her mother's high school yearbook page and a certificate of adoption. "I can't find any death records for her or any proof that she's still alive."

"Interesting. But wouldn't a private investigator be a better fit for getting this information?" Tanner asked.

"Maybe. But I know this is a small town and you're an entrenched local. And I understand that attorneys can get whatever information they need for their cases. I have money and can pay you." Lisa was a sharp woman.

"That sounds like a good approach." I applauded her tactics.

"Why not ask around in town or hire an older attorney who might have known your mom?" Tanner asked.

Lisa hesitated. "This happened at least thirty years ago. A younger person has no skin in the game, which is a good thing. I'd like fresh eyes on this."

"Are you sure she's not still among the living?" I wanted to be sure what we might be dealing with.

"If she's still alive, I would be very surprised. She would have to be a ghost or have completely acquired a new identity, which I know is possible, but not likely." Lisa didn't seem especially emotional over the thought that her birth mother might be dead—more like…resigned.

"What about her family?" Tanner asked.

"I honestly don't know. I can't find anyone listed here in town with the same name. She doesn't seem to exist beyond giving me up for adoption so far as I can tell. Obviously she lived here before and had an entire childhood and life until then, one that began here in Cypress Bayou. Of course, my thoughts have gone through some weird scenarios."

I had to agree with Lisa. "No, people don't usually up and disappear, especially nowadays, with all the ways to find someone." I made a couple notes on my yellow pad. "Have you done any asking around in town?"

"I just got here. I've done some searching on Google, but so far, I've not come up with anything. If I do find new family, I wouldn't want to face them alone."

I nodded. "I've recently had a similar situation in my own family, so I understand how uncomfortable finding new family might be."

Tanner had been making notes. "You mother's full name was…is Justine Chaffin?"

Lisa nodded. "That's all I have. I couldn't find any Chaffins in Cypress Bayou though."

"I can't think of any either." I'd been here my entire life and wasn't familiar with that surname.

Tanner glanced over at me as if to check and make sure it was okay to take this on. I understood the silent question in his eyes and nodded briefly in agreement.

"Since we're getting the practice established, we'll agree to work with you to solve your family mystery. The hourly rate is two hundred and fifty dollars. That includes local travel and expenses. We can bill biweekly or monthly."

Tanner was smart to put the rates out to Lisa in such a no-nonsense way where there wasn't any doubt as to how our work would be done and how we would bill the hours, but it also gave a little flexibility on invoicing.

Lisa's shoulders visibly relaxed. "I can pay your rate.

Thank you both so much. I knew you were the one for the job. I've been researching all the attorneys in town. You get top marks for your compassion and being thorough. That's what I need. I realize what I'm asking is a little outside the normal attorney skill set, but I don't know if any laws have been broken. And I don't know what it will take to solve this mystery."

Tanner reassured her. "I appreciate your confidence. We'll do our best to help you maneuver this…situation. Send us any information you uncover. We'll do some additional looking into the family and ask around, starting with people we know and trust."

"I can't tell you how much of a relief it will be to have support, as I'm kind of short on family support these days."

"We're glad to be able to help you," I reassured her.

"Since we're going to have to share your mother's story while asking questions of the locals, there won't be a lot of privacy. We'll need to use your name and your mother's name, so the usual privacy clause won't exactly apply here."

Lisa nodded. "I guess that's what I'll give up if I'm going to find out what happened to her. And just so you know, my family—the Henry family who raised me—they aren't especially thrilled about my search, so we won't get a lot of help from them. They are a rather affluent bunch from uptown New Orleans and would rather I didn't do this."

"Do the Henrys have information regarding your birth mother? Did they know her?" This was an interesting twist.

Lisa frowned. "I don't think so. At least my mom says she didn't know her. But every time I bring it up, she throws drama my way and says if I loved her, I wouldn't do this to her."

I barely controlled the snort. "My mother is rather dramatic, so I get it. Maybe as she gets used to the idea, she'll be more willing to help." I put my hand over Lisa's. "We're on your team, Lisa. Call anytime. We don't yet have business cards, but here is my personal cell phone." I handed her my generic card that included my cell number and email contact.

"Yes, we're working on that, along with all the other things involved in setting up this office. Don't hesitate to email or call." Tanner stood as Lisa did.

We all shook hands and saw Lisa out the door.

I stepped out on to the sidewalk as she made her way toward a very nice late-model BMW 6-Series sedan and climbed in. Tanner had walked outside with me. "I like the idea that our first client is able to pay our fees without hesitation." Even though this wasn't the kind of work they'd likely be doing moving forward with the business.

"Yes. Having money coming in is definitely a good way to pay for all the things you're going to need to get this place up and running." I looked up then, remembering the new sign had been the thing that had brought Lisa here. "Sign looks great." I pointed upward.

It was oval and hung from two chains. The letters were bold and simple: **Tanner P. Carmichael, Attorney at Law**. "Yes. It's good to see. Makes some of the headache in doing this worth it."

I nodded. "I can't wait to dig into Lisa's mother's background. What an odd client request." We walked back inside, and Tanner locked the door so not just anyone could enter off the street while they we were getting set up.

"I'll get the security system installed ASAP. It's got a doorbell with a camera where we can unlock the front door remotely to let in visitors."

"I still like the old-fashioned bells," I said.

"Noted. We can keep them."

We went back inside the conference room and sat down. "So, tell me what you want me to do to get started on Lisa's case."

Tanner gave me an odd look. "Are you deferring to me?"

"You're the boss." I stated the obvious.

"Am I?" He didn't appear angry. Maybe amused.

I frowned. "Of course. Why do you ask?"

"You seem to be one step ahead of me. I'm a little in awe of your precise planning, I must admit." He sat back in his chair. "And very impressed."

"I'm too direct, huh? Bossy?" These were things I'd been called in the past. I hated that Tanner might believe these were bad traits. Maybe he *was* like all the other men I'd known, which would be a real disappointment. It was true. I was a little direct, and maybe a little bossy, but I was also super excited about helping him. And maybe a little overwhelmed by him, thereby making me talk a little faster and behaving a bit like a Chihuahua.

"No. Not at all. I can't think of a single thing you've suggested that isn't a solid idea."

"So, do we have a problem?" I was confused by the conversation, except maybe I wasn't. Tanner was an alpha all the way. And I'd known alphas during my time in law school. Students who were alphas and professors who were as well.

They liked to be in charge. I liked to be in charge too.

"No. We do not have a problem. Keep up the good work." He held his hands up as if in surrender.

I liked to get cracking, as it were. I realized I was less experienced when it came to the law than Tanner, but my planning and perfectionism were my strengths, and I tried to keep myself from being too much.

"Okay. I won't apologize for being organized and a perfectionist then. But you'll need to let me know if I get on your nerves. I'll work on things in my own space. I take direction well, but you've got to tell me what you want me to do."

His eyebrows went up, but I could see that he wasn't angry. "Deal. I've got no problem with your being decisive and working hard. You impress me but don't intimidate me, Carly."

I shrugged and nodded. "Good. I do intimidate some men."

"I admire a woman who knows her mind and isn't afraid to speak it. I'm glad you're here with me. It makes this journey a hell of a lot smoother."

"So, I'll make my plan of action notes and get back to you on Lisa's case, then?"

"Sounds good. I'm going to do a little digging on the grandmother."

"ALLISON SAID SHE would come for the vow renewal. Isn't that exciting?"

I'd gotten home around six o'clock to find Momma there in the kitchen with Nana. Planning. "It'll be great to see her again." Yes, it would be nice to see my new sister again.

Nana slid a bowl of something that smelled heavenly in front of me. And a piece of crusty French bread. "I'm assuming you haven't eaten yet."

"No, I haven't. Smells great."

"It's a potato leek soup. I got the recipe from Inez down at the pharmacy. It's got a little lemongrass in it. Let me know what you think."

I tasted the soup. "Mmm, it's good. Unusual, but good." I think that almost anything would've been delicious right now. I was starving. The warm bread and melted butter made my brain go fuzzy. But I knew I would be leaving shortly to go and meet up with Jo and Sue for oysters.

"You look exhausted. Tough day?" Momma frowned at me.

"Long day. Or it felt like one. We have a lot to do to get things running like they need to be. Website, social media, and all the other things that will make Tanner's law firm show up to the public when they search for attorneys in the area. It takes a while for the algorithms to catch up on the internet once a new business is entered."

"Sounds like a lot of work, and it sounds complicated. Glad he's got you to help him with all those things, darling." Nana puttered in the kitchen while I finished my bowl of soup.

"Thanks for the soup. I'm gonna run upstairs and change into jeans before I head out to meet my friends."

"Oh, okay." Nana would never say if she thought I

shouldn't do something, but I could tell she was concerned that I'd had a long day already.

Before I'd managed to leave the room, Momma spoke. "I guess you'll be glad to know we've decided on the date of our vow renewal." Momma wasn't to be ignored. "June twentieth will be the big day. We'll invite around a hundred people. Not too big, but not a tiny event either."

I tried to retain my patience. Momma knew I wanted to go upstairs and change, but she delayed me anyway. This was information I could get anytime between now—and anytime. But I took a deep breath and indulged her.

"It sounds pretty big." I knew my input wouldn't be taken with any real weight.

"You know we couldn't get away with inviting any less than that. Feelings would be hurt." Momma's idea of hurt feelings meant that if the event were any smaller, it wouldn't make a dent socially. And if she went to the trouble of having an event, it should be noticed in town.

I controlled the eye roll. I wished Leah was here to back me up.

"I'll add it to my calendar."

"You, Leah, and Allison will be my attendants."

"Your attendants?" This was sounding a lot like a traditional wedding. I was getting a bad feeling about my part in this thing. And my sisters' parts.

"The only way I could get Allison home was to include her in the ceremony."

"You *extorted* her?" This didn't surprise me in the least.

"Well, I wouldn't call it *that*." Momma sounded only slightly ashamed.

"Did you consider that Allison might not want to come back right now?"

"I don't think it's too much to ask that she be included in our ceremony. She's my daughter, after all."

I shook my head in sympathy for my new sister. She was getting the "baptized by fire" treatment into the family. Allison would learn about Momma's need to get what she wanted from her daughters by emotional manipulation, or by any means necessary really. Her love often came with strings. I'd hoped she wouldn't do that to Allison, even though in some twisted way, Momma believed she was doing all this in Allison's best interest.

Leah and I should reach out to Allison and give her permission to decline the summons back to Cypress Bayou for the vow renewal and give her the heads-up that it was all a ploy to bring her back to town. It would level the playing field so that Allison could make her decision to return based on whether she wanted to come back.

"I've gotta go. I won't be late, Nana."

CHAPTER SIX

"SO, WHAT ON earth made you want to come back here? Aren't there much better opportunities in Baton Rouge and New Orleans?" Jo asked me once we'd gotten seated and started on our first round of oysters.

"It felt like the right thing to do for now. Leah's back home and I'm tired of being four hours away from home. But I do have some feelers out in the bigger cities, so I guess we'll see how things go in the longer term." I laughed. "I did get a job with Tanner Carmichael, so that's something, I guess." Since he'd officially broken off with Carson, the secret would be out.

"Get *out*! The one and only guy you've ever shown any real interest in your entire life?" Sue whooped and slapped her thigh. "Score!"

"It's not like that. We're both attorneys and he's just starting a solo law practice and needed an associate. It kind of…worked out."

"I'll say it *worked out*." Jo managed a smile then. "You're like a cat, aren't you? Land on your feet every time." The smile wasn't exactly a warm and friendly one, I noticed.

"Are you upset with me, Jo? I know I didn't exactly keep in close touch while I was living in Baton Rouge, but did I do something I'm unaware of?" I had to ask or let this fester further.

Sue jumped in then. "Lay off, Jo. She's gotten in touch now and we're all together. Not every single slight has to be fed and watered until death."

"Slight? What are y'all talking about?" I couldn't remember an actual slight. These were my friends, and I wasn't going to let them hold grudges behind my back that I wasn't even aware of.

Jo stared hard at me and took a swig of her beer. "It was graduation night, if you must know."

"From high school?" I blinked. "I don't remember."

"That's the problem. It was one of the worst experiences of my life and you don't remember. You had a date. Sue had a boyfriend—if you want to call him that."

"Hey—that's not fair—" Sue protested, but Jo held up her hand and shushed her.

"I was with a group of our classmates at the after-party on the bayou. I'm not sure where you were, but you missed the part where Jason Mosher tried to kiss me in front of everyone. He was drunk—"

"He was always drunk—" Sue imparted, but again Jo silenced her with a hand.

"Everyone got super quiet when I punched him in the nose. Of course, his go-to was to call me a lesbian, which we know now that I was. I guess several of our classmates probably did too at the time. But I hadn't come out yet and I'd had a couple beers—enough to be shamed and horrified. I left the party with a bruised hand and no friends who had my back."

A tear spilled down Jo's check from her left eye. "Where

were you?" she asked me.

Tears filled my eyes, and the oysters suddenly weren't sitting well. This was the first I'd heard of this. "I didn't know. Why didn't you tell me what happened?"

"You should've been there. We were always together at parties. It was our last night."

I thought about that night specifically then. "I'm pretty sure I was making out with Tommy DuBois in his new truck." I said it before I realized how ridiculously *high school* it sounded.

The three of us burst out laughing at the stupidity of it. "Okay, you're excused then. Tommy was *hot*." Jo shook her head and wiped the tear away. "But I've carried that around for a good long time, as far as grudges go."

"I know and I'm so sorry. But just so you know, Tommy was a horrible kisser." Jo was sensitive but she also had a sense of humor, thankfully.

Tanner

TANNER WONDERED HOW much research Lisa had done on her own before bringing the case to him. To them. It shouldn't be too hard to dig some information up on Lisa's family, being that they were from Cypress Bayou. One thing was certain; somebody knew something here in town. He wished he still had access to Carson's filing cabinets filled with everybody's dirty secrets.

But Tanner had traded working for dirty Carson for

working with the exceptionally efficient Carly, who'd become his right hand in a matter of days. He couldn't imagine moving forward without her. It had happened so quickly. She'd texted several times to get his opinion on website text and graphics, so he knew she was working on getting that set up. He'd sent her a headshot and a few candid photos for social media. They were supposed to meet at the office later today.

The entire time he'd worked at Carson's law offices, he'd been on his own, both personally and professionally, so it was nice to have someone to bounce ideas off and get opinions.

Plus, he had to admit, she wasn't hard to look at and she smelled nice. That was something Tanner hadn't been expecting. An attraction to Carly Bertrand. Little Carly Bertrand. He'd remembered her as a child, always. But now, it was impossible to ignore the fact that she'd grown into a smart, gorgeous woman. He'd need to be careful on that front because it was imperative that he stay a hundred percent professional. They were at the beginning of a very good thing.

Thunderstorms had moved into the area early in the day and as Tanner was working in his trailer currently, the weather was something he had to keep a close eye on. Mostly he was good with rain and a little thunder, but high winds, close lightning, or tornado warnings put him on high alert. He would've gone to the office, but the painter was doing some work there today. If things got much more extreme, he'd need to make a move either to Jake and Leah's loft or the office. Paint or no paint.

A text came in then from Carly: *What do you think about this one?*

He saw that it was a sample graphic from a web developer. Clean, professional, and updated compared to Carson's old-fashioned one.

He responded: *Looks great.* And then, on impulse, he included a thumbs-up emoji, something he never did. He'd hired her on a gut instinct, and so far she'd shown herself to be far more proficient than he'd imagined.

Carly

IT WAS STORMING today. The summer months in most of Louisiana brought frequent afternoon showers as the heat and humidity rose. Today, I worked on my to-do list from Nana's house. Tanner suggested we work from home since so much of what we were doing right now was online research. He'd hired a painter to freshen up a few areas in the outer office today, though the high humidity wouldn't help with the paint-drying process. Imogene was put in charge of taking inventory and stocking fresh supplies. Office supplies, cleaning supplies, coffee, et cetera.

Since today was Friday, we would reconvene Monday morning at the office.

Tanner had texted a few times to check in about some of the things we were working on, which made me feel connected to what was happening with Lisa Henry and the information he'd found so far. I couldn't wait to dig in and research the family, but I was prioritizing websites and social media for the practice.

I so wanted to be involved with the actual hands-on personal side of things. But I realized my job was to wait until I was asked to participate.

"Hello, darling. It's come up a bad cloud out there hasn't it?" Nana had entered the kitchen and gazed out the window above the sink. She was wearing her pink raincoat and polka-dot rubber boots.

"Aren't you cuter than a speckled puppy under a red wagon in the rain." She really was.

"Well, I don't see any reason to get drenched in the weather. And I won't let it keep me from getting my business done either." She was practical like that.

"I'll be here when you get back. Too wet and stormy for me. Be careful out there." I was sitting at the kitchen table with my laptop and iPad. Both were needed, along with my own yellow legal pad for jotting down random thoughts and notes as they hit my brain.

"Looks like you're neck deep in it." Nana waved a hand toward me.

"Yes, we've got a long list of things to do before the practice is fully functional."

"Let me know if there's anything I can do to help." I wasn't sure what Nana thought she could do to help with Tanner's practice, but nothing would surprise me. Nana was a woman with many skills.

"Unless you can design a killer website, I think I'm on my own for today." Nana pulled out her big umbrella. "Where are you headed?"

"There's a small leak in the attic and I've got to get a bigger bucket at the hardware store until I can get somebody out here to fix it."

The very idea of Nana up in the attic attending to a leaky roof made me cringe. "I wish you'd told me about it. Let me go up and deal with that, okay?"

Nana sighed. "Those stairs *are* pretty steep, so when I get back, you can replace the small bucket I've got catching the drip with the bigger one."

I knew she hated deferring anything to her age, but she wasn't a stupid woman either. "Should I call Daddy and have him take a look?" Daddy was a pretty good fix-it guy.

"No, it's going to take a roof professional. Fortunately, the rain is supposed to stop by morning. I'll get someone out in the next day or so."

The thunder shook the house and I cringed. "Are you sure you want to get out in this weather?"

Nana gave me a stern look. "I agreed to let you help with the attic, but I'll not be kept home by the rain like a doddering old woman. Let me do my business, granddaughter. Plus, there are groceries to get. Got to put my chili on."

I couldn't argue with that. "Okay. No offense."

"None taken." She smiled and winked at me, showing that she still had a deep dimple on her left cheek.

Beau the calico cat jumped on my lap for a snuggle and maybe for security from the storm. He purred and settled, making pretend biscuits by kneading his soft paws against my leg. So long as his claws didn't come out, we were good.

Now, back to websites. Not the most exciting part of my current job, but necessary. I believed I'd finally found a couple of website designers that would work for Tanner's practice. They had great reviews and appeared to be very flexible. I sent a query to both sites and would wait to hear back. Since it was the beginning of the weekend, I realized that might not be until Monday.

The leak in the attic was distracting me. Now that I had one of the biggies checked off my list for the day, I decided to go up and have a look at how bad things were up there.

I was dressed in leggings and a lightweight Tulane Law sweatshirt with my hair in a ponytail. Perfect for climbing up in the dusty, and now leaky, attic. I slipped my sneakers on without socks and went upstairs where the pull-down for the attic was located.

The pull-down took a little muscle to handle. The small rope cord hung barely low enough to get hold of and lower the rectangular-shaped trapdoor from the ceiling. A set of wooden stairs unfolded all the way to the floor as the spring-hinged contraption worked its creaky magic.

I hated the idea of Nana climbing up there without anyone knowing it. Now that Leah and I both lived in town, we were available to help her do more of the heavy lifting. Plus, Jake was there if the lifting was heavy.

I couldn't recall the last time I'd been up here. The thunder rumbled again as I fumbled for the light switch once I'd cleared the opening at the top of the stairs. There was a window, but it had blinds that matched those on the rest of the house, and they were closed, so the space was dark. I flipped the switch and a single bulb illuminated the room.

It was as magical as I'd remembered. Old furniture, trunks, racks of vintage clothing that Leah and I had played dress-up in as kids, and the ancient record player still sat in the corner. I heard the *drip, drip, drip* sound then and made my way through the cluttered area to check and see how full the bucket was. It was a single drip coming down from where the roof was steeply pitched.

About two inches of water had been captured by the bucket so far. Plenty of time until Nana returned with a new, bigger bucket. I looked around quickly to check for any other possible leaks.

Once I felt confident there was only the one, I allowed myself the indulgence of reminiscing in this dusty attic from my childhood. There were so many books. Leather, hardbound ones on old bookshelves of various heights and finishes shoved against the edges of the room, forming a perimeter. I spotted some children's books I remembered from when I was a kid.

The rain continued as I saw this place through my grown-up's eyes instead of a child's view. There were unopened trunks and drawers that hadn't interested me during my younger years. Leah and I had loved reading stories up here when we were able to sneak away.

I'd developed a love of history during law school. In all my reading of case files for school, so much of learning Napoleonic Code involved historical documents that established our current legal system, which Louisiana still abided by today, though much amended.

Nana had once told me that some of what was in the attic had been here for a century or more untouched. Some documents had been donated to the preservation society through the years, likely before Nana's time even. But the amount of preserved history in Cypress Bayou, because of the age of the city, was overwhelming. People here sometimes took all the old things for granted because they were so plentiful, which made them less precious in some ways.

Of course, I assumed some of it was Nana's stuff from her past as well as some older items. She said everything was fair game when I'd asked her about digging around up here, so I wouldn't worry about snooping where I shouldn't.

As I scanned the shelves and stacks, a small trunk caught my eye. It appeared to be something one would've used as a suitcase for travel decades ago. I pulled it from the top of one of the bookcases. It wasn't too heavy, but it was covered in dust, and I searched around for something to wipe it off. But everything was dusty.

I sat down on one of the old settees, which I rolled back the dust cover on, revealing the faded brocade fabric. I laid the trunk beside me to inspect it. The latches weren't locked, but they were a little stubborn after being frozen in place for such a long stretch of time.

Anticipation buzzed through me as I lifted the top.

Tanner

TANNER PLANNED TO get as much information about Justine Chaffin as possible without causing a stir. After a scan of the yearbook photo Lisa had provided, he learned that she'd been in the same graduating class at Cypress Central High as Carly's mom, Karen Bertrand. So, right there, he had someone loosely within his circle he could mine for information.

Karen Bertrand might not be the most reliable narrator, but hopefully she could give him some insight about her former classmate. Tanner had gotten hold of one of their early yearbooks at the library and noticed several candid photos of Karen and Justine together. So, it appeared they'd been friends.

It was something, but he would discuss with Carly how best to approach her mom about this. It might be best for her to do it alone, depending on what she knew. Could be that Nana had some information as well.

In this instance, Carly could be closer to getting what they needed than him. At least it was a starting point. A quiet one.

The bolt of lightning was so close, Tanner ducked, just before the crunch and boom rattled his trailer. He'd managed to ride out this especially nasty thunderstorm tucked away in his mobile home, but that was too close. Maybe it was time to rethink this idea of living temporarily on the bayou and saving up to build his forever home. Today was a test of his nerves.

Are you okay, man? It was a text from Jake.

Tanner: *That one was close*

Jake: *Head over to the loft*

Tanner: *I can go to my office if it gets worse*

Jake: *Dude, take cover. Storm's bad*

Tanner decided after having a quick look at the local weather radar and seeing the warnings for tornadoes approaching this area, he would head to the office.

Tanner: *Will do*

Tanner grabbed his rain slicker off the hook beside the door, shoved his laptop inside the backpack next to it and took the power cord just in case. The rain was coming down so hard, he was soaked by the time he'd made it to his truck. *Damn!*

Tanner pulled his phone from the pocket of his rain jacket and a text came through at the same time from Carly. *Are you okay? Come on over to Nana's house. She's making chili*

That sounded way better than smelling paint fumes at the office where there wasn't any chili. *Made it to my truck to avoid being taken out by a tornado... That sounds good. Thanks*

Carly: *See you soon*

CHAPTER SEVEN

Carly

J UST AS I'D gotten lost in the past, I heard Nana call my name from below. I'd texted her some time ago to make sure she was okay. She was, of course, but still I worried. I'd found a treasure trove of old photos in the trunk I'd opened, but the dim lighting upstairs didn't do them justice, so I brought the photos, trunk, and all, downstairs and into the kitchen—after I'd swapped out the buckets once Nana had gotten back from her soggy outing.

As I sat at the kitchen table, sorting through the pictures while Nana started the chili, I mentioned my invitation to Tanner. "Tanner's coming over here. I was concerned about him in that metal trailer by the water. I hope you don't mind."

It had been a while since I'd texted. I wondered what was keeping him.

"Of course I don't mind. I hope you invited him to eat with us." Nana was currently browning a blend of ground pork sausage and beef. I knew this because I'd learned how to make her chili recipe a couple years ago. It, like everything she cooked, was special and delicious.

I nodded. "I did. We've got some work things to go over

anyway, and since the weather's so terrible today, I figured here was as good a place as any." I never worried if people were welcome at Nana's house, because they always were. I couldn't imagine her ever turning anyone away. Even someone she didn't particularly like. Plus, she always made enough food for a small army.

"I expect your parents in about an hour, and maybe Leah and Jake. I hope that won't put a damper on your work with Tanner. Feel free to use the den should you require quiet."

I figured the rest of the family would show up at some point, but since the rest of the family included Tanner's brother, it wouldn't be uncomfortable. "No, that won't be a problem."

Nana's house had enough rooms that there was space for a private discussion should one be required.

"So, what did you find in the attic?" Nana peered over her glasses to see what I was doing.

"A bunch of old photos. They look like some of yours, and maybe of Momma's when she was young." There were some degraded envelopes from the drug store with actual negatives and black-and-white photos, but most were old color photos, the kind that were thick but faded with time. Most had writing on the backs of them. I hadn't taken time yet to look at any of them. I was sorting them by time stamp. Basically, by decade.

"I love looking back at old photos. I'm sure your momma would love to go through those with you."

"Yes, a lot of these were from when she was growing up. When she was in school and as a little girl."

"Look in the drawer behind you, Carly. There's a magnifying glass. So many of the old pictures are blurry and hard to see clearly." Nana pointed to the old piece of furniture against the wall.

"Oh, good idea." She was right. I noticed how hard it was to see faces in the photos.

I gently transferred Beau to the chair beside me, but he continued to purr, so no harm done. There was a knock on the door as I stood to grab the magnifying glass.

"I'll get it." As I suspected, it was Tanner.

And he was soaked. Hair, jacket, jeans. "Goodness, boss. Did you stop and take a swim in the bayou on the way?"

He wasn't amused, based on his expression.

"Let me get you a couple towels." I ran upstairs and grabbed towels and some of my giant sweatpants and an oversized double-X T-shirt. Stuff I still had from an old boyfriend. I rarely wore either item but hated to get rid of them.

"Here, put these on and I'll throw your clothes in the dryer." I handed the items to Tanner, who eyed them with doubt.

"Oh, just do it. Nobody here cares. Your stuff will be dry in thirty minutes." Had that sounded bossy?

He toweled his hair and pulled off his boots. I forgot how tall Tanner was, as he towered over me. I was barefoot-ed. We usually sat together while we worked, so I guess I hadn't thought about it much. For some reason, I thought about it now.

"The bathroom's there." I pointed.

I stood outside the door while he stripped and handed me his wet shirt, socks, and jeans. That felt kind of—

intimate. And I was again thrown back to wanting to sniff his shirt when he handed it to me. "Um, are you soaked through to your skivvies? You can give those to me too." I'm sure my face was an unbecoming shade of red, but I was a grown woman, and it would be stupid not to ask.

"Uh—yeah. They're wet too."

"Give 'em up."

I was rewarded with a very warm and very damp pair of boxer briefs. I wanted to hold them with two fingers and run super fast to the washing machine. Like a middle school girl with a crush might. Oh, yeah.

I had all the wet things in my hands and controlled my urge to run to the laundry room. It was so stupid. They were wet clothes, not a bomb. I threw everything in the dryer and set the timer for forty-five minutes to be sure.

When I returned, I tried, really, not to laugh.

The pants were six inches too short. And they were— snug. As in, *wow*. I tried not to stare. The T-shirt was also snug, but holy moly, did it do him justice. How much working out did a man have to do to look like that in a well-fitting Tulane tee?

"Not a word or you're fired."

I might have snorted a tiny bit after I turned my back.

"Smells amazing in here." The subject change was a welcome one.

"Nana's chili never disappoints."

We entered the kitchen as Nana pulled a tray of corn bread from the oven. "Tanner, if you're hungry, y'all can serve a bowl. The others will be here in a little while."

"Thanks for having me, Ms. Elise. Sorry about my appearance." He turned to me as a dog whose owner dressed him up in the most ridiculous costume might. A mixture of shame and embarrassment. "My clothes were soaked."

"Honey, you look fine. We don't worry about such things in this house. Can't have you catching a cold." But I saw the twinkle in Nana's eye just before she turned around.

Tanner had fished out the laptop from his backpack and carried it to the table where I'd been pulling out pictures. "What's all this?"

I explained about the leak in the attic and about all the treasures.

"Can I help with the leak?"

"I don't think there's anything to be done until it stops raining. And it's only in the one spot."

He nodded. "But please let me know if there's anything I can do."

Nana agreed that she would.

I showed him the photos I'd been going through in answer to his question about what this all was.

"Oh, I haven't told you the news yet. Your mom was a classmate of Justine Chaffin's." "Mom will be here shortly for dinner. We can ask her about Justine when she arrives."

Nana had heard our conversation. "Yes, Justine was a nice girl. Haven't heard anything about her in many years. There was some scandal from what I recall."

Tanner and I looked at each other, and then we both turned toward Nana. "What happened?" Our words were simultaneous.

"Oh, I don't really remember the particulars. She went off to college somewhere down South. New Orleans. Yes, that was it. Her sweet momma, Marie, worried so about her heading to the big city, you know?"

We nodded. "Do you know what happened to her while she was away at college?" I prodded for Nana to continue.

"Got into a little trouble with a boy as I recall. But I'm not sure how it all turned out. Marie and I were friends, but as soon as Justine had difficulties, she didn't want to talk about it. Then, not long after, Marie's husband was killed in an offshore oil rig accident. So tragic. We lost three young men from town in that accident."

"What about Marie and Justine? Whatever happened to them?" I pushed.

Nana shook her head. "Marie remarried about a year later, and I never heard anything else about Justine. Marie and I never communicated after that."

Tanner asked Nana, "Do you know where Marie is now?"

"No, I don't. She and her husband moved to another town not far away, but I'm not sure exactly where. I haven't heard anything about Marie in years. Not since she moved." There were a dozen small towns in the area surrounding Cypress Bayou.

But I realized how important this might be, so I stayed with the questions. "Nana, do you know what Marie's new husband's last name was?"

"Trichel. He was a transplant and didn't have family here, which is why they moved later. Most folks in Cypress Bayou stay in the area. But I guess he didn't have any reason to stay, and when Justine got in trouble and Marie lost her husband, she didn't want to stay here either. You know how people talk."

I looked at Tanner and raised my brows. "Should we fill her in since Lisa gave us the okay?" Since we weren't bound by attorney–client privilege, we had to decide how much to tell people when asking around town. And I knew Nana was trustworthy.

Tanner nodded. "Yes, I think this might be our first break in the case."

So, I said to Nana, "Somebody came into the office and hired Tanner to find out what happened to Justine."

"Hmm…may I ask who hired you to find this information?" Nana asked.

I glanced at Tanner, then answered. It felt odd being able to discuss a client so freely. "Her daughter, Lisa. Apparently, she was given up for adoption while Justine was in college. Lisa never knew Justine and wants to find out what happened to her mother. She's not been able to locate any death information or to find her."

Nana let out a low whistle. "Sounds like a real mystery."

Tanner spoke then. "We're not sure what happened to Justine after Lisa was born, and now we're wondering who might have some information. Justine didn't list a father on the birth certificate."

Nana cut big fat squares of yellow corn bread as she suggested to us both. "You might look for Marie. I know she's not here in town, but I don't think she's far, if she's still with us. I'm guessing she would know who her daughter was seeing."

Still with us, meaning not dead.

Tanner

WHEN TANNER ARRIVED, he'd not expected to be handed the name of Lisa's grandmother. He'd also not expected to be sitting with Carly at the kitchen table, barefoot and commando in tight sweatpants that would be better suited for a teen boy. But here he was.

"So, I'm thinking my clothes might be dry now." Tanner didn't want to wear damp clothing, but he also would rather be damp and back in his own jeans before the others showed up for dinner.

"I'll check on them." Carly scooted her chair and slid behind him to go have a look. When she did, her hair grazed the back of his neck, and he caught a whiff of her shampoo. She smelled clean and female. Not a good time for an arousal considering his weird state of dress. He was thankful when she returned and gave him an update. "About ten more minutes."

Unfortunately, his brother and sister-in-law came bursting into the kitchen right after that. Tanner groaned.

"Dude, what are you wearing? Did the little boy down the street loan you his clothes?" Jake had a good laugh at his expense.

"Leave him alone, brother-in-law. His were soaked from the storm when he got here. I couldn't let him sit in wet clothes all evening." Carly stuck up for him, thankfully.

But there was no way to disguise the fact that he wasn't

wearing underwear once his clothes were dry and he'd have to stand up eventually. Jake wouldn't let him live this down, he was sure of it.

"Jake, can you help me with something out here?" Nana was suddenly elevated to sainthood in his eyes. Tanner had no idea if she pulled Jake outside for a legitimate reason, or if she was sly enough to understand how badly Tanner needed to make a clean getaway the minute Jake crossed the threshold to the sunroom.

"Excuse me, ladies." He wasn't nearly as embarrassed to hear Leah and Carly snorting with laughter behind his retreating backside as he would've been had Jake caught sight of him. It was rather comical, he realized, but he knew they would have a laugh and let it go.

Once he was back in his own—albeit, warm—clothing, Tanner felt his manhood return. Somewhat. He didn't put his boots back on, rather stayed in his socks instead. Everyone else had kicked off their shoes at the front door due to the wet weather.

By the time Tanner sat down again at the table, Bob and Karen had entered. "Wow, it's a real turd floater out there, don't you know?"

"Don't I know it, son-in-law. I went out earlier and thought I might need a pirogue to get home." Nana Elise laughed at Bob's description of the heavy rain. Karen, on the other hand did not.

"That was rather crude, Bob." Her face was pinched with distaste.

Everyone else laughed and ignored Karen, who clearly didn't care to be ignored. She huffed and plopped down on a barstool. "I swear, he just says anything that pops into his head."

"Momma, it was funny." Leah leaned close and chided her mother.

"Momma, we need your help. Tanner and I are working on a missing person's case and learned that you went to school with the woman we're trying to find." Carly gave Karen the distraction needed to change her focus.

That snapped Karen back into the spotlight. "Oh, who is it?"

"Her name is Justine Chaffin. Do you remember her?" Carly got high marks for introducing the subject at the right time.

"Why yes, I remember Justine. We were pretty good friends in junior high and into high school. She—well—she was someone I trusted when, you know, I got into trouble." Karen ducked a little when she said it, like she was uncertain of the subject.

"It's okay, Momma. You can talk about it. We're all family here." Carly tried to encourage Karen. Bob did appear a little uncomfortable, but Nana handed him a longneck beer and that seemed to help a little.

"Well, Justine was there for me when it all happened. But I left town for several months to have your sister, and when I came back, we weren't as close. I didn't tell her who the father was, of course. I didn't tell anyone. In fact, now that I think of it, she's the only one I ever told about my pregnancy, and I swore her to secrecy."

"You told Justine about being pregnant?" Nana held her hand over her heart as if she were shocked by Karen's admission.

"You know, I just remembered it. Things are a little fuzzy from that time. But, yes, Justine knew about the baby. She never said a word to anyone as far as I know." Karen shook her head. "I can't believe I told her now that I think back. I didn't remember trusting anyone with my secret."

Bob made a coughing sound. Tanner wondered if that was intentional. Because he hadn't known about Karen's secret baby. And he was her husband.

Bob's noise hadn't slipped by unnoticed by Karen. "Shut it, Bob."

"So, anything you can tell us about Justine would be helpful. Have you heard from her over the years?" Carly tried to help Karen stay focused.

Karen shook her head. "No. She went to college in New Orleans. I didn't go off to college. I'd met Bob by then and we were engaged my first year after high school." She eyeballed her husband then. It was hard to say if it was in a good way.

"Did you ever communicate with Justine while she was in college?" Carly tried again.

"Maybe. I can't remember. I'll have to give it some thought." Karen's focus was waning, Tanner could tell. Her eyes were straying toward the photos on the table. "What have you found here?"

Carly nudged yet again. "If you think of anything else about Justine, would you let us know, Momma? It's important."

"Oh, sure. She might have come home after she started college. I'll think about it. It's been a long time." Karen had picked up a small stack of photos and started looking through them. "Oh, Momma, remember this?" She held out an old photo to show Nana Elise.

Carly gave up then and shot Tanner a look, as if to say, *We're done here.*

Tanner shrugged his shoulders in understanding. Karen was somewhat flighty. They were lucky to have gotten the information today to kick-start their case. The name of Lisa's grandmother would hopefully be useful in helping find the first clues to Justine's disappearance.

Carly set to clearing the table of everything, and Leah helped their grandmother get the bowls down from the cupboards and the food ready to serve. How big did a pot of chili need to be to serve that many people? A Nana-sized pot, apparently. There were also bowls of shredded cheddar cheese, finely chopped onions, sour cream, and large squares of crumbly corn bread piled high on a platter. Tanner hoped his stomach hadn't growled loudly enough for anyone else to hear.

Tanner was satisfied here for the moment eating well with this loud, odd, and weirdly close family that was so different from his own. He thought about his and Jake's own mother and missed her then, but he was pleased for Jake. That he'd finally married Leah and found happiness and family.

CHAPTER EIGHT

Carly

"I FOUND HER. I found Marie Trichel!" I was searching Google first thing Monday morning. I'd wanted to get to it over the weekend, but Momma had us busy helping her plan the vow renewal. By planning, I meant choosing our matching dresses and flowers. And *that* had been a nightmare.

Tanner was in his office but came to where I worked in the conference room as soon as he heard me. "You found her?"

"I think so. At least I found where she *was*. I'm assuming it's the same woman. She and her husband were living outside Alexandria in Leesfield."

"That's a small town. The one with the lake, right?" Tanner snapped his fingers as if trying to place it. "Jake and I went fishing there once a few years ago."

"Yes. But it appears that her husband, Jay Trichel, passed away a couple years ago from a heart attack. The home was sold by the bank. No mention of what became of Marie." I read from a short newspaper article if one could call it that.

"Hmm. That's odd."

"Here's the obituary for Marie's husband, Jay Trichel. It

states he left behind his loving wife, Marie, was a veteran who'd done a couple tours in Iraq during the Gulf War, had no children, and attended church regularly. No mention of which church. Cut and dried."

Tanner was perched behind me looking over my shoulder, staring at the screen. I could feel his breath on my hair. "Not much to go on. Certainly doesn't say anything more about Marie."

"Do you think it's time to give Lisa a call?" I dared not move a muscle, or I'd be pretty much face-to-face with him. Being this near to Tanner, I was close enough to feel the heat emanating off him. The former crush kicked up at the least convenient times. My heart rate increased, and I felt a little breathy.

"I believe it might be."

"I'm keeping a dated and timed log of my hours dedicated to Lisa's case."

"I assumed you were. We can tally those weekly."

"Okay."

I could tell the second he backed away. His heat left and I was able to breathe normally again. "I'll give Lisa a call. It might be worth a visit to Leesfield to do some asking around about Marie."

I exhaled. "Let me know what Lisa says and I'll keep digging into the court records." Some of the death records might be parish or church ones. In Louisiana, we had parishes instead of counties, unlike every other state in the union. Part of the Napoleonic Code thing. Lawyers here really did have a different bar exam to pass. Like a different country almost.

"I'll call Lisa now."

But before he could make the call, the bells on the office door jingled, so Tanner went to check it out.

I could hear male voices. Not friendly ones.

The bells sounded again, and the door shut.

I stood to go see what was happening.

Tanner showed up at the conference room door before I made it outside. His expression was thunderous. He held a packet in his hand. "I've been served."

Tanner

"SAYS HERE, I'M to cease and desist from the practice of law within the city limits of Cypress Bayou, per the court order of Judge Keller. Pursuant until the complaint by the litigant, Carson Carmichael, is heard before the court."

"How can he do that?" Carly's outrage on his behalf was obvious in her stance and tone. Hands on her hips in clear defiance as if she were ready to go to battle.

"He did it." Tanner had been expecting Carson to do something foul, as he'd promised.

"Is it legal?"

Tanner pulled up a chair in the conference room at the table. "I'm going to read through the summons. I doubt it's a bluff."

Carly paced as he read. Tanner couldn't blame her, and her pacing gave an outlet to the inner emotions he couldn't afford to let out right now. "Did he name me in the suit?"

"No. Thankfully. He didn't have grounds since you never worked for him." This was all utter bullshit though. "Says I didn't give his practice reasonable notice to recover from my leaving. That I harmed clients by leaving with no notice. That I have court dates still scheduled under his business's umbrella and it would be a conflict of interest to operate a separate law practice while I'm still doing business as his associate."

"But you gave him a letter of resignation, right?"

"I did. And I made copies and had them notarized. I also mentioned that I no longer intended to represent those clients in the cases unless he specifically wanted me to continue to do so."

"So, the ball was really in his court to respond to your letter of resignation and what his decision was with regards to the cases you were involved in already on the books. This sounds like a way to keep your business from getting paid for any work until he has his day in court."

"Yes. There's nothing here that can stick legally. He's doing what I thought he might. Throwing a monkey wrench into my plans and causing me as much pain as possible." And that was a relief on the one hand since it was a nothing burger. Except Carson had a way of getting what he wanted within the corrupt little circle of politics here in Cypress Bayou.

Carly paced and frowned. "Is there a way to beat him at his own game?"

"Do you have a plan?"

"No. But maybe there's a way to shame him into withdrawing the suit. It's such a childish thing to do. Is there anyone we could tell about this that would embarrass him? Someone he wouldn't want to know?"

"Carson doesn't shame easily."

"No, I'm certain of that. But can we threaten to discredit him for doing this? This is childish and obvious. He thinks he's got some big-shot reputation. Doesn't he sit on a couple boards around town?"

"Why, yes he does. Carly, you are devious. And brilliant."

She took a mock bow. "I've been called both before. What are you thinking?"

"There's a fundraiser coming up for the Rotary Club. It's all about promoting goodwill and integrity. It's also mission-oriented toward supporting new businesses. If it were to come to the attention of the governing board that Carson was actively undermining his own son's fledgling law practice, it wouldn't shine a positive light on him."

She grinned at him. It was somewhat cunning. "Whoa, I see where you're going with this, and I like it."

Tanner tapped his pen on the notepad that was beside him. "Threatening him with exposure in the Rotary Club is important because they are a national organization that reaches far beyond all the local BS and politics that go on in town. Carson doesn't much care what the locals think of him, but to throw shade on his reputation and his law firm at a state level would do some real damage."

"I *am* brilliant. So, how do we do it?" Carly's eyes held a sparkle at the idea of this most devious plan.

"First, I'll answer the legal complaint with a letter directly to Carson, answering point by point, making him aware that I know nothing in the grievance is legitimate. That I understand he's doing this to stall my business, and I'm waiting for him to answer whether he wants me to see the cases through that I'm already involved with for his clients. I'll also copy Judge Keller on that email, so the judge understands how all this has really gone down."

"I like that idea. The judge doesn't want to fall on the wrong side of things. He's an elected official. Then?"

But Tanner was concerned about how close Carson and Judge Keller were and how they manipulated people with Keller's judiciary power. "Then, I'll fill out an official Rotary Club complaint form listing exactly the ways Carson is prohibiting my business from operating. And I'll include that he's threatened to do everything in his power to ruin me, and that I've got a witness to his threats. I'll also include that we never had a signed contract of employment terms."

"Sounds like he knows it won't work, but it's something he can do to cause you pain and retaliate for you leaving."

"Classic Carson, but I'll have all the documents to support my claims. I won't file the complaint yet but show it all to Carson and strongly suggest he drops the suit immediately."

Carly nodded. "That might work. But keep in mind how angry you're going to make him."

"Maybe he should keep in mind how truly angry he's making *me*. And how by pulling these underhanded schemes, it's only going to get worse for *him*. He's bullied half the people in this town to get what he wants, but nobody will stand up to him. He's not used to that."

"He wants a big reaction. He thrives on getting under

people's skin. I suggest you do what you're going to, but don't speak a word to anyone else. He's waiting for a phone call from you right now. He's sitting there anticipating one. It will drive him nuts if you don't give him a response for a day or two. Then, meet him with your counter."

"You're right. There's nothing I have to do about this immediately. So, let's call Lisa. We can focus on that for now."

So, I put the call on speaker and dialed Lisa's number. "Hello?"

"Hi, Lisa, this is Tanner and Carly. We've got you on speaker."

"Hello there. Is there anything new happening?" Lisa sounded upbeat.

"We've done some research here in town and gotten what might be a lead on Justine's mom, Marie. It seems she remarried after her husband passed away and they moved about an hour south just outside of Alexandria to Leesfield around the time of your birth."

"Well, that's something, isn't it?" Lisa spoke up.

Tanner continued. "Her married name was Trichel, but then he died a couple years ago leaving Marie a widow. I'll send you a copy of the article in the local newspaper. It is ambiguous and doesn't contain much in the way of details for finding Marie, your grandmother."

"So, there's no record of her dying?" Lisa asked.

Carly had a few thoughts on that. "I've been combing through local church records and parish courthouse documents, and so far, I can't find a death notice filed anywhere. I looked her up in the state database as well. And she isn't listed as having a current address that I can find."

"What do y'all suggest we do next?" Lisa's voice had a hint of excitement Tanner hadn't heard before.

"I think a day trip to Leesfield is the likely next step." Tanner spoke into the phone then. "You are welcome to accompany us."

"So, we go there and start asking around about her?"

"We start at her last known address, which was sold by the bank when her husband died, according to the newspaper, but there might still be a neighbor or two who will remember her."

"Yes, I'd love to come and try to find out what became of her."

"How does tomorrow around noon sound?" Tanner suggested. He lifted a brow in question to Carly.

She nodded with a smile. He could tell she was eager to get out and help find Marie Trichel.

"That sounds fantastic. I'll meet you both at the office."

"We'll see you then."

Tanner disconnected the call and suddenly felt relieved that they were refocused on helping their client instead of worrying about the summons from Carson.

Carly

"I'LL MAKE A list of all the places we can check to see if Marie might still be around town. Or, if anybody might know where she went." I was still smarting over Carson's unexpected serving of a lawsuit to Tanner.

He seemed less angry and worried over it than me now. I guess that might be the age or maturity thing. I wanted to do something about it *right now* despite what I'd said about not giving Carson the satisfaction of an immediate response. That sounded good and rational, but it was eating at me.

"You okay?" He must have noticed my frown. I could feel it indenting my brow.

I huffed a big sigh. "Yes. I guess so. As much as I know there's nothing to be done about it this second, it burns me that Carson served you with a cease and desist."

He nodded. "It burns me too, but you're right about him wanting a big response. We've got a good plan and I'm going to do my best to stick with it."

I stood and started pacing again. And frowning.

"Nope, let's not do that again. I'm getting you out of here and into the fresh air and sunshine. C'mon, we're going fishing."

"Fishing?" I couldn't compute what he was saying.

"Yes. Go home and put on fishing clothes. Something you don't mind getting dirty and stinky. And some sunscreen and a hat."

"I've got work to do. Who goes fishing in the middle of a Monday?" This plan sounded terribly irresponsible.

"We do. I'm the boss and we can discuss work stuff in the boat."

"The boat? We're going fishing in a boat?"

"Yes, and don't forget the hat. It'll keep the sun off your face. Wouldn't want to burn your face." He stared at me then. Right into my eyes, as if he liked my eyes. *Had he lost his mind?*

I got that old crushy feeling then out of the blue. Like I was thirteen. But I wasn't thirteen, and I knew what I felt wasn't crushy, it was a bolt of desire. For. My. Boss.

"Okay, fine. I'll go fishing with you, but I think it's the wrong move. We've got a lot to do to get this place up to full steam. I realize we're not official yet, especially now, since Carson has essentially shut things down until we deal with his bogus lawsuit, but there's still a *lot.*"

"Shhhh...now, go." He made a circle motion with his finger for me to turn and then pointed toward the door.

Thankfully, that stopped my idiotic babble and had me retreating out the door. I babbled because I wanted to throw myself at him and do all the things with him that young associates should *never* do with their older, very hot bosses.

Tanner called at my back. "I'll see you on my dock in forty-five minutes. Feel free to pick up lunch on the way over if you're hungry."

"Are *you* hungry?" I turned back around as I asked the question.

"Always." He grinned.

I got my bearings as I drove the short distance from the office to Nana's house. The leaves on the trees even sparkled after the heavy rains over the weekend. Cypress Bayou was bursting with every kind of bloom. Magnolias, gardenias, hydrangeas. The sky was bright blue with a few puffy clouds. A perfect day for fishing since it wasn't too hot.

The unexpected burst of pure lust for Tanner had been unnerving. I'd been on edge, sure, but when he'd looked at me like that—well—something had changed. And he *had* given me a look. I knew that I was physically attractive to men, despite my personality flaws. Tanner didn't seem to have that problem with me. But I also knew that our crossing a professional line was not smart. It was really the worst possible thing we could do for our relationship. So, I would ignore whatever that was.

And I guess I didn't blame Tanner for wanting to get our minds off the lawsuit and enjoy the day. Plus, I was kind of driving him crazy with my pacing and fretting about it.

"I didn't expect you to come home this time of day." Nana entered from the direction of the sunroom when she heard me in the kitchen.

"Tanner's decided we should go fishing."

To Nana's credit, she didn't seem to think this was an unusual idea. "I've got half a sweet watermelon balled in a container you can take with you. Also, make a couple turkey and honey-mustard sandwiches. There's fresh turkey from the deli. Oh, and don't forget those Zapp's potato chips you like from the pantry."

And just like that, we had a killer lunch for our unexpected fishing trip. I grabbed a small cooler and ice pack and a couple root beers and waters from the fridge. "Thanks, Nana."

She handed me a floppy straw hat from the hook inside the back door. "Protect that flawless complexion while you've still got it, my girl."

I'd changed into jean shorts, a pink cotton tank, and white deck shoes. And yes, I had a bottle of sunscreen and my sunglasses, along with a beach towel. Where there was a body of water, there was always a possibility of getting wet.

Growing up along the bayou and near Lake Breaux, we understood how easy it was to plan to not get wet and still end up in the water. Often, it was intentional and part of the fun of getting together with friends. Louisiana was hot and muggy a good part of the year, and swimming, waterskiing, floating around on rafts or whatever we could find to cool off was a part of our growing up. So, yes, I always brought a towel with me.

CHAPTER NINE

D ADDY LOVED TO fish, and we'd had a small aluminum boat with an outboard motor he kept on a trailer for fishing days. Leah and I both fished with him, sometimes together. We wore our bikinis so we could get some sun and take a dip in the water when it got hot. Momma, on the other hand, did not like to fish, but she was agreeable to cooking whatever we caught that was within the legal limit. Fishing got us out of her hair, and we got to spend time with Daddy.

I carried the cooler and slung my blue-and-white-striped beach/pool/lake bag over my shoulder when I got to Tanner's place. His land was gorgeous. Well, his and Jake's. Mature oaks shaded the slow-sloped banks. I vaguely remembered the old house that had once been there. Land like this was valuable along the bayou.

"What've you got there?" Tanner emerged from his shiny silver Airstream trailer wearing a ball cap, a pair of blue swim trunks, and a T-shirt that appeared to be older than me, judging by the faded purple logo from Northwestern State that was barely discernible against the heather-gray background. On his feet were a pair of water sandals that had also seen better days, or years, as the case might be.

"Nana fixed us up with a picnic lunch."

"Gotta love that." He grinned from behind the classic Ray-Bans, and my stomach kicked. He was a gorgeous man. I wondered if he knew it because he didn't act like a guy who knew it. I didn't know if I'd ever seen him out with a woman here in town.

"Yes, she never misses an opportunity to feed me well." Tanner had a small aluminum boat with only a trolling motor at the front tied to the dock, which told me he didn't go far to find his fish. "What are we fishing for today?"

"White perch, if they're biting, and maybe some bream." He had four rods with reels in the boat already. Two with red and white corks to float the hooks to catch bream, and two with weights to pull the hook to lower, cooler depths for catching the perch.

"Crickets and shiners?" I asked. Shiners referred to small bait minnows used to catch white perch, or crappie, as they were also called. The minnows had to be kept in a Styrofoam bucket in coldish water so they would stay alive and active. The crickets were, well, crickets.

Casual looked good on Tanner, and discussing bait and gear gave my tummy a little tingle. This was a different side to him, and I liked it.

"I stopped by the bait store on my way home." He held up a little screened bucket to show me the live crickets crawling around inside. "The shiners looked pretty good. Big."

He grabbed the bucket with the shiners still in the plastic bag filled with air and water for safe transport from the store.

"If we catch any, you get to clean them." I drew the line at fileting fish. I remember helping Daddy as a kid, but it was a skill I'd never become proficient at.

"Deal. But you've got to stay for dinner." His eyebrows lifted.

"Only if we fry them." There was nothing like fresh, cornmeal-crusted, fried fish from the lake or bayou. What we called the bayou had some pretty fresh water and moved enough to keep from becoming too marshy, especially in the area where Tanner lived. There were some parts farther down that were a tad bit swampier. But cypress trees, hung with moss, grew along most of the banks, giving the appearance of a slower-moving traditional bayou.

"Deal."

We climbed into the small boat—much smaller now with the two of us and all our gear. Tanner was a large man. And he smelled like sunscreen and sunshine.

Tanner

"I'M IMPRESSED BY your skills."

Carly's cast landed her wiggly cricket a foot from a floating piece of dead wood beside the bank. "We fished a lot as kids with Daddy."

"That's obvious. Not everybody has such a way with a rod and reel." Had that sounded suggestive?

She shot him a look that said it had, but he was spared her comment when she got a hit on her bait. "I've got one." She reeled and pulled the slack, reeled, then pulled, handling the catch without a lot of drama. Like an old pro. Tanner grabbed the net when she got the fish close enough.

"Looks like you've got a good-size bass there." They'd caught a half-dozen bream between them so far. This was the first bass.

"Not bad for a cricket as bait."

"We can rig up a couple rods for bass fishing if they're biting." The hooks for bass fishing were significantly larger and more substantial than for bream since the mouths on the fish were much bigger. Bass fishing was a little more involved, mostly using rubber worms and a lot of casting outside the boat, but when bass were biting, you had to get them when they were hot.

Carly struggled a little to reel in the fish. "He's a big guy. Should feed us both." Tanner could tell Carly was excited about her catch. He scooped the fish the moment she'd reeled it close enough as it flopped to avoid capture. They both laughed as the fishy lake water hit them square in the face. "Might want to put on a little more sunscreen. Looks like your nose is getting a bit pink."

"Yes. I guess if we're going to be out here awhile, I'd better." Tanner had stared at her nose for a second too long and he hoped she hadn't noticed.

Tanner snapped the live well that held their catch shut and used the foot pedal on the troll motor to guide the boat back toward the dock.

"Oh, are we going back?" Carly seemed surprised.

"Um, nature's calling me. I thought we might want to wash our hands and use an actual bathroom. If I were out here by myself, I would do things a little differently."

Carly laughed. "Yes. I guess I could use a handwashing

too." Code word for bathroom.

By the time they'd both gone to the bathroom, washed hands, and unpacked the food, it was almost three o'clock. They ate under Tanner's retractable awning in the shade. He had a small picnic table set up outside.

"This is nice." Carly did indeed have a bit of sunburn on her face.

"Thanks. It works well most of the time. I like the solitude." And he did, most of the time. But he had to admit that it was nice sitting here with her having lunch. The fishing was fun too. How long had it been since he'd shared anything with a woman? Too long, probably. His history with women and dating wasn't anything much worth sharing.

He'd had a serious girlfriend, a fiancée even, but Kerry-Ann had gotten a better offer. She'd gotten into Harvard Law after a deferral at the end of their first year at LSU. So, she went. A long-distance relationship hadn't been an option at the time. The workload and time required by school was all-consuming. She'd chosen her career over Tanner. And he hadn't blamed her. But it had hurt, badly.

His heart was worth protecting, though it was probably time to allow himself to ease up on the care he took with not getting hurt. At some point he wanted what his brother had. He wanted a family. Maybe a couple kids. He'd heard from a former classmate that Kerry-Ann was living her best life practicing law in Boston. It only caused a twinge now.

"The watermelon is sweet for this early in the season." Carly wiped a drip of watermelon juice from her chin. "Nana says it's a Sugartown melon from Beauregard Parish. They're the best."

"Yes. Mom would drive as far as she had to for those when we were kids. I remember how happy she was when they put up a roadside stand off the highway between here and Alexandria." He reached over and grabbed a small ball of ripe, red melon. Despite Carson, their mother had worked hard to make a nice home for them, always doing fun things with her boys.

"Your mom was a nice lady." Carly smiled as if she was remembering. "One time she came over and brought Momma some yellow roses from her garden. They sat and drank coffee in the kitchen, and I eavesdropped on their conversation."

"That sounds sneaky."

Carly laughed out loud. "They were trying to figure out how to keep Jake and Leah from having sex, or how to keep them from getting pregnant maybe. I was *scandalized.*"

"Talk about a fly on the wall."

"So, you know my momma, right? She was all: 'They need more Jesus!' And your mother was such a lady about it all. She was like: 'I'm not sure Jesus is going to fix what's happening here. Maybe we should make sure they're being responsible.'"

Tanner was so entertained by Carly. He could picture her hiding and listening to their mothers' conversation as a young girl. And she was right about the very different perspectives of their mothers. His mom was all about responsibility and kindness.

"Now that we know Momma had a secret baby when she was sixteen, I get why she was so nutty about things like

Leah and me having sex as teens. She turned to her religion to absolve her from all her sins, so it makes sense she would've done the same when it came to us."

Tanner nodded. "It does put things into a better perspective now, doesn't it?"

"If she'd only been able to share her big secret and unburden herself all those years ago, maybe she wouldn't have ended up such a hot mess."

"At least y'all know now and can take her past into consideration in certain situations." Tanner didn't want to speak harshly about her mother even knowing how oddly Karen Bertrand acted in certain situations.

"You're too kind." Carly rolled her eyes. "We appreciate how you and Jake overlook her bad behavior when she gets cranked up."

"As long as you don't hold Carson against us."

"I think it's time to go back to fishing since you've said the 'C' word."

"I think you're right."

Carly

I COULDN'T BELIEVE how much fun I was having. I'd always enjoyed fishing, but I was seriously enjoying Tanner's company. He was funny. This wasn't the serious, alpha dog I'd always known Tanner to be.

Among our family, he was known to be overly protective, serious, and a bit of a pain when it came to having fun. And though he'd been pleasant since we'd been working together, I'd gotten only glimpses of a different side of his personality. But he'd been stressed since hiring me, so there hadn't been a lot of opportunity thus far, until today, for Tanner to lighten up.

Today, he'd made the effort to pull back from the stress and dedicate this afternoon to having a nice time. For my sake. I'd been the one pacing and frowning, after all.

By the time we pulled back up to the dock, our live well was almost full to the legal limit with bass, bream, and white perch. We were sweaty, hot, and smelled like fish. It was a little past five o'clock and the sun was dipping below the tree line.

"I'm going to call Jake and Leah to see about getting some help cleaning these. Plus, there's no way we can eat them all ourselves." Tanner transferred the still-alive fish to a Styrofoam cooler. They flipped and flopped, and I helped him corral one that almost gained its freedom.

"Do you need me to get some ice for those?" I asked, knowing it was best to clean them almost immediately once they came out of the live well. They could stay on ice for a while, otherwise.

"I grabbed a couple extra bags at the bait store. They're in the big cooler."

"Look at you assuming we'd catch something."

"There's beer in there too."

"Win-win."

"Why don't you go on home and take a quick shower? I'll clean the fish and set up the cooking pot."

A shower sounded marvelous right now. I couldn't remember the last time I smelled so bad. "Okay, text me a list to bring back from the store."

"Great. I think I'm low on cornmeal."

I gave him a thumbs-up and headed up the hill to where I'd parked. I laid my towel across the seat to avoid any possible fish contamination from my stinky self. Within seconds of pulling onto the street, my sister called. "Y'all went fishing on a Monday?"

"Are you surprised by that?" I rolled the window down halfway because I refused to turn on the AC and get the smell sucked into my car's air filter.

"I'm surprised he took you fishing is all. I'm having a hard time picturing it. Tanner doesn't often take Jake fishing. It's his alone time thing he does when he's stressed."

I would only share a little about that. "He is stressed right now, but I think he took me fishing to de-stress me more than him. I was pacing and it might have gotten on his nerves."

"Why are y'all so stressed? Has something happened?" Leah suddenly sounded suspicious.

"Can't really talk about it right now. He's the one having to deal with some stuff." It wasn't my place to discuss the lawsuit and Carson's shenanigans.

"Uh-huh. Something that's got *you* pacing enough that he took you fishing on a Monday?"

"I'd hoped you were calling to tell me that y'all are coming to eat fish with us tonight at the trailer. I'm headed home to shower and get more stuff for dinner."

"We're coming, all right. What can I bring?"

"Hmm. Dessert? But *not* Jell-O salad. Nobody likes that

but you and Momma. Maybe get something up in town if you can."

"Everybody loves Jell-O salad but you. Anyway, I just picked up some mini peach cobbler Bundt cakes from Sheri's on Washington Street. I saw she had them on special on her Facebook page. I've been craving peach cobbler lately."

"Sounds like a winner. Wait, why are you craving peach cobbler? Are you pregnant?"

Leah laughed at that. "No. Of course not. Wait. I don't think so. No, of course not. I like peach cobbler is all."

"Well, bring it with you. But you might want to check into whether you're pregnant." Pregnancy for Leah was a sensitive subject, as she'd had a miscarriage several years ago, well before she and Jake had gotten back together for good. "Leah?" She'd gone silent. "Are you still there?"

"I'm here. I'm pretty sure I'm not pregnant."

"Okay. I'll see you soon."

I invited Nana to our impromptu fish fry as soon as I arrived at her house.

"Darlin,' y'all go on and have a nice evening. I've got a couple programs I'm planning to watch on the Netflix tonight." But of course, by the time I'd showered and was ready to leave, she sent me on my way with a homemade jar of tartar sauce and a fresh lettuce and tomato salad with chopped red onions and crumbled feta cheese. She was a magic food lady.

CHAPTER TEN

TANNER HAD CLEARLY taken a shower while I'd been gone. His hair was still damp, and he smelled like soap and deodorant as he helped me carry things from my car. I'd noticed that about him in the office, that he wasn't a cologne wearer, but he always smelled good.

He'd gotten some sun today, same as me. At some point this afternoon, he'd taken off his shirt in the boat, with my permission. So, I assume, he'd gotten plenty of sun on his back and torso. His lean, muscular torso. Taking off shirts is what guys did out in the boat, so it wasn't unexpected. But, dang, he was getting under my skin, and I swear he didn't have a clue.

I could smell the seasonings and spices as the hot oil did its magic, crisping the cornmeal crust. Frying fish was a rite of passage around here. Everybody did it. We all had a big fry pot that doubled as a crawfish pot setup and a tank of liquid butane so that the messy cooking could be done outdoors. He'd made hush puppies and french fries.

"Do you think Nana would share her tartar sauce recipe?" Tanner asked as we all sat together eating at the picnic table outside.

"Nana doesn't believe in keeping secret family recipes, so sure she will," Leah answered. "But I'll let you know that hers is always better."

"Are you accusing your sainted grandmother of leaving out an ingredient or two when she shares her recipes?" Jake placed his hand over his heart as if the shock might kill him.

We all laughed at that idea. "I can't say she would do it on purpose, but since she doesn't actually use written recipes, the retelling of them might lose something in translation."

A shadow fell over the group. "Well, well, looks like I wasn't on the guest list."

In our laughter, we hadn't noticed Carson's approach. His arrival was the proverbial wet blanket on the evening, as all laughter ended abruptly like the sudden scratching on a vinyl record when the music is interrupted. Tanner stood from his seat at the end of the table, towering over the older man. "What are you doing here?"

"I didn't hear from you, so I decided to stop by and make sure you got my message." Carson's smile was as dead eyed as the fish heads in the bucket that sat waiting to be disposed of some twenty feet away.

"What message?" Jake stood up and moved next to his brother.

"You didn't tell him?" Carson's surprise couldn't be masked in that split second before he slipped back into his slimy, satisfied grin.

"Carson had me served with papers today in a childish attempt to keep me from running my practice. But since he's got no claim on anything I do, I went fishing. I decided to deal with it tomorrow." Tanner waved a dismissive hand toward Carson as if he was nothing more than an irritation.

Jake narrowed his eyes at their father, then wrinkled his

nose in distaste. "Are you afraid your clients will all move to Tanner's law firm and leave you? What a cowardly thing to do."

Carson obviously hadn't expected this response. He was accustomed to people cowering in fear at his big and powerful threats.

"It's okay, Jake. When people in the Rotary and on the state bar association get wind of what he's trying to do to me and my business, he'll be even more disrespected than he is now. And *that's* saying something." Tanner pointed a finger at Carson to make his point.

Carson blanched for a second. The bar association. Carson had power here in Cypress Bayou and maybe he had some pull here and there beyond, but not in the state bar. The hint of disbarment would shrivel him.

I had to give it to Tanner for slinging that threat, along with the Rotary Club, of course. But I kept silent, not wanting to add more gasoline to this potential fire. I could tell Carson had been bested, and he knew it too. But someone like Carson could never back down.

"I guess we'll see who comes out on top, won't we?" Carson narrowed his eyes at Tanner, and then shifted them toward me. "Too bad you threw in with this lot. He'll take you down with him."

I stood and stepped forward, my anger ignited. "I'm not afraid of you, Carson. You might be able to intimidate other people, but not me. Be careful with your threats and remember that I know the law. You're not the only one who can litigate."

Carson's eyes flashed with an ugly anger. He pointed a

long, bony white finger at me. "Be careful, little girl. Just be careful."

He then stalked up the hill without acknowledging Leah at all.

Tanner

TANNER STIFLED THE strong urge to follow his father and physically drag him back down the hill and beat him to a pulp. Of course he wouldn't, and could never, because that would give Carson the kind of sick satisfaction he longed for.

Jake demanded of both him and Carly, "Why didn't y'all tell us what Carson had done?"

Tanner and Carly shared a look. "We refused to let him get to us. We decided on a plan and then went fishing." Tanner tried to explain it to his brother. "It didn't require anything other than what we did." Jake, he knew, was protective of him and of Carly.

"Looks like it worked. He left here pretty riled up, didn't he?" Carly pointed toward where Carson had gone. "Attention was what he wanted and when he didn't get any, he came here to see why not."

"Pretty smart thinking, you two. That kind of restraint is remarkable. I don't think I could have done it." Leah despised Carson for all the things he'd said and done over the years while she and Jake had been together, so she tended to get a little hotheaded in her response to him. The fact that she hadn't said a word as she watched the exchange this evening amazed Tanner.

"I guess our surprise when you told us about the lawsuit worked in your favor. His face. I mean, that really was priceless, man." Jake laughed and slapped Tanner on the back.

So few times throughout the years had Tanner or Jake been able best Carson when it came to a battle of wits or cunning. This was a small victory they could both appreciate.

"Anybody want peach cobbler and ice cream?" Leah offered, changing the sour subject.

They all chimed in and gathered back together at the table for dessert. But Tanner knew this wasn't over by a long shot. With Carson, nothing ever was. At least for now, they could celebrate this small victory. What might it be like to have a father who behaved as if he truly cared about his children? The thought made Tanner more determined than ever that if he did have his own kids someday, they would come first in his life. Their hearts, emotions, and their well-being.

"So, any luck with finding the mystery woman for your client?" Leah asked once they were all eating the delicious sweets.

"We're going to Leesfield tomorrow with Lisa to do some looking around for her grandmother, Marie Trichel," Carly answered her sister.

"Wasn't that where we caught all the catfish that time, Tanner?" Jake asked.

"We nearly sank the boat, they were so big." Tanner laughed as he held his arms wide, emphasizing the size of the catfish they'd caught. It had been a stellar fishing trip.

"A fishy tale if I ever heard one." Leah scoffed at his exaggeration.

It hit Tanner how happy and relieved he was that Jake had come home to stay. He'd recently signed a contract at Cypress General for a permanent staff position. Before that, Jake had traveled all over the state to help diagnose cases with his team. Now, doctors came to him for help with tough cases. They sent him blood work, test results, scans, and anything else needed to help their patients.

Jake's team had a home base here and worked to help others without traveling, except on rare occasions. Now that Leah was back from Paris, they were always available as added support. Tanner hadn't realized how much he'd missed them being together. As a family. Plus, it meant Leah's family came as part of the network.

Before, Tanner had been here in his hometown, and sure, he had friends, but he wasn't a super social guy. But being here now, with a larger network of support, was likely why he'd had the courage to make the break and start his own law firm. It felt like going to battle with an army at his back instead of nearly alone. Timing was everything.

Carly

BY THE TIME we'd cleaned up and gotten everything back to normal, it was around ten o'clock. Jake had an early meeting at the hospital and Leah was headed to New Orleans in the morning to do some work on her new art gallery. Since she'd moved back home from Paris, Leah had bought an art loft in the Bywater area on the Mississippi Riverbank. She had plans to assist local artists by giving them a place to paint and show their work.

The loft had a living space upstairs, so Leah was able to make trips there and stay on the premises while she got the place ready. The local manager she'd hired lived a couple blocks from the gallery, so they worked for a few days at a time together when Leah was in town.

This commute had been the trade-off for selling her half of a popular Paris art gallery Leah had inherited from her boss and best friend, Alaine, when he'd passed away a year ago. Leah was using the money as his legacy to do the most good for artists. New Orleans was a gold mine for talent in the state and was only a four-hour drive from Cypress Bayou.

I hated that she was gone so much, but it was better than her being in Paris and never coming home like before.

"Thanks for hanging around to help clean up." Tanner pulled me out of my thinking. He was holding a garbage bag that held something that appeared heavy and wet.

"What kind of friend would I be if I left you with the mess after such a great dinner?"

"Well, I appreciate it. I'd better get these into the freezer before the flies get wind of them." He indicated the bag he was holding. I assumed they were the fish guts. Daddy always double-bagged them and put them in the freezer until he could bring them to the dump.

I gathered up the remaining items sitting outside on the table and brought them inside his Airstream trailer. I had to admit it was nice. Since I hadn't been inside it before today,

I wasn't sure what to expect.

It was small, but clean. Obviously newish. There was a flat-screen TV, a leather sofa, a tiny kitchen area with a banquette nook that looked like it might somehow double as a sleeper if one needed it. At the front end, there was a queen-sized bed, made up with a down comforter and several pillows. I'd used the little bathroom earlier and wondered how a big guy like Tanner managed to shower in there.

For a single person who had a temporary plan, it wasn't a bad one. Plus, the outdoor living here was pleasant. The weather was mild most of the time, except in the hottest part of the summer. Or when it rained, which right now was often, but only for an hour or so, usually in the afternoons.

I noticed Tanner had a bug zapper that trapped flies and mosquitoes. A must for someone who enjoyed the outdoors in such a bug-rich environment. There was a colorful oversized hammock strung nearby between two hardwoods that appeared especially comfortable. The whole setup was cozy and inviting. Plus, he had no neighbors. Perfect for a somewhat introverted guy like Tanner.

A couple acres over, however, Jake and Leah had recently started building their home. It was far enough away to not bother Tanner, but close enough for him to hear the construction and for the trucks and workmen to enter and exit the same drive. They were building their own dock, so I guessed that was a good thing.

Tanner and Jake were a lot like Leah and me, as siblings went. We were all each other had. We appreciated that the other was different but got along most of the time and were each other's best friend. So, living pretty much next door would likely be a good thing for the brothers.

I did wonder how things would change for Leah and me though once Allison became part of our lives on a regular basis. *If* she really were to move here permanently. She was older than us by a few years and hadn't had the shared experiences we did. So far, Allison wasn't showing a strong interest in becoming an equal third sister.

She'd been here for a short time while she recovered from the bone marrow transplant several months back. The family had brought her food, checked on her, and texted. I was still living in Baton Rouge at the time, so I'd been more distant than the others, and I knew her the least. She seemed like a strong personality though. Had traveled as an army brat, was a great cook, apparently, and loved to paint and do crafts and such, from what I was told.

I guess there were worse things than getting to know my older sister. Time would tell for sure. Change was inevitable now that Allison was part of our family tree. And if Momma had her way, we would see her in June.

Speaking of Momma, we were scheduled to have another planning session tomorrow night at Nana's house, where Leah and I would show our picks for dresses. Momma had decided on shades of lavender and purple as the color for the ceremony. My least favorite.

But tomorrow was also our day trip to Leesfield, so that was a far more interesting thing to look forward to.

WE MET AT the office at nine o'clock sharp. I decided jeans

and a lightweight top were best for our purposes. Not sticking out was key. Too dressy in a rural town wouldn't serve us, but then neither would too casual, as we wanted to appear professional. Tanner wore boots and dark jeans paired with a button-down shirt. I was glad to see that Lisa's shoes were sensible for walking today. I could tell she was accustomed to high-end brands. Her slacks and blouse weren't showy, but they were clearly expensive.

"Good morning, ladies. I cleaned out my truck for our short trip today." Tanner's truck was big, but it was new and nice. I decided to let Lisa choose where she wanted to sit.

"Thanks, Tanner. I'll let Carly ride shotgun, as I'm sure the two of you have things to discuss."

"Are you sure?" I hated sticking her in the back. Lisa approached the truck and used the running board on the side of the truck to get inside before Tanner could assist her. Case closed, I guess.

"Ready?" He lifted a brow at me.

"Let's do it." I didn't wait for his gallant assistance either, though I believed he would provide it should I show a need.

The truck's black interior was spotless. "This is very nice, Tanner." Lisa commented on it as I was thinking the same thing. I'd had the same thoughts when I was in his trailer; he was neat for a single man.

"Thank you."

He smelled of the same clean soap and deodorant I'd noticed when I'd arrived last night. But now, we were together in close quarters. Maybe I should have insisted Lisa sit up front. I felt myself wanting to lean closer to his big man body. More and more.

"So, what's our plan?" Lisa sounded upbeat and ready for the adventure.

"I thought we could start by stopping by Marie's home and looking around, maybe speaking to a few neighbors, and asking around about Marie and her husband." I'd made an agenda. Mainly ideas of where we might go in town. "Next, we can go to the courthouse and ask for any documents that were filed with her name. Those folks tend to know everyone in town, so even if there aren't any documents on file, we might get something."

"Sounds like a good start." Lisa was quiet during the ride south on I-49. I spent my time working on my iPad on office business. I'd set up Tanner on Instagram and Facebook with business pages last week. He already had over a hundred "likes" on his professional Facebook page. I'd added several photos of the office and of him. He insisted that I add myself on the page as his assistant and include a headshot as well. It made sense to show an accurate representation of his firm, what kinds of cases we would handle, and who clients could expect to handle them.

I noticed a small red notification badge on the Facebook page. Someone had commented that they were aware the firm was being sued for Tanner's breach of contract for leaving his previous place of employment, and did anyone really want a lawbreaker to represent them?

"Did you see this comment on Facebook?" I quietly brought it to Tanner's attention.

"No. I haven't checked the site. What does it say?"

I quietly read it to him. "Looks like Carson's doing, or one of his minions."

"Can you get rid of it?"

I nodded. "I'm not sure if I should be transparent and address it or delete it."

Tanner frowned but kept his eyes on the road. "Delete it and maybe block the person who wrote it? And if it comes back, then we can address it."

I made a note of the name—no one I recognized—and deleted the comment, but not before I clicked on the commenter's name to try and figure out who he was. The guy had a private account, so I couldn't see anything about him. "Private account. Do you know a Joe Davies?"

Tanner shook his head. "Doesn't ring any bells."

"Probably a phony account." I blocked the user from making any more comments on the page.

I shut the laptop after about an hour and looked around. Everything was green in Louisiana now. So many shades of green. Pines, hardwoods, and every kind of grass and flowering plant. Thankfully, the yellow pine pollen that blew through earlier in the spring was long gone. My allergies had come and gone with it. There was no avoiding them for most people throughout the South. Leah suffered with terrible migraines during allergy season. I was fortunate to never have had them.

"Everything okay?" I looked over at him and realized he was talking to me.

"Yes. Just enjoying the green."

He smiled. "It's my favorite time of the year. Not too hot yet."

"It's gonna get hot soon enough. It was eighty-five down in New Orleans last week," Lisa chimed in.

"What part of the city do you live in?" I admitted to being a little curious about Lisa. She hadn't overshared about her personal life.

"I live uptown just off Napoleon Avenue." She said it like it was no big deal, like someone not trying to impress.

"That's a nice area." Tanner had gone to law school at Tulane, in New Orleans, so he also knew the city well. And Napoleon Avenue was one of the nicest parts of New Orleans. Expensive old mansions mostly. Lisa did say she'd grown up in a family with money. I'd spent quite a bit of time in New Orleans as well since it was only an hour from Baton Rouge and LSU, where I attended school.

"Yes. My husband, Doug, is a doctor at Touro. An oncologist." Again, her tone wasn't trying to impress; only stating the facts.

"Oh. I look forward to meeting him." I honestly didn't know what else to say. This was the first time she'd mentioned a husband, though I'd noticed a wedding ring. A gorgeous one.

"He's calling this a *wild goose chase*. He's not against my doing it, but he's worried I'll be terribly disappointed if I don't find what I'm looking for. And he's a little worried about how much it's going to cost. Good thing I've got my own money to spend."

She sounded somewhat sad that her husband wasn't enthusiastic about her search. She didn't sound especially angry, though. Just disappointed.

I tried to sound positive. "Hopefully, we'll get lucky today and learn something."

"That would make this a good day."

CHAPTER ELEVEN

Tanner

TANNER FOUND THE address using the GPS navigation. It was still wet here, but the rain had moved on. Marie and Jay Trichel had lived in a small shotgun house set back from the packed-shell road. These narrow houses had one hallway down the center length of the structure, with all the rooms on either side of the hallway. The idea was, if a bullet from a shotgun were to enter the front door, it would pass through the entire house without hitting anything before passing out the back door.

There were loads of shotgun houses all over Louisiana, but mostly in the southern part of the state down in New Orleans and throughout the rural bayou areas. This was farther north, but plenty could still be found. Built in the time of the Civil War until around the 1920s, they were a thing of necessity during hard times, but enduring all the same.

"This is the house?" Lisa stood staring at her grandmother's house on Lemon Street. There was a tiny pond out back that a few other homes backed up to as well. The homes were well spaced, not exactly a neighborhood, but not completely rural either.

It was clearly old, the paint peeled and cracked where it once had been painted white. The number seven on the house had lost its top screw and was hanging like an L. "This is it. Number 227 Lemon Street."

"It appears empty now." There were several cracked and broken windows, but still there were curtains that hung inside. The full porch seemed a sad protector of the home at this late stage.

They stood on the white packed-shell driveway where the grass grew in a strip between the old tire tracks. Weeds and dandelions were mixed with the grass. It was…unkept.

"Says on Zillow that the property is for sale, but I don't see a sign." Carly looked it up on her phone.

"I guess it doesn't really matter, does it?" Lisa sounded disappointed.

A large, noisy, truck pulled up, its engine vibrating without a muffler, the stink of exhaust nearly overwhelming. "Y'all folks looking for something out here?"

Tanner had to look up to see the occupants of the truck. Two males, dirty, covered in tattoos, leered at them. "We're looking for my friend's grandmother. She's been out of touch for a while."

"Now, how'd you go about losing your granny, little missy?" The passenger asked his question of Lisa, then spit a long stream of tobacco juice not far from Tanner's boot, but he didn't flinch.

Lisa's eyes narrowed, and Tanner hoped she wouldn't lose her cool with these two, who were clearly troublemaking. "Not sure. Did you know her? She lived here." Lisa pointed to the house.

"Naw, un-uh. That there house has been empty for a few years. Just some kids doin' dope up inside sometimes. Don't know any grannies who lived there."

"Thank you for your help." Tanner lifted a hand to the two guys and made eye contact with both Carly and Lisa and cut his eyes toward his own truck, hoping they got the message to move that way.

"Y'all sure you don't need anything else? We've got *resources* if you know what I mean." Drugs, for sure.

"Thanks, but we're heading out now. Appreciate the information." He unlocked the truck and both Lisa and Carly both didn't waste a second getting inside. Tanner climbed in before things could escalate with the drug dealers.

"Nice truck. Them's expensive." He hooted to his buddy. "I'd like to have me a nice truck like that someday, wouldn't you, Darrell? And some pretty ladies to ride in it with us."

Darrell, aka, tobacco-spitter, howled with laughter. "I'd like me some tail like that, for shore."

Tanner was certain these two were armed to the teeth inside that monster-polluter truck of theirs. "We've got an appointment at the courthouse in a few minutes. Nice to meet you both." Tanner had heard both women buckle their seat belts as soon as they'd climbed inside, so he threw up a wave and took off.

"Are they following us?" There was an edge to Lisa's voice.

Tanner kept one eye on his rearview mirror as he drove at top speed directly toward the courthouse, which also housed the parish sheriff's department, as was common in small towns across the state. Fortunately, these guys weren't likely to want to race Tanner to that destination.

"Looks like we're in the clear." The courthouse was only a two-mile drive from where they'd been.

"Maybe you shouldn't have told them where to find us." Was that a touch of sarcasm from Carly?

"Yes, but what outlaw's going to follow somebody to the police station?"

She snorted. "Touché. But you might consider parking out back among the patrol cars."

That wasn't a bad idea. The back lot had several large black SUVs with the parish law enforcement logo on them. Tanner's black truck could easily be missed among them. "Good call."

They looked around before heading inside the rear entrance of the courthouse. No outlaws in sight. "What an adventure we're having today." Lisa gave a nervous laugh.

Once inside, they made their way to the front desk inside the lobby. A woman with large glasses that hung on a chain greeted the trio. Well, she mostly greeted Tanner. "Well, hello, sir, and how may I help you on this fine day?"

He stepped forward and gave her a quick head nod and noticed her nametag. "Hi there, Rose. We're from Cypress Bayou in Natchitoches Parish and wondered if you could help us. My friend Lisa here is looking for her grandmother, Marie Trichel. She lived on Lemon Street several years ago, but we can't figure out where she's gone."

The woman's brows knitted, and her expression was almost comical. "Your grandma's gone and disappeared on you?" She directed the question at Lisa. It was slightly reminiscent of the outlaw's same: *How'd you lose your granny?*

Lisa cleared her throat. "The sad truth is I never knew her. It's a bit of a search for my history. I was so hoping somebody here could help me find her." Lisa's plea was a little over the top. But it seemed that a bit of drama was called for here.

"Oooh. Like a DNA search or what have you? Everybody looking for their people. Well, let's see what we've got, darlin'. Trichel with a *ch*?" Lisa nodded, then the woman's fingers flew across her keyboard.

They waited a few minutes while Rose made some noises as she searched. A few grunts, *hmmphs*, and *wows*.

"Well, this is strange, Miss Lisa. Looks like your grand-momma's been taken over by aliens."

"Beg your pardon?" Lisa replied.

Rose gave a little snort at her clever response. "Well, she was here, and then she might as well have been beamed up by the Good Lord himself, or aliens, because somebody sold her house and took over her finances, like a trust or something. But there's no record here of her dying."

That *was* strange. "Is there an institution listed who we might contact?" Tanner asked. I stood back and let him and Lisa ask the questions.

"Hmm. Looks like there's a reference to a credit union listed, but it's not familiar to me. I'm sorry to say I can't give out the information unless it's a public document. You know, birth, death, that kind of thing." Rose looked around and then over her shoulder. "I already said too much, you know?"

"Is there anything you might tell us that will lead somewhere?" Tanner asked.

"I'll just say that this poor lady appears to have been hijacked. Did she have a mental problem or something? 'Cause that's what they do to people when they lose their minds, you know? They pluck them up and put them someplace."

Rose nodded and winked at us like we should catch on.

"But you didn't hear nothing from me."

She gave a little turn of her fingers and pulled them across her lips, as if to say her lips were sealed. "O-okay. Thanks, Rose."

The three of us started to move away, but Tanner turned back. "Rose, there were a couple guys we ran into on Lemon Street. Guys with lots of tattoos in a big, loud truck. They gave us a bad vibe. Might want to have a couple officers check it out." This was a small town. Characters like that would be known to law enforcement.

Rose frowned. "That's Jimmy and Larry, our local weed dealers. They just got out of jail again. Probably looking for some new customers. Those two are mostly bark and no bite, but the sheriff keeps them on a short leash. Best to stay out of their way if you can."

"Got it. Thanks again for your help."

Carly

I HADN'T GOTTEN in on the conversation with Rose in the courthouse, but I'd been listening hard to what had transpired. I heard what she hadn't said: "Something strange is afoot here."

"It sounded like that woman was telling us that someone took Marie, or took over her finances. Or both." Tanner appeared thoughtful.

"How does somebody do that?"

"I'm wondering what happened when her husband passed. Could she have been sick or maybe not in her normal state of mind? Maybe we should go back and knock on the neighbors' doors where she used to live. Surely she had friends in the area. Larry and Jimmy should be gone by now, right?" I was annoyed we'd had to leave so quickly because of those idiots.

"We can go now and give it a try," Tanner agreed.

We drove back to Lemon Street. Thankfully, there wasn't any sign of Larry and Jimmy. "We should split up. Lisa and I can go together. Most of the cars are older models with no after-market modifications, so chances are, it's an older crowd."

Tanner indicated the house across from Marie's. "This one has more vehicles in the drive, so I'll take it. Not to be sexist, but if there are any more Larrys or Jimmys around, I'd rather be the one to face them."

"No argument here." Lisa shrugged.

Lisa and I approached a small duplex and rang the doorbell on the left-hand side first.

Dogs barked. Big dogs, by the sound of it. "Hang on, I'm coming." A rather feeble voice answered. "Let me get these dogs put away." There was some shuffling and banging and then the door opened. A tiny black woman, not five feet tall, stood before us. "How y'all doing today? Can I help you?" But she kept her screen door open barely a crack.

"Hello, my name is Carly Bertrand, and this is Lisa Henry. She's Marie Trichel's granddaughter. Do you remember Marie? She used to live right there across the street." I pointed to the little shotgun house and then turned back to watch as the woman assessed us. Our clothes, our manner, our words. Who could blame her?

She squinted her eyes at us, and at some point decided we meant her no harm, because she opened her screen door wide. "I'm Jean. Marie was my friend. Y'all want some sweet tea?"

It would be poor manners to refuse such an invitation, but also I hated to leave Tanner on his own out here without knowing what his current situation was. "Thanks so much. Let me text our friend so he knows where to find us."

I texted Tanner: *Join us when you're done. We've found a friend of Marie's.*

He replied: *Will do*

"Tell him to come on in. We're all neighbors here. Y'all have a seat, ladies." Jean disappeared into the kitchen and there was much banging around until she returned with a tray that held an iced tea pitcher, a bowl of sliced lemons, and a lovely sugar dish with a tiny spoon. Oh, and four glasses.

"How nice, Jean. You said you knew my grandmother, Marie?" Lisa began to serve herself from the offered tray.

Jean smiled at them then. "She was my *best* friend here in the neighborhood. We played a lot of gin rummy together. Marie had some tragedy in her life, you know? Her daughter just up and disappeared one day. But not after she'd had a baby by a low-life scumbag who'd knocked her up and done away with her."

I tried to stay calm, and I noticed that Lisa's hand had paused in the stirring of her tea, but she laid her spoon down and looked Jean in the eye. "Well, I'm sorry to say that I'm late in meeting Marie. I'm that baby her daughter gave birth to while she was in college."

Jean's eyes grew large and round. "You don't say?"

"Do you know what happened to Marie? We can't seem to find her." Lisa had established a connection, so she continued the conversation.

"Like her daughter, she just up and disappeared. We played rummy on a Tuesday before. Of course she'd recently buried her husband, and she was sad about it. I say, good riddance. Jay was a nosy one. Always up in my business. Didn't like Marie out of his sight. Never hurt her though that I could tell. Marie said he was a bit possessive was all."

"So, she disappeared not long after Jay passed? Did you notice anybody hanging around who didn't belong around that time? Strangers?" I was trying to wade in gently so as not to upset Jean, but she seemed to be our best lead to finding out about Marie so far.

"Marie said there were people asking what she knew about her daughter, Justine. Said Jay had moved her out of her hometown to get away from people asking questions." Jean stopped for a moment and sighed. "You know what I think upset her the most? It was that nobody would tell her anything. She said she'd tried for years to find out about her girl's disappearance, but every time she went to the law, they told her Justine had done run away. So, they wouldn't call it a crime. She finally got them to file her as a missing person, but I don't think they followed up."

I had to ask. "Do you believe Marie was afraid of Jay for any reason?"

Jean shook her head. "I don't think so. But she didn't act how a wife ought to be with her husband if you ask me. It was like she'd married him to take care of her, you know, to have a man in the house. They didn't seem real in love, I guess, even though he kept her on a tight leash."

That was an odd answer. One with no real specific information attached to it. The doorbell rang then. Tanner.

Jean looked up when she heard it and squinted her eyes as if she weren't wearing her glasses. "Must be your friend. We don't get many visitors around here."

"I'll let him in if that's okay. His name is Tanner."

Jean motioned with her hand toward the front door that I should.

Tanner was standing outside and appeared no worse off than when we'd left him. "Hey there. You okay?" I opened the door for him.

"Not much help from the two houses where I stopped." I could tell there was something else, but we would discuss it later.

I led Tanner toward the seating area where we'd gathered with our tea. "Hello, young man. I'm Miss Jean. Would you like some sweet tea?" Jean welcomed Tanner, a gracious Southern hostess, she was.

Tanner, I could tell, was immediately charmed. "I would be honored."

Jean motioned for him to sit and join the group. I quickly brought Tanner up to speed as to what he'd missed. Tanner nodded.

"So you're trying to solve a mystery here, yes?" Jean's eyes brightened.

Lisa spoke. "I came to Tanner and Carly and asked them to help me find my mother, which would have been Justine, Marie's daughter. I was adopted at birth and never knew her or Marie. So, this is where it's led me. I'm so glad we were able to meet you, Miss Jean."

Jean covered Lisa's hand with her own. "My kids are long grown and gone from here. There's nothing a lonely old woman appreciates more than some young people to sit and drink tea with. I hope you find your grandmama, dear. And what happened to your momma."

"We won't forget your kindness and your help. And if you think of anything else about Marie or Jay, please let us know." I handed her one of my new business cards.

We all stood to say our goodbyes. Jean paused a second, as if she weren't sure whether to speak. "You know, Marie wasn't that old. She was smart and funny, and knew her mind, but Jay told her all the time that she was speaking nonsense, and nobody would believe her crazy talk about her daughter going missing, so she ought not be going around telling people about that."

"Sounds like he was gaslighting her." Tanner kind of muttered this.

"What?" Jean appeared confused.

But Tanner clarified. "It's when you know your mind, but somebody else tries to make you think you don't by telling you you're crazy."

"You know, that's exactly what he did to her. But she never did let him convince her she was wrong, even if he kept her from finding out the truth."

I thought about Tanner's dad and what a professional gaslighter he would've been as a husband. A father too.

CHAPTER TWELVE

E VERYBODY WAS ALREADY at Nana's waiting for me by the time I got there. "Did you find out anything about Marie on your outing today?" Nana was in the kitchen as usual. She'd made crawfish étouffée to serve over fluffy white rice. It was one of her favorite go-to dishes when we gathered. It was made with only the tail meat of the crawfish, which she kept in frozen one-pound packages in the freezer year-round.

"Maybe. But nothing solid. We met a neighbor of hers who held no love for her second husband, Jay Trichel."

Nana frowned. "I didn't know him because he wasn't from Cypress Bayou. They left town soon after they married."

I glanced over the side of the pot on the stove. "Mmm. Smells yummy." My stomach growled. We'd stopped for a quick bite after leaving Miss Jean's house, but then we'd gone on to do some further looking around town and asking around about Marie and Jay, so by the time we drove home, it was nearing dinnertime.

"It's ready. Just waiting a few more minutes on the garlic bread."

"Why don't you show me your picks for your dress?" Momma was sitting at the table with several magazines open.

I would have sworn she was planning an actual wedding.

"Okay." I grabbed the iPad from my bag and sat down between her and Leah.

Leah was placing bright pink stickies on pages in a magazine. She rolled her eyes when I raised my eyebrows in a silent, *Don't ask.*

"I like the style of this one, but I don't know if the color is quite right." I slid the device toward Momma.

"*That* one?" Momma stabbed a finger at the only one on the page. "But it's so short. This isn't a cocktail party."

"But it's not a wedding, is it?" I couldn't help but raise the question. "And it's almost touching the knee."

"No, it's not a wedding, as you well know, but it is a nice event. I was hoping you girls would honor it as such since it will be officiated by a priest."

"It's not like I'm going to show my panties, Momma."

Leah snorted beside me and I elbowed her in the ribs. "Ow."

"There's no need to get snarky with me, you two. I don't know why you think you must poke fun at me and your daddy because we want to rededicate ourselves to each other."

Leah spoke up then. "Momma, it's not the rededicating. It's the big hoopla you insist on everybody participating in. I would think with the situation as it is, putting on a big show and drawing attention to the past would be the last thing you'd want."

"I'm not ashamed of what happened to me. I was a victim of *men.*" Her statement, while somewhat true, carried the slight stench of the dramatic, wounded, long-suffering kind of stuff Momma was darn-near famous for.

"Oh Lordy, Karen. This is a celebration of your love for your husband and his for you. Let's not make it about revenge or showing anybody up." Nana had clearly had it up to there with listening to Momma ramping up her tale of woe. "I was there. I know what happened and it was terrible. But we're here now, and it's best not to beleaguer the tale with angst and drama. Let's keep the attention where it belongs. On the happy couple."

"Of course we're happy. Hmmph." Momma's *hmmph* made that statement laughable. None of it was funny, obviously, but our mother could drive a priest to cuss.

"Where's Daddy?" Leah's voice held an innocence I didn't believe for a second.

Momma blew out a breath. "Says he's tired of hearing about flowers and dresses and vows." That made perfect sense. He was not a man who dressed up and spoke his heart aloud real often.

"Ah. Well, he'll show up in his suit where you tell him and say what he's supposed to, I guess." Leah smirked a little, but Momma didn't see it.

"He'd better." Momma's voice held the promise of serious consequence.

"So, should we do a call with Allison and loop her into all the fun here?" Leah suggested.

"Absolutely, we should. I want to see her dress choices." Momma forgot about all the angst then.

"I'll try her with FaceTime. Let's use the iPad so we can see her." I slipped the iPad over so Leah could make the call.

"Hello?" Allison's voice, so like Leah's, as well as her face, came on the iPad's screen. "Oh, hi, everybody." She appeared somewhat disheveled and pale.

"Hey there. Everything okay?" Leah asked.

"Oh, yes. Just working on some paperwork for the house. How are you all?"

Momma grabbed the iPad and pulled it close. "We're having a planning meeting for our vow renewal. Have you found a dress yet?"

Allison's face said it all. She hadn't even looked. "Gosh, I'm sorry. I haven't had much time to think about it."

I tried to throw her a lifeline. "I'll send some links over for some sites I've been going through." I could see a spark of laughter in her eyes, even through the iPad.

"Thanks, Carly."

"You bet."

"Honey, you'd better find a dress soon, in case it needs to be altered. I'm happy to pay for it if you're short right now." Momma said the cringy words before we could stop her.

Allison, bless her, didn't cringe. "I'm good. I'll find something. Purple, right?"

"Lavender." Leah and I both burst out laughing because we corrected her at the same time.

"Oh. Lavender. Got it." Allison laughed, and when she did, she looked so much like Leah, it nearly took my breath away.

"Is everything all right, Allison?" Momma asked. "You know we miss you and hope you're doing well."

"Um, I'm okay. It's been hard trying to sort through my mother's things and have the house on the market. And I've got a boyfriend; Hank's his name. But I'm not sure how that's going right now, so, I'd have to say that it's a strange time. But I'm looking forward to seeing everyone in June."

"Well, okay. Please tell us if you need anything. We're here for you, you know."

Nana came over to where we were crowded around the iPad. "Darlin,' it's your nana. I'm working on getting your trust set up, okay? So, if you need anything in the meantime, you call or text me anytime."

Allison's face crumpled then, and she burst into tears. "Oh, Nana, I can't thank you enough. All of you. I have to go now." The call disconnected, leaving us staring at each other.

"I hope she's all right like she says." Momma's eyes filled with tears. "I'm not getting a good feeling about this."

"Maybe she was a little overwhelmed. We can be a lot for some people when we're all together. She might have been embarrassed with all the money talk." Money was something we discussed in a practical way. As in: *Do you have enough? Do you need some? Make smart decisions with your money. You'll get your trust when you turn twenty-five.*

I figured that it was probably easier for people who didn't have real money worries to discuss money than those who struggled more. But we always shared our benefits within the community. It was part of privilege. We volunteered at every opportunity as a family, and we gave our time and our efforts as individuals to help others without anyone else knowing about it. It was never enough, but Nana always made sure we tried for it to be enough.

I hated that Allison was put on the spot like that with all

of us watching. She didn't know how our family shared information so freely and I'm sure she was mortified. I would text her later and try to smooth it over.

Leah spoke up then. "Sounds like she's got a lot going on right now dealing with her mother's estate. And who knows what's going on with that boyfriend of hers. Doesn't sound like things are going very well there. Let's give her some space. Oh, and maybe not ambush her like that again." Leah's statement was her admission of the idea being a bad one.

"It sounded like a fine idea when you came out with it." I didn't want her to feel bad about it. "I'm sure she appreciated being included."

"Of course she did, darlin'." Nana patted Leah's shoulder.

"Who knew one of my girls could be so sensitive?" Momma shrugged.

We were all sensitive people, but where Momma was concerned, we'd grown elephant skin, so she didn't see us that way.

Tanner

TANNER RECEIVED AN email from Judge Keller's office first thing Wednesday morning that stated that Tanner must defend any claims made by Carson on their court date. The hearing was set ten days from today, which didn't give them much time to have Carson drop the suit. But Tanner assumed that his father feared the retribution should Tanner bring this before the state bar association.

If Carson called his bluff and drew out the lawsuit, even though the evidence was on Tanner's side, it meant time and money that Tanner didn't have to spend, of which Carson was aware.

"Good morning. Everything okay?" Carly arrived like fresh air and sunshine, bringing with her a dozen doughnuts from Shipley's across the street.

"Tell me you've got something with chocolate in there." He pointed to the heavenly-smelling box. "And I'll fill you in on the latest."

Carly flipped open the lid to display his choices, which were limited to a half-dozen glazed and a half-dozen chocolate frosted. "Ah. Perfect."

The back door opened and closed. Imogene called to them, "Good morning, all." She then poked her head in through the doorway where Tanner and Carly were staring into the box. "I'll get us come coffee made to go with those doughnuts."

"Okay. What's up?" Carly eyed Tanner as encouragement to spill the info.

"The reply from Judge Keller's office says we've got to defend the charges on our court date. Period."

"Any word from Carson yet?"

"Not since Monday night's drama when he stomped up the hill."

"Maybe you should send a copy of the letters you intend to send to the bar association and to the Rotary Club, just to make certain he realizes what's at stake if he continues on this path. Because we all know the law is on your side."

"Yes. I'll show him that going through with his bluff will have real consequences and cause problems for his firm. And the last thing Carson wants is somebody digging into his business dealings." Tanner began scratching out notes on his legal pad while he bit into a chocolaty, warm doughnut.

"Okay, we've got a plan for Carson. What about Marie? Something about the woman at the courthouse made me think she had a gold mine of information pulled up on her screen that she was waiting to divulge, given the right permission." Carly tapped her stylus against her iPad.

"Since we can't get the information ourselves, maybe we should get law enforcement involved and have them request the information," Tanner suggested.

"Yes, if Marie disappeared, then she's a missing person. If they've got information about where she is, they would be compelled to share it, wouldn't they? Maybe the local district attorney would help with this since Marie lived here for so many years."

Tanner liked the idea of going this route because it was official and there was less opportunity for hiding evidence. The downside is they would be bringing other people into the situation and could lose control over the investigation and search. If something underhanded was afoot, who knew what they might be getting themselves into? "We'll need to discuss this with Lisa. Bringing law enforcement into this changes everything."

Carly said what he was thinking: "It might be our only way of getting to the truth, unfortunately."

CHAPTER THIRTEEN

TANNER HADN'T GOTTEN this far in his career without making a few friends in city hall. He and Alan Litrell, the newly elected district attorney, were downright friendly, as luck would have it. Litrell had grown up in Cypress Bayou and played football with Tanner in high school. He was an amazing athlete and had gone on to be a solid quarterback at NSU before heading to law school at Southern in Baton Rouge.

Carson didn't have the younger generation of politicians quite so tidily wrapped up in his grip like the older ones. In fact, on several occasions Tanner had heard Carson cursing Litrell's disinterest in becoming a political lackey of his.

Tanner called the DA's office and asked to speak with him. After being put on hold and some shuffling around of phone lines, they were connected. "Hey, Tanner, how's it goin', man?"

"It's going all right, all told. Listen, I don't want to take up your time, but I've got a unique situation brewing here and I'd hoped we could sit down and discuss it."

"Sure. How do you feel about a lunch meeting? I can't seem to get anything done without interruptions unless I'm eating." Tanner understood what he meant. Sometimes, when he was at Carson's practice and juggling a full load of clients, he'd had to leave the office to get anything accomplished. Not so much now since he couldn't bill anyone.

"I get it. Lunch sounds great. Let me know when and where and I'll meet you."

"Great. I'll have my assistant contact you once she checks my calendar. Good to hear from you, Tanner."

Fortunately, Alan had an opening for lunch today. His assistant called right back to confirm their meeting for noon at Laborde's Meat Pie Kitchen. Tanner's mouth watered thinking about it.

"I'm meeting with the DA for lunch to discuss our next move to open a missing person's case for Marie," Tanner called out to Carly who was working in her own office. They'd begun a habit of projecting somewhat loudly down the hall if the other person wasn't obviously on the phone or nobody was in the office.

Tanner heard her footsteps coming down the hall after she'd pushed back her rolling chair, with its slight squeak, from her desk. He could identify every sound and movement in the office. Imogene was tapping away on her keyboard up front entering client information.

They'd had lots of phone calls in the past few days since the website had gone live. The schedule was booking up for new client meetings. Since the court appearance with Carson and Judge Keller was scheduled in a week, they'd pushed all the new potential clients until the following week.

Carly stood in front of his desk. "How do you plan to present this to the DA?"

"Have a seat." She sat, folding her long legs into the chair across from him. Tanner worked hard to accustom himself to having a young, gorgeous associate in his line of vision during business hours. But sometimes, when she appeared in front of him, with that long, dark, wavy hair and sexy body, he couldn't help but react...just a little.

"I'm thinking to ask a favor after filing the missing person's report. Tell him that we've done some asking around and are getting nowhere. I've made a list of our efforts so far."

Carly grinned. "You know how I like a list. Do you think we should have Lisa go ahead and file the missing person's report or do you want a chance to speak with DA Litrell first?"

Tanner considered that. "She went missing for a reason, and I'm a little skeptical as to whether her husband, Jay, was looking after her best interests during their marriage. Yes, he's dead now, but was he keeping her in line for someone before that?"

"Okay, so I guess that means you'll want to speak with the DA first to fill him in. Probably a good idea before announcing it to the world that we're doing an official search. Sometimes things get done around here with a simple phone call, even if it's not quite right." Carly shrugged a shoulder.

"I'm meeting him at noon, so there isn't time to do much before I see him. I'll ask his opinion on whether we should file the report, or at what point Lisa should do it."

"Makes sense. I'll help Lisa open her adoption records so she can be officially declared a family member of both Justine's and Marie's. She's going to have to work with her mom to help her there. It's going to depend on how helpful she chooses to be."

"Lisa has her birth certificate and adoption records showing that she was born to Justine Chaffin. She could get Justine's records with that documentation while we work on getting a copy of Justine's missing person's report that Marie filed here in Cypress Bayou. Now that Marie is missing, we should be able to file a report on Lisa's behalf. Or have Lisa do it."

Carly nodded. "I'll go make some calls."

The room lost its air and energy when Carly left. They did their best work when the two of them sat together and made plans. At least he did. Maybe she did too? Tanner enjoyed her presence. Even though his new endeavor was fraught with pitfalls and stress, because of Carly, it felt like an adventure. He doubted any of this effort would be half as pleasant without her.

Carly

LISA HAD RENTED a short-term apartment in Cypress Bayou while she investigated Justine Chaffin's mysterious disappearance so she could be available if we needed her at a moment's notice. I was glad for that now since we were going in this new direction of filing paperwork that would require Lisa's participation.

We agreed to meet at one of the picnic tables along the bayou on Front Street. Today was gorgeous and the weather begged humans to step outside and enjoy the low humidity and cloudless skies.

Lisa held a couple shopping bags from the soap store and one of my favorite boutiques in town. Clearly she'd been out already appreciating the nice weather. "Did you find anything fun?"

"That soap store is a new weakness of mine, I've got to say. And I adore the accessories at these little shops. I'm bored hanging around while nothing is happening, so I'm getting acquainted with all the merchants here. It's probably not a good thing for my bank account."

I nodded. "The soap store is my absolute favorite. I love the new cucumber avocado body butter. Last year, I was nuts about the coconut milk bath bombs. I could spend all day in there."

"Yes, I just discovered the cucumber avocado line." She patted the outside of her bag.

"I thought meeting out here would be a nice change. Tanner is having lunch with the district attorney now. We're hoping he can guide us on the next move as far as finding Marie."

"Can't I file a missing person's report since I can prove to a pretty good degree that I'm her granddaughter? I'm wondering why we didn't try getting more information that day when we were in Leesfield."

Lisa seemed a little frustrated that we weren't farther along. "Yes, well, that was a strange day if you remember. Being threatened by drug dealers and all...but mostly, we needed to get the lay of the land there. Demanding information at that moment without all the proper credentials wasn't the right time. When we do go back and insist they turn over their records, let's be sure nobody has any advanced notice to hide anything."

"Do you think they're hiding something over there?"

I shrugged. "I have no idea, but if they are, we don't want to take the chance they'll have the opportunity to deny us." I tried to sound reassuring. "Honestly, we have no idea what happened to Marie, but she got lost someplace in the system. Maybe on purpose, maybe not."

"Yes. Even more reason to get some good advice from the DA Either we do it the good ol' boy way, or we do it all by the book. He'll tell us which might work better. And if we try it one way and that doesn't work, then we'll go in with warrants and such."

Lisa nodded. "You see? *That's* why I hired attorneys instead of private investigators."

We both laughed at that. Just as a text came in from Tanner.

Alan knows the DA in Rapides Parish. Says he's going to be doing some quiet snooping into Marie's whereabouts.

I showed Lisa the text.

"So, it's gonna be the good ol' boy route for now, huh?" Lisa shook her head and rolled her eyes. "I guess we little women need to sit tight and wait for the menfolk to handle things."

Boy, did I get her frustration. "Looks that way for the moment, unfortunately. If I thought there was a better way, I'd go rogue and do it." Lisa was right. This was a small town in Louisiana and the patriarchy here was still well in control of most politics in the state. It had been that way going on a couple hundred years and counting. "We have our uses and our power. Until men can give birth, we're still in control."

"Ha. Isn't that the truth. But my mother gave birth and then gave me up, most likely because of a man. I'm on a mission to find out why and who my father really is. My adoptive mom, who will always be my mom, finally agreed to share the records."

"Why now?" I was becoming more fascinated by this family story by the minute.

"Probably because I threatened to make a public stink about it and file for them myself. Like I said, they're a family of means in New Orleans. She doesn't want that kind of publicity. Daddy's a lawyer and he refuses to help me with this."

Something about this made my eye twitch. Why didn't her family want to give Lisa peace about her birth parents? Why would they even try to prevent her from getting it? "I'm sorry you've had to go out on your own with no support. What about your husband? You said he's not big on you doing this either?"

"He's not big on me being away from home for so long and spending money on it. He's not a bad guy, just busy and thinks I'm going to get hurt."

Double whammy. Shitty parents and a possibly shitty husband. "Sorry."

WE WERE BACK in the office. I needed to do something productive while we waited to hear from Alan Litrell, so I was going through the prospective clients and prioritizing them as to which cases might be quick and easy. There were a couple estate disputes within families. Those could drag out and be super messy, so I put those in the long-haulers' list. When money was involved, it was always messy, which made me think about my own recent family situation. As I got distracted by this, Tanner flew down the hallway to the front door of the office.

What on earth? Curious, I followed, but not as hurried, noticing that Tanner had gone outside but hadn't come in yet. I glanced over at Imogene, who was wearing earbuds while she entered data. She shrugged her obliviousness, same as me, so I stepped outside to see what was up.

Tanner was down the street, past the printer next door and near the corner. Had he followed someone? I walked toward where he was, trying to get some idea of what was going on, but his back was to me. "Tanner?" I called out.

"He's gone." Tanner appeared out of breath and a little red in the face.

"Who?"

"The guy who left this on our front door." He held up a small piece of paper with some writing scrawled on it. I was too far away to see what it said.

"What's that?"

Tanner looked all around him again and dropped his shoulders in defeat. "I couldn't catch up with him. No idea which way he went."

"Wait. What does the note say?" We walked together back toward the office.

He handed it to me. In a heavy black scrawl, it said, *Don't go digging up the dead. Or you might end up like them.*

"What on earth—" I couldn't even finish the sentence. I was so shocked at the threatening tone of the note. Not just the tone. It was an actual threat. "This is a death threat, Tanner."

"Yeah. I got that."

We re-entered the office and Imogene looked up from her computer. "Everything okay?"

Tanner showed her the note.

"Oh my. Did you get the person on camera?"

"I need to check. I saw the notification that there was movement at the front door and went to see what was happening. It takes a minute or two to load the video, so I haven't had a chance to pull it up yet. When I opened the door and saw the note, I went racing down the street one way and then the other, hoping to figure out who left it."

"Did you see anybody?" I was trying to piece it all together in my mind.

"No. I'll have a look at what the camera captured now."

We moved into the conference room and waited for Tanner to pull up the security app on the larger screen of his laptop. My heart rate had kicked up and it was the first time since the drug dealers in Leesfield had threatened us that I'd experienced such distress. Actual fear. *Don't go digging up the dead. Or you might end up like them.*

"Here we go." We gathered around behind Tanner to view the video.

The deliverer was a lanky young man, from what I could see. He wore a black hoodie, but his face was distorted by the poor video quality, and he'd kept his head down. "Can you sharpen the image?" I wanted badly to see more definition.

"I can't, but maybe the security company can." We watched the video several times. Pretty much all that was visible was the guy's nose as it was closest to the camera when he attached the note to the door.

The note had a regular piece of clear tape attached to it. Nothing special there. "Maybe there are fingerprints," Tanner said.

"Who should we go to with this to get it analyzed? I mean, you *just* spoke with the district attorney and this happened."

Tanner shook his head. "I don't think he's got anything to do with this."

"Then who?" I was getting angry now. Somebody had the audacity to threaten us.

"Maybe his asking about Marie? His inquiring about her might have tipped off somebody involved. You know what kind of crony network we've got going on around here." Tanner stood and paced.

"It sounds conspiracy-theory-ish, but who sends death threats these days? What on earth would compel somebody to do that?" It was like a suspense drama from Netflix, but it wasn't.

"Someone with a big secret. One they would kill to keep." Tanner picked up his phone and dialed. "I'm calling Alan Litrell. I'm betting money he isn't in on this."

"You're betting with our lives. I hope you're right." I hated the drama in that statement, but it was the truth. "But I trust your judgment." I didn't want Tanner to think I didn't have his back.

Tanner's expression was grim as he went through the assistant and finally got the DA on the line. "Alan, someone left us a note on the front door. It was a note telling us to back off 'digging up the dead' or we could end up just like them. I need to know who you told about our conversation."

Tanner was silent while he listened as Litrell spoke.

"Okay. Can you get that done today? Oh, and for my peace of mind, can you ask Judge Watkins instead of Judge Keller? I've got my reasons." He waited. "Thanks, man. I appreciate it. I'll wait to hear from you."

"He's sending over a couple of patrol cars to sit outside the front and back of our office."

I exhaled hard. "I can't believe this is where we are."

"Should we leave and go home? Stop what we're doing for now? Or do we sit tight and wait?" Imogene, who was normally so confident, didn't seem like it now.

"We wait until we hear back about the warrant."

I was not a fan of waiting...

CHAPTER FOURTEEN

Tanner

T ANNER PEEKED OUT the front door of the office. There was a patrol car sitting front and center, which made his shoulders relax just a bit. Alan had followed through on his promise. Hopefully they would get word soon about the warrant.

Having Imogene and Carly to worry about made this so much worse. And Lisa. He'd hated calling Lisa to tell her about this. She'd agreed to check out of her lodgings immediately and come over to the office. At least there was a police presence here.

They'd all gone upstairs, as it was more comfortable there. Tanner joined them once he double-checked the doors again.

"Can we get you anything, dear?" Imogene was a comfort to Lisa right now. She usually knew instinctively what to do during stressful times, but this seemed to have her rattled a little. After working with Carson, Tanner figured not much would.

"I'm fine, thanks. I wonder where I'm going to stay now. I hate the idea of heading back home now that we're on the verge of finding what happened to Marie."

"You could stay here if you'd like. It's small, but the police are nearby to keep an eye on things." Tanner motioned to the small efficiency apartment space where they sat. "There's a pullout here and the kitchenette has a microwave and a toaster oven. There's a shower in the bathroom."

"Hmm. Yes, I guess it's a good solution for the present. It's nice. Thanks, Tanner." Lisa smiled a little sadly. "I just hate that my coming to you has put everyone in danger."

"I'm not sure a threatening note means the sender would actually carry out the threat, but it's a chance we can't take until we learn more." Carly paced the edge of the room. Tanner could tell by the tone of her voice and her body language that she was anxious.

Tanner had a loaded gun in a holster strapped on to his person now. He was licensed to carry one though he rarely did, but now seemed a good time.

"Are your bags in the car, Lisa?" Tanner asked.

She nodded. "I don't have a lot with me, so packing up didn't take long."

"I'll turn the TV on if that's okay." Carly used the remote and flipped channels until she got to the home and garden network. The hosts of the show were renovating a turn-of-the-century craftsman-style bungalow. Perfect.

"Oh, I've seen this episode. Wait until you see what they do with the backyard." Imogene sat down beside Lisa. At least it was something to get their minds off the current dilemma.

Tanner and Carly slipped downstairs to discuss what was happening. Tanner shut the door so they wouldn't be overheard. No sense upsetting either of the other women.

"What next?" Carly asked him.

He was about to speak when his cell phone rang. He looked at the screen. "Hey Alan, what've you got?"

"Listen, I don't know where the leak came from, but I've got your warrant. There's some interesting stuff on Marie Trichel's whereabouts. You were right to keep Judge Keller out of it. Can you come over here to my office? I don't trust anybody at this point."

I'd put him on speaker so Carly could hear. She raised her eyebrows. "We'll be there in a few minutes. Carly, my associate, will be with me. I know for certain she's to be trusted."

"Tanner, don't say a word to *anyone* about where you're going, and tell Carly the same."

Basically, Alan was telling them to *trust no one*.

So, after he'd hung up with Alan Litrell, Tanner spoke, "Let's take his advice and not tell Lisa and Imogene where we're headed. Only because he said to keep it quiet."

Carly nodded. "Okay. We can fill them in later."

The fewer people who knew what was happening here, the easier to keep a lid on the information that was spread. "Let's tell them we've got an errand and leave it at that."

Imogene wanted to know where they were headed.

"Just checking on something." Tanner didn't cave on telling them.

Carly

I HATED SNEAKING around and keeping secrets, but our situation clearly required that we make sure nothing got out until we found out who or where the leak came from. It might even be a phone tap, so saying nothing was best. As we headed over to the district attorney's office, I couldn't help but wonder how Judge Keller was involved in all this. He was my newly discovered sister, Allison's father, we'd found out. The man who'd gotten Momma pregnant when she was sixteen.

Alan's office was in the courthouse building—as were Judge Keller's and Judge Watkins's—so security was as tight here as anywhere. Now, it appeared there was a clash within the city's governmental forces. And judges always outranked other officers of the court. Fortunately, we had Judge Watkins on our side in this since he issued the warrant.

Once inside, we made our way toward the DA's office quickly. My heart pounded as if I were racing against the clock for something. Once again I reflected that this felt like something out of a suspense movie. A door opened down the corridor and someone waved to us. "Come here. Quickly." It was the DA's assistant.

We entered the outer office, where the DA's assistant, Jeff locked the door behind us, flipped the sign to "closed", and then turned off the lights and lowered the blinds, before ushering us into the inner office of Alan Littrell.

He was waiting to shut the door behind us. "Thanks for coming right over. If this wasn't shaping up to be such a strange situation, I wouldn't have seen the need for such cloak-and-dagger behavior."

"This is Carly Bertrand, my associate." Tanner introduced us.

Alan nodded. "No one knew you were coming here?"

We both shook our heads.

He flipped the lights off and turned on his computer for presentation on a pulldown screen against the far wall of the office. "Okay, here's what we've found from the sharing of the computer files released from the Rapides Parish courthouse just an hour ago."

There was a document signed off on by Judge Keller that allowed someone permission to become Marie's legal guardian. But the name had been redacted—as in, there was a solid black line marked through the name. "What the hell—?" Tanner growled.

"You see why such expedience was necessary. It appears there's collusion to commit Ms. Trichel to an institution between the judge and someone else. This seems especially important because somebody is trying to cover it up."

"Where did they put Marie?" Not to mention, why? I was barely keeping up.

"It appears she's a patient at the Central Hospital in Pine Hill."

"But that place has been pretty much shut down for years. It's mostly used for the criminally insane now." I was aghast at the idea they'd put Marie there. "Is she mentally incompetent?"

"There's nothing to lead us to believe that's the case except a doctor's signature. A Dr. H. R. Miller. But until then, nothing. We're working on pulling her medical records with the warrant."

"As far as Pine Hill is concerned, there's a small area on the hospital campus dedicated to research for elderly patients with different types of dementia. It was endowed by a family many years ago specifically for that purpose, so it continues to operate as such. This is apparently where Marie has been a patient since her husband passed."

"Is there a way to go and see her? Try and get some idea of her condition?" This was screaming conspiracy...more by the minute. But I didn't understand why the judge and whomever he colluded with would do such a thing.

"What's the connection between Marie and Judge Keller?" Tanner said it out loud.

"Clearly the judge and the mystery guardian have gotten wind that you're asking questions about Marie. The threat must have come from one of them. The safest thing to do would be to take custody of Marie Trichel if she's in a condition to travel. But legally, someone is her guardian, so he or she must authorize any visitors or transfers."

"But we have no idea who that is until we speak with someone at the hospital." I wanted to try and figure out a path to help Marie, first and foremost. We were assuming she was still alive.

"Unless we show proof that she has a family member to take control of her guardianship, which we have. What started all of this is her granddaughter from New Orleans looking for her long-lost birth mother, Justine Chaffin, if you'll remember?" Tanner clarified.

"Do you have the court documents?" Alan asked Tanner.

Tanner pulled them from his briefcase and handed them over.

"This should do it. We'll need the granddaughter to file for guardianship immediately and quietly. Hopefully, we can expedite the process through Judge Watkins, since he was the one who got the warrant for Marie's information. Rapides Parish will do whatever we ask. They have no skin in this and would prefer it went away without a public stink."

Judges Keller and Watkins were both district judges, which meant their jurisdiction covered several parishes, Rapides included. That's how Keller was able to sign off on Marie's guardianship. "Is Judge Watkins in the building?" I asked Alan Litrell.

"Yes. We can get him down here as soon as the paperwork is completed by the family member."

"We'll take care of that piece." Tanner spoke then.

"How do we stay safe while we pull all of this off? And how do we keep Marie safe? What's to stop someone from moving her someplace else?"

"I'm going to make some calls to the Rapides Parish DA's office. The hospital doesn't have the best reputation. There's corruption at every level, which is likely how the poor woman got shoved there in the first place. It might take a rescue by somebody higher up. Does she have a place to go if we spring her?"

"We'll get her taken care of if you can get her out of there before her mystery guardian figures out what we're up to." Tanner sounded determined and very angry.

"Okay. Get the paperwork done for the guardianship. I'll get Judge Watkins to sign off on it. We'll get a tail on Judge

Keller. This must be done privately and very quietly, you understand. To get a judge investigated officially takes weeks and it's not a quiet affair."

We left the office as stealthily as possible, with the assistant showing us out a side door. Neither of us said a word until we were back in Tanner's truck. And it took a minute then. Tanner finally spoke. "I can't believe this is happening."

"And why would one name be redacted but not the judge's?" I wondered this aloud. "Maybe whomever is being protected doesn't care about the judge."

"I'm guessing there's a third party involved in the cover-up." Tanner started the truck and we drove toward the office.

"How much of this do you think we should tell Lisa? I mean, we obviously can trust her, right?" But something was eating at me.

"I think we should say nothing about what's happening except that we need her to fill out the paperwork to become Marie's guardian as her only living relative to get the information from the courthouse."

"But she's the client. I'm not sure keeping this from her is fair." I couldn't quite reconcile it all.

"It's for her safety. And the less anyone knows about any of this, the better we can control what gets out."

"Imogene too?" I asked. Because Imogene worked so closely with us, I couldn't imagine that she wouldn't at least overhear something.

"Yes. For sure. I trust her but I can't be sure she won't share the info with her husband. And if there's going to be an internal investigation of Judge Keller, this will all be privileged information soon. The less risk the better."

"Okay. So, we only talk outside the office?"

"Might be the best plan."

The rain started so suddenly—as if the crack of thunder caused it. I hadn't even noticed the clouds gather, we'd been so focused on what was happening. Tanner and I ran the few feet between the truck and the back door of the office, but still got soaked.

"My goodness, can you believe this weather lately? Came outta nowhere." Imogene met us as soon as we got inside. "Is everything all right, you two? Here, let me grab a couple hand towels from the bathroom." She disappeared for less than a minute but came back with the promised towels.

"Everything's fine. We've got some paperwork for Lisa to fill out requesting guardianship for Marie."

"I hope that won't make all this more dangerous." I touched Imogene on the shoulder. "This has rattled us all, Imogene. No one will judge you if you decide to sit this one out."

"No. No way. If y'all are in, so am I." But she still didn't appear too convinced. "Plus, won't you need a notary to witness the paperwork for the guardianship?" Imogene smiled then, as if she'd made her peace with the idea.

"Yes, indeed we will." I nodded.

It was getting late in the afternoon, so I fired up my computer and loaded the PDF files for Lisa to complete digitally. This was our next step toward legally wrestling Marie from whomever held her captive. Not knowing what her medical condition was, we couldn't say if she was placed in Pine Hill because she had legitimate dementia or because she was being held for a more nefarious reason.

"Lisa, how about I grab your things from the car now that the rain has let up and you can get settled." Tanner suggested and Lisa handed over her keys and followed him outside.

"Do you think one of us should invite her to our house to stay while we figure this out?" Imogene asked me.

"I'm living at Nana's, and Tanner lives in his Airstream, so that's not an option. Of course, we wouldn't impose on you and your husband." It was a little awkward, I had to admit. Lisa was a client, and we really didn't know her very well.

"Well, I certainly have room for a guest. Maybe we can try this and see how it works. I guess it seems like a logical solution for the time being. I'll go with her to the store tomorrow and we can make sure she has anything she needs. It's probably best to travel in pairs out in public, don't you think?" Imogene's suggestion had merit.

"I think that's a great idea, Imogene. It's not a bad idea to stay together in public for support."

"Tanner can monitor the security system here from his phone, right?" Imogene bit her lip, as if she were still worried about Lisa's safety.

"Yes. He can, and there are the patrol cars as well, so she should be safe here." Lisa would likely be safer than any of us. In fact, I was concerned with Tanner's being a sitting duck out there in that trailer on the bayou. If anyone meant harm, he would be the most vulnerable.

Tanner and Lisa returned with a small suitcase, a tote

bag, and some clothes in a zipped hanging bag. All matching. I would call that goals in my world.

CHAPTER FIFTEEN

Tanner

A<small>FTER</small> I<small>MOGENE HAD</small> gone home for the day and Lisa was settled in the tiny apartment upstairs, Tanner and Carly exited together and walked toward their vehicles. It had been a long, emotional day. "You wanna grab a beer?" Tanner wasn't sure why he'd suggested it, but he wasn't quite ready to be alone. Or maybe he wasn't quite ready to leave Carly.

"Oh, uh, sure. Do you think we're being watched or followed?" They both looked around. The back parking area was practically empty besides Tanner's truck and Carly's car. There were a couple catering vans that were obviously empty.

"I don't see anybody. Do you?"

She shook her head. "Nope."

"We could sit on the dock at my place. I've got beer." Tanner decided that might be better than going out in public.

"Works for me. I'll meet you there." She pressed the button on her key fob and unlocked the door to her car.

It didn't occur to him until he climbed into his truck that she might think anything weird about his inviting her home with him. Weird, as in out of the bounds of their professional co-worker friendship. They'd developed an easy camaraderie and he quite simply enjoyed her company. And they'd known each other most of their lives, so he let that go.

She followed him to the family property. He noticed Jake's truck parked on the lot where he and Leah were starting to build their house. Might as well invite Jake to join them. He stopped, and Carly stopped right behind him.

The slab had been poured for the footprint of the house. The framing was supposed to begin in a day or two. Tanner figured the rain had delayed things, as rain always did. Louisiana homes rarely had basements, as most of the land here was at, or sometimes below, sea level. One didn't have to dig far to hit water. Often homes were built on stilts to allow for flooding. Fortunately, this property was on slightly higher ground, being that it was on the bank of the bayou.

North Louisiana was hillier than south, and they were almost right in the middle, so there were some hills, but not many.

"Hey you two. What's happening?' Jake was still in a pair of scrubs from the hospital.

"We're gonna sit on the dock and have a beer. Wanna join us?" Tanner asked his brother.

"Sounds like heaven. Leah's meeting me here any minute. We're checking out the progress on the place. Not much of it today, as you can see." He motioned toward the bare slab.

"This rain. Every day. I guess it's no surprise, huh? Like every other year here in Louisiana." Tanner shrugged. "I imagine that's how folks in Seattle feel most of the year."

"Let's head to your trailer and grab those brews. I'm done here," Jake said. "I'll text Leah and tell her to meet us there."

Tanner was certain he had at least a cold six-pack of amber ale to share with his guests. He'd determined it was something he and Carly shared—a love of the same beer. That made him smile.

"What are you grinning about?" Leave it to Jake to catch him with a stupid grin on his face that he didn't care to explain.

"I was thinking that I was glad I had enough of the right kind of beer to share." Partly true. Enough true that his brother wouldn't question it further. Jake knew him so well and could tell if he was lying.

"Good thing since you invited us over." Jake punched him in the arm just hard enough for it to require a little return shove.

"All right, you two, I'm thirsty. I say we don't wait on my sister." Carly had grown up with the two of them doing the push-and-shove guy thing. Girls used words. Guys were physical. Tanner chose physical any day. That cerebral warfare between women was fearsome.

They drove the length of the packed-shell drive to the end, where Tanner's trailer and the dock sat. It was humid after the rain, and now the darker clouds began to move aside and allow the sun to radiate the late afternoon. It wouldn't be dark for another couple hours, so the heat and humidity would climb until then.

Carly wore a sleeveless turquoise top with a knee-length cream-colored skirt. She didn't seem to struggle with the heat, though she had twisted her long dark hair into a clip. Her medium-heeled shoes weren't exactly the best for trudging through the shells and pathway down to the dock. But neither were bare feet.

Jake and Carly took a seat at the picnic table under his awning while Tanner disappeared into the trailer to snag the beers for the small group. He pulled out a six-pack cooler and added an ice pack to it to keep the bottles cold.

"Hey, Jake, grab those chairs." Tanner pointed to the two lightweight aluminum chairs with mesh webbing leaned against the trailer. There were already two permanent Adirondack chairs on the dock.

Tanner offered them a beer, which they took.

Leah drove up as they were heading toward the dock, beers in hand.

"Not gonna wait for me, huh?" Leah kissed Jake on the cheek.

"Glad you're here. It's been a bear of a day." Carly said to Leah.

"What's going on? Is it Carson?" Leah, of course, asked what was happening.

Tanner wasn't sure how much to share with their respective siblings since they'd decided to keep the circle of information very small.

Carly must've realized what she'd done and darted a glance over at him. "Let's go have a seat where we can discuss this situation." Tanner figured there wasn't any way around letting the siblings know what was happening. Jake might even be able to shed some light on the medical part of things where Marie was concerned. There wasn't anyone they could trust more than these two.

Once they'd set up the folding chairs and made a circle-ish, they seemed to all let out a sigh of sorts. The air was warm and heavy but being with family and sitting on this dock together helped to lighten the burden for Tanner.

"What's going on now?" Jake started the conversation. "You two seem a little stressed."

Tanner nodded. "Yes, but this stays between us. You know we've been searching for Marie Trichel, our client Lisa's grandmother?" Jake and Leah both nodded. "Well, someone has been tipped off, and that person sent us a threatening note today warning us to back off."

"Warning you? Warning you how?" Leah asked before Jake got the chance.

Tanner quoted the note. "But who really knows if it was serious. It's unlikely anyone would follow through with it."

"I wouldn't be so sure about that. This place has some ugly secrets, or so we've found out recently. Who knows what lengths someone might go to, to protect them?" Jake's tone was grave.

"What did you do exactly to cause someone to send such a threatening note? I mean, what bear did you poke?" Leah asked.

"We got a search warrant to compel Marie's health, property, and financial records from Rapides Parish. It seems Judge Keller is involved with a doctor and a lawyer in town to have Marie committed to Pine Hill as a mental patient."

"That would do it. Why would Keller have an interest in Marie? And who are the doctor and lawyer involved?" Jake leaned forward in his chair, fully engaged.

"The lawyer's name has been redacted from the files, but the doctor on record is a Dr. H. R. Miller. You know him?" Tanner asked his brother.

"I know him. He's an older doc. Doesn't have hospital privileges anymore though. He's a psychiatrist. Still sees patients in his office over by the hospital. He's a buddy of Carson's."

"Somehow that doesn't surprise me. Carson's name hasn't popped up with regards to this yet, but I guess it was only a matter of time, given his connection to Judge Keller. Those two grew up together, were roommates in law school, and still hide each other's dirty laundry." Tanner shook his head. "And Carson has no problem issuing threats around town."

"Do you think Carson's the third person in the paperwork, the one who's Marie's legal guardian?" Carly asked.

Tanner ran a hand through his hair. "It's a decent theory. A place to start, I guess. It takes all three to declare someone legally incompetent: a judge, a doctor, and a lawyer. The trifecta of dread in Marie's case. Once it's done, it would be hard to undo legally."

Carly shrugged. "We're having to do this dance with what's legal and what's right. Finding out what Marie's mental status immediately is what's right. But there's no quick legal way to do that. We're at the mercy of her court-appointed guardian to get access to her. But we don't know who that is. We'll have to show up and try to see her, but if we do that and they refuse us, who knows what might happen to Marie until we can find a better way to gain entry."

Tanner spoke up then. "DA Litrell is working with us, along with Judge Watkins in expediting things. They believe us that Keller is involved in taking away Marie's personal liberties against her will. But getting Marie out of the facility will take some finessing since we don't know if she's got some legitimate mental deficiencies. Also, we don't know how many people within the hospital system are involved."

"Can't you just spring her?" Leah suggested what Tanner assumed was an idea born of watching too many crime dramas.

Tanner shook his head. "Ha. I wish. We're hoping to get a court order that will allow Judge Watkins to appoint an interim guardian until it's settled. Also, we need to get a medical evaluation for Marie immediately. Dr. Miller is at the top of tomorrow's list of people to contact."

"This is a whole lot more complicated than it was last week when we were looking through photos at Nana's house, huh?" Leah's question was rhetorical and obvious. "Maybe Nana knows more about the family than she realizes, or maybe Momma does."

"We really don't want anyone else involved now that there are actual threats to us. I certainly don't want your family members more deeply committed to this case." Tanner would do anything he could to protect the family, including *not* asking questions if he believed it would keep everyone safe.

They all sat quietly for a few minutes. Such a conundrum. "So, we're sharing this information with you both so you know what's going on, but please don't tell anyone, including family, what's happening. There's a leak someplace and we're trying to keep the circle who know about all this as small as possible, so when we do decide to make a move, no one will get a jump on our plans ahead of time." Tanner had to let them know not to say a word.

"You can trust us, of course. You wouldn't have said anything if you thought you couldn't, but we get that you had to say it." Leah smiled. "Now that we know about it, let us help where we can. Don't hesitate to call on us if you need partners in *investigating*. I won't say partners in crime because we can't have Jake doing sketchy stuff. He has his medical license to think of."

"Exactly." Carly nodded at her sister. "No sketchy stuff for either of y'all, got it?"

Leah rolled her eyes.

Carly

LAST NIGHT, AFTER Leah and Jake had gone, Tanner and I sat together on the dock. Not for a long time, but long enough that something shifted between us. We'd been relaxed, finally, after the day we'd shared, and the moon was big and bright over the water. A fish, or something, splashed nearby, breaking the sounds of crickets and frogs that echoed through the nighttime.

I was comfortable with Tanner; safe and secure in way that I'd never felt with any other man. I could be myself and I knew he wouldn't judge me. When I compared my childhood crush with the utterly crushy feelings I was currently having, I really couldn't tell where one ended and the other began. I reached over and put my hand in his. The urge had been almost overwhelming to touch his warm skin.

He responded by curling his fingers around mine. We didn't speak. It wasn't necessary in that moment. I'd sighed, so content. With everything happening in our lives, I was relaxed and happy to sit beside Tanner on a moonlit night by the water and hold his hand. The thrill—the romance of it—ran through my fingers and straight into my soul.

We sat like that for half an hour before I stifled a huge yawn, which made Tanner laugh. "We've got an early morning. You'd better get some sleep."

"Yeah. I guess I'd better get going. Thanks for inviting me over. It's been a nice evening."

He nodded and smiled. "It has."

He and I walked up the dock together and I got in my car while he cleaned up the bottles and battened down his hatches for the night. I'd only had one beer, so driving wasn't an issue.

The house was dark when I arrived at Nana's. I assumed she was already asleep since it was well past her bedtime. I set my alarm and fell into bed exhausted but somehow excited about the connection Tanner and I had made. It was subtle, but somehow it seemed important, like the ground had shifted between us.

I'd barely closed my eyes when my alarm went off...or so it seemed. I was still in the same position as when I'd gone to sleep.

This morning we were headed to meet with Dr. Miller. Well, *ambush* him really. Instead of calling him ahead of time, we'd decided not to give him the opportunity to slip away without talking to us. If we were going to get information on Marie's situation, this guy could hold the key.

I showered and dressed quickly for the day. When I got downstairs, Nana was already in the kitchen in her robe. "Egg sandwich?"

"Sure." Since she already had it made and on a plate for me, I wasn't going to refuse the delicious sustenance. I grabbed a mug and poured a cup of fresh-brewed Community Coffee. The dark roast chicory blend was a staple in the state for so many folks. I'd gotten hooked on it when I lived in South Louisiana while I was in law school.

"What's happening with Lisa and Marie? Anything new?" Nana's tone was conversational.

I hadn't filled her in on the latest and thought better of going into it now. "We're working on a couple things now. I'll let you know how it goes." I also didn't want to worry her.

Nana nodded. She wouldn't pry into my professional life beyond asking. "Y'all stay safe out there. Something about this is crawling up my spine, darlin'."

Nana had a wicked sixth sense. Call it gris-gris or juju, or whatever. Nana had a touch of it in her soul. She'd learned about herbs and some of the healing arts as a young woman, but I didn't know much about that. Only that when Nana said she had a funny feeling about something, I listened.

"I'll be careful." I took a second to lay my head on her shoulder and give her a quick squeeze. "Thanks for making breakfast."

"I like to send you out there ready for the day. I miss the

days when you girls were little and I could spoil you." She kissed the top of my head.

"I miss those days too. I like being spoiled." Momma wasn't much for spoiling us as kids, but I was so grateful we'd had Nana in our lives to take up the slack.

I wrapped the other half of my sandwich in a napkin and took it with me as I hurried out the door. Being late wasn't an option this morning—well, any morning. But especially this morning. I was excited to find out what Dr. Miller knew about Marie. Excited and a little anxious. Was it wrong to thrive on this kind of excitement? It was kind of like watching a thriller on TV. I guess it was a little depraved, but my heart was beating fast, and I couldn't wait to find out what happened next. Also, there was last night's hand-holding thing. That might be part of this morning's anticipation. Maybe.

When I arrived at the office, Tanner's truck was already parked outside, along with Lisa's BMW. I didn't see any sign of Imogene's car yet. I hoped Lisa was an early riser since we would be bursting in every morning around seven thirty to start the day. It seemed to be the time both Tanner and I had adjusted to naturally over the past couple weeks since we'd begun our venture together.

Lisa was up and dressed, which had me breathing a sigh of relief. She and Tanner were having a cup of coffee together in the conference room when I came in. "Good morning." I greeted them both, but my eyes darted immediately to Tanner without hesitation. He was smiling at me. *Whew. Good.* I didn't want to see regret about our handholding in his gaze because I had none.

"What do you think about Lisa's going in to speak to Dr. Miller alone at first while we wait in the car and listen in?" Tanner spoke as soon as I'd put down my bag and sat down at the table. "We could be ready to come inside at a moment's notice." It was legal by law if one party gave consent to listen or record conversations.

I nodded. "Good idea. Maybe he's innocent of anything besides being manipulated. It's worth a try." This was a good strategy to begin with.

"I could bring my adoption papers with Marie's signature on them to prove I'm her granddaughter," Lisa suggested.

"We'll have to be ready for the doctor to tip off the others as soon as Lisa leaves the office. Unless the doctor agrees to work with us." Tanner frowned. "Our main goal is to keep Marie out of harm's way."

"We've got to figure out a way to get to her before someone else does." I tapped my iPad. "How soon do you think we could gain entrance to Pine Hill?"

"That depends on a lot of things. I suppose we'll take it a step at a time."

"I guess Imogene will be her shortly." Imogene was oddly late, and since she wasn't there, they locked up the office.

Carly scanned the small parking area once they were outside to make sure nobody was hanging around. It was getting to be a habit whenever she entered or exited now.

CHAPTER SIXTEEN

Tanner

THEY USED LISA'S phone as an open mic for her impromptu meeting with Dr. Miller. Tanner and Carly listened on speaker in the car with a plan to record every word, in case the good doctor said something that could incriminate himself or anyone else.

"Good morning. I'm Lisa Henry to see Dr. Miller."

"I'm sorry. I don't see you on Dr. Miller's schedule. Do you have an appointment?" They heard a woman's voice, whom Tanner assumed was the receptionist.

"No, but please tell him it's with regards to Marie Trichel, so he'll want to speak with me immediately." Lisa pulled out an intimidating voice Tanner had not yet heard her use. He and Carly exchanged an impressed look.

Tanner wasn't sure what to make of his and Carly's hand-holding last night. It was like something new and different was introduced to their friendship that was more than friendship but not anything that needed discussing—yet. As nice as it had been, Tanner wasn't sure yet if it should go any further. But he'd felt something between them—a closeness that went well beyond their working relationship—even beyond a close friendship.

We heard some shuffling and muffled voices. "Ms. Henry. Dr. Miller will see you now. Right this way."

"Thank you."

More shuffling. Doors opening and closing. "Good morning, Ms. Henry. How can I help you?" An elderly male voice asked the question. Was there an edge to his gravelly voice? Maybe nerves?

"Yes. Thanks for seeing me on such short notice. I need to see my grandmother, Marie Trichel. I understand she's committed at Pine Hill and is under your care?"

There was silence for a few seconds. The doctor cleared his throat. "Um. Well, that might be a problem. I understood Miz Trichel didn't have any blood kin after her husband died. She's been assigned a court-appointed guardian."

"I have proof that I'm her granddaughter." There were sounds of shuffling papers. "I'll need to see her medical records and have you sign off on allowing visitation at Pine Hill."

Silence again. More throat clearing. "I'll…uh…have to check on that, Ms. Henry. Legally, everything goes through her guardian."

"Who might that be?" Lisa's question was more a demand.

"Well, I'm not at liberty to say, exactly." Dr. Miller's anxiety was coming through the phone's speaker loud and clear.

"Exactly, what *are* you at liberty to say?" Lisa's chair scraped as if she'd stood and was possibly towering over the doctor. Man, she was good.

"Well, you know, there's a process for this type of thing."

"*This type of thing?* I've been advised that my grandmother's rights have been violated. Are you a party to that, Doctor? Are you going to let others let you take the fall for that, sir?"

"Oh now, hold on, ma'am. I don't want any trouble here. Let's figure a way to work this out."

Tanner looked over at Carly. The phone on their end was muted. "He's ready to save his own skin. Let's go."

They got out of the truck and headed inside, ignoring the protests of the receptionist on their way into the office from the reception area. It took about two seconds to find where Lisa was in conference with the doctor. "Hi, I'm Tanner Carmichael, counsel for Lisa Henry. This is my associate, Carly Bertrand. We're also representing Marie Trichel. You've been recorded at the behest of Lisa Henry."

Dr. Miller was old. Like in his seventies, old. Tanner experienced a twinge of conscience at bombarding him like this. He likely was a true patsy in all of this. "Like I told Ms. Henry, we can work this out." He held his hands up as if we were pointing a gun at him. It probably felt that way.

"I'm glad to hear it, Doctor. We have court orders and an investigation started on the judge and attorney who helped you secure Marie's guardianship. What we need to learn from you is her state of mind and to understand why she was mandated to Pine Hill."

The man was visibly shaking. "Th-they'll harm me. They'll harm my family if I go against them. They said they would."

Understanding washed over Tanner. He nodded at the

doctor. Tanner couldn't promise his safety—yet. "Okay. If we get proof of their guilt and protection for you family, will you testify against them?" *Them* being at least Judge Keller and the attorney.

Dr. Miller nodded. "If you can guarantee our safety." He pulled off his glasses and pinched the bridge of his nose. "I will tell you that Miz Trichel shouldn't be there—in Pine Hill. That's all I'm gonna say. But that's for your information. Don't tell anyone I told you." Then his eyes widened. "You're recording this, aren't you?"

"Don't worry. This is need to know only."

It was what they'd come to find out...mostly. Marie Trichel was alive, and she wasn't insane or infirm. She didn't belong at Pine Hill. She was being kept there against her will. And it was all on tape.

Next stop...the DA's office.

Carly

"I HATE THAT we had to upset him like that." I couldn't help but feel awful about it. The old doctor seemed to be truly terrified. Not that he hadn't done wrong. He had. But it appeared he'd been placed in an impossible position.

"So, my grandmother is not only alive, but she's mentally okay?" Lisa's expression was one of wonder. "I honestly can't believe it."

We were driving toward Alan Litrell's office. He had no idea we were on the way. With the likelihood of phone taps and such, no one could be trusted aside from our closest family at this point. Well, besides Momma. She could unintentionally blow it with a careless word. "Here's hoping the DA is in his office." Tanner's jaw was set. He wasn't jumping for joy just yet.

We pulled in and circled to the back of the lot, parking the black truck alongside the other larger black vehicles, like last time. "We have no idea who's in the tank with Judge Keller, so let's split up and take separate ways to Litrell's office. I'll take the stairs, and y'all grab the elevator. Look around before you head up."

The office was on the third floor, so this bait and switch may or may not be necessary. It would help to see who noticed our coming and going and give us an idea who paid attention and took notice. We arrived about the same time as Tanner, who didn't seem winded. Surely he'd sprinted up the stairs.

Nobody had seen us so far. Well, unless there was a camera in the elevator, which was a good possibility. The administrative assistant, Jeff, who we recognized from last time, nodded when he saw us and showed us back to the DA's inner office immediately.

Alan Litrell put a finger to his lips and motioned for us to step out onto his small balcony that overlooked the city. He shut the door before speaking. "I can't assume no one is listening, so sorry for the cloak and dagger. I'm assuming you've gotten some new information."

"We paid Dr. Miller a visit, and we've got him recorded saying that he and his family have been threatened should he share any information about Marie Trichel's guardian or how that came about. But he did tell us that she's of sound mind and doesn't belong in Pine Hill. Says he'll testify if we can guarantee his safety and that of his family." Tanner filled the DA in quickly.

Alan nodded. "Dr. Miller's got to be willing to get out of town immediately for a few weeks to make sure he's safe. We'll help with that. The wheels won't turn at a state level quickly enough to keep him out of harm's way here in town. District judges get the benefit of the doubt…always."

"What about the court order for Lisa to get legal custody of Marie until we can get her re-evaluated?" I asked.

"Now that I know from the doctor's own lips that she's mentally stable, I can do a temporary order. Problem is, we still don't know who her guardian is."

"Can we go to the hospital with a temporary order immediately and have her released to our care?" Lisa asked.

"Theoretically, yes. But it will help to have a physician there to assist with transport and to assess the patient's condition. In case you get resistance from the facility, we'll send some state police. They're the only ones who would have jurisdiction to escort her back here on short notice. I'll give a call to Rapides Parish and find out if we can get a couple deputies to meet you there." The DA let them back inside. He pulled out an official-looking document from his desk drawer and signed it, and then called in his administrative assistant to notarize it. Clearly he'd been waiting on our next move. We'd sent in the paperwork from Lisa proving she was legally Marie's granddaughter and applying for custody. For it to be truly legal, there had to be a hearing. But judges could do temporary orders in emergency situations.

"I've already had Judge Watkins sign it. He trusted we would get the go-ahead from the doctor. I'll use the next two hours to fulfill my promise to handle what we discussed, while you round up whomever you need to do your part." He used cryptic speech in case anyone might have bugged his office.

The DA and Tanner shook hands. "Thanks so much."

"Best of luck. I can't stand corrupt politicians." He nodded toward Lisa, who had tears in her eyes. "So, let's get busy."

"Thank you, Mr. Litrell."

WE ALL TOOK the stairs on the way down since there didn't seem to be anybody lurking around the building. Once we got outside, Tanner pulled out his phone and called Jake.

"How's your afternoon looking?" I couldn't hear Jake's reply, but it was probably along the lines of, *Why? What do you need?* Jake had a team of specialists who worked under him, and he could make himself available should the need arise.

"We're doing a jailbreak in about two hours from now for Marie Trichel at Pine Hill. Do you have a psychiatrist on hand who might be able to help?"

Jake spoke for a couple minutes.

Tanner replied, "There will be law enforcement present, and we have a court order signed by the DA and Judge Watkins. We're as legal as we can be for now... By ambulance? I hadn't thought about that. Yes, it's probably a good idea."

Tanner disconnected the call. We'd climbed into the truck and were heading toward the office now. "Jake says he'll have the psychiatrist who's not on call head over to Pine Hill with us in an ambulance. It will cover our bases legally in case Marie isn't herself."

"What do you mean, 'not herself'?" Lisa asked.

"We don't know what the situation might be when we arrive. If she's there against her will, the facility might have her drugged to keep her compliant."

Lisa didn't reply, only stared out the window. I couldn't imagine what she must be feeling right now. This search of hers must be taxing emotionally, especially since she had no real support from the people who were supposed to be her main source of it—her family. So far, she'd shown few cracks in her façade of strength.

"I know if somebody put me in a mental health facility against my will, I'd require drugs to keep calm. I'd probably be trying to escape every day of my life." I said this because it was likely that Marie wouldn't be in the best condition. It had been a couple years since her husband, Jay, had passed away. And I was concerned about her having been locked up with no hope, even though she wasn't in the throes of dementia.

"I guess I'd best be prepared then." Lisa's voice was sad. Not the same excited tone she'd used when we'd found out Marie was alive and *well*.

I hoped and prayed Marie hadn't been abused in that place.

We made a quick stop by the office before heading to Pine Hill. Imogene's car was now parked in the lot. "Sorry I was late this morning. I stopped by Walmart to pick up some coffee. Where've y'all been?" Imogene met us as we got halfway down the hall. "I was worried when nobody was here. What's going on?"

"We're headed to Pine Hill to hopefully pick up Marie Trichel. She's been committed to the facility under false pretenses. We've gotten a court order for her release." Tanner filled her in.

"Wow. How did you find out all this?" Imogene's eyes were wide.

"It doesn't matter. We've got to get on the road now so we can meet Jake and the doctor there with the ambulance."

"Ambulance?"

"Just a precaution."

"Oh, dear." Imogene had gone pale.

"What is it, Imogene?" I put my hand on her shoulder. "Are you all right?"

"Yes. This is just so shocking."

Tanner's phone buzzed with a text. He read it and then looked up. "Dr. Miller is on his way out of town. We're not being told where for his safety."

I nodded, feeling relieved on that front at least. "That's probably a good idea."

"Are y'all ready to spring Marie?" Tanner asked us.

CHAPTER SEVENTEEN

WE MADE THE drive in silence. The three of us were obviously tense and concerned about how this would go. When we pulled up in front of the somewhat Gothic Greek Revival building that looked more like a timeworn mansion, a throwback to asylums of old, the ambulance pulled in right behind us. There were several law enforcement vehicles as well. Two sheriff's cars and two state troopers.

All were still sitting in their cars. Waiting for us, I supposed. Tanner grabbed his leather portfolio case that contained all the appropriate legal paperwork. "Give me a minute."

I noticed as soon as he got out that the others did too. Jake approached from his personal vehicle not far away. It was nice of him to come for support. The two brothers spoke for a few seconds before the law officers joined them, along with the paramedics and the psychiatrist. They were clearly planning. Tanner was pointing and speaking.

He opened the door and said, "Okay. Lisa, you, Jake, and I are going to go inside and ask to see Marie. We'll see how it goes from there. The officers and Carly will hang at the entrance and will advance if needed. We'll do this with as little commotion as necessary."

I hung back with the law officers as they entered the front door. The lobby had a chandelier and a round entry table with a large floral centerpiece in keeping with the old Southern mansion look of the exterior. I wondered why they bothered, because just beyond the entryway, the place became all institution with buzzing doors and lots of cameras. Jake spoke to a woman in a pair of scrubs at the first window. She picked up a telephone to call someone. Jake, Lisa, and Tanner backed away from the window and waited.

Tanner walked over to me. "They've called the director, so we're waiting." He touched my hand lightly, sending a thrill through me, and I wanted to lean toward him. I could feel his breath brush my cheek as he spoke near my ear. I shook my head to clear it when he stepped away.

A good ten minutes later, through some awkward pacing and shuffling, the woman called through the plexiglass to Jake. "Dr. Carmichael, you can come through the door when it buzzes. No one else."

"I have a court order signed from a district judge." Tanner held up the document as if to argue with her about their only bringing in Jake.

"Dr. Hart will start by speaking with Dr. Carmichael. Bring the documents." The woman's nasal tone was firm.

Tanner handed them over and spoke in Jake's ear. Jake nodded.

I raised my eyebrows when Tanner stepped over to where I was waiting. "He's going to record the conversation. He can't patch us through due to patient privacy." Again, he leaned in close and spoke softly. And again, my entire being recognized his closeness.

Jake was buzzed through and disappeared into the bowels of who-knew-what. My heart rate kicked up and my palms got sweaty. Leah would kill me if I let anything happen to him. Something about this place made me believe in every horror movie ever filmed surrounding creepy asylums. Nurse Ratched came to mind unbidden.

The place smelled of alcohol and pine cleaner. At least I didn't detect urine here in the reception area. I hated to think of what was behind the buzzing doors. "Hey, are you okay?" Tanner asked me.

I nodded, but I realized my mind had been going down a dark path of worry. I looked over at Lisa. Her expression likely mirrored my own. Big-eyed and struck with worry about what was going on back there. I moved toward her and took her hand. "It's going to be all right," I tried to reassure us both.

We waited for a half an hour before Jake reappeared. "They're going to let us see her while the director makes some phone calls to the state board."

"I hope he realizes we're on the right side of the law." Tanner kept his voice low.

"He seems conflicted but not corrupt. He's got two sets of paperwork. One says Marie's committed legally by a board giving full authority to do so. Ours says he should go against that. I tried to explain the situation, but I couldn't even give the name of her legal guardian."

"He wouldn't give you the name of her guardian?" I wondered at the continued absence of this mystery person's identity.

Jake shook his head. "Says the guardian never comes

here. Just a signature on a page, but he can't give out the information. Says Marie is sedated most of the time or she raises Cain."

"Okay, y'all can go back now," the woman at the desk called out.

Lisa, Tanner, and the psychiatrist were allowed back.

I sat in one of the lovely brocade chairs in the initial entry, where there was classical music and finery. I'd remembered about the endowment for this building that housed dementia patients. This small allowance of beauty must have something to do with that. I did wonder what the rest of the place looked like behind the doors.

Losing one's faculties must be terrible, especially if you knew it was happening. Not in Marie's case, but I'd seen it with some of the families whom I'd worked with during law school. Those who'd been caregivers as they worked and cared for children and elderly as single women in poverty. How hopeless their circumstances. I hoped this facility, besides housing Marie Trichel against her will, was one that did good work for those who couldn't advocate for themselves.

I made a mental note to do some digging once we had Marie settled. To find out who the patients were who lived here. I would make certain there hadn't been any other cases of abuse against residents. The elderly were especially vulnerable, but the elderly without full control of their faculties were utterly helpless.

I thought of Nana and how lucky we were that she was healthy and independent. And how horrified I'd be if anyone were to ever treat her badly. I hoped for Lisa's sake she found

Marie in decent shape.

Tanner

THE FACILITY WAS clearly quite old, maybe built in the fifties, but Tanner could see there had been some improvements implemented since then. The paint was relatively fresh on the walls and doors and, from what he could tell, the equipment appeared modern. But despite its exterior, this was an institution for patients with dementia. He could see attempts here and there to brighten things up, but still, patients were locked up tight at night due to necessity.

The slamming doors echoed, as did their footsteps on the worn gray tile. The floors were shiny, but old. "Ms. Trichel gets agitated very easily so we've had to keep her somewhat sedated during her stay."

"The entire time she's been here?" Lisa sounded appalled, and looked to our psychiatrist, Dr. Gill, for his reaction. He simply gave a barely discernable nod, which could mean anything. He'd looked over Marie's chart as soon as the doctor here had allowed it. Dr. Gill hadn't said much thus far. Tanner assumed he'd decided to wait until he met the patient before assessing things. Tanner assumed that anyone Jake sent would have been brought up to speed and be good at his job.

"It's not unusual for our patients to function on some level of sedative, depending on their state of mind. Dementia often causes a constant state of anxiety that can't easily be controlled without medications."

"You do realize that Marie doesn't have dementia, right?" Lisa narrowed her eyes at him.

"Dr. Carmichael has explained a rather outlandish scenario that I find very hard to believe. We are not in the business of stashing away perfectly functioning people for nefarious purposes here at Pine Hill."

Dr. Gill finally spoke up. "How did you find the patient when you met with her initially?"

"She was quite vocal about not being incompetent, but I must admit that I've never had a patient say otherwise. She also swore there were people trying to silence her by putting her here." The doctor blanched. "That has also been a common claim."

"I need you to understand that we firmly believe, with the backing of a court order and four lawmen, outside that this is the case. There has been collusion between a judge, a physician, and an attorney to lock this woman up, and since she's got no family, it was successful."

"But why? Why would someone go to such lengths?" The director, Dr. Hart, asked, shaking his head as if this were all nonsense.

"We believe she has information at least one of them doesn't want her to tell anyone. It's an ongoing investigation so we can't share. But you won't have any legal liability in releasing her to us. Dr. Gill is here to determine if that is the best thing for her. We aren't doing this lightly, Doctor, though I know it sounds farfetched."

"Well, here she is. She mumbles about her daughter being taken from her and something about a baby—how she must find the baby. We try to have her interact with the other patients, but she sometimes upsets them, so she spends a lot of time alone." This had Lisa and Tanner exchanging glances.

Dr. Hart unlocked the door of a room with only a small square window on the door. Tanner's stomach clenched. Everything he'd said about Marie matched with what they knew so far.

"Let me go in first so I can tell her what's happening. I don't want to bombard her without warning." When the door swung open, they saw her.

Tanner grabbed Lisa by the arm to prevent her from rushing to Marie's side. He leaned down and whispered, "Let's give him a second." So far, despite being unconvinced, the director had seemed to be playing it straight with them. At least they'd gotten this far.

Marie was a small woman, her dark hair cut short. She was slumped a little in her wheelchair. The director was speaking softly to her. Something he said must have struck a chord because she turned her head and made eye contact with Lisa. She raised her thin arm and pointed. "It's the baby."

Tanner couldn't stop Lisa then. She was beside Marie in a second. "Hi there, Marie. I'm Lisa."

"I'll give y'all a few minutes. Let me know if you need anything." The director shut the door behind him, leaving the four of them in the tiny room with a single window with the thin Venetian blinds that were pulled all the way up to allow some sunlight to radiate the sparse room.

Marie blinked at Lisa and grinned. She was a little out of

it but not so much that she wasn't conscious. "I've been trying to find you, honey. They put me in this place to keep me quiet, you know? But nobody believes me."

"We believe you, Marie. That's why we've come. We're doing our best to get you out of here today," Tanner told her.

"Well, what took you so long?" Marie asked them. They laughed in response.

Dr. Gill cleared his throat. "Let me have a look at Ms. Trichel, if you will."

Lisa spoke gently to her grandmother as she held her hand. "Marie, this is Dr. Gill. He's our friend and he's here with us to make sure you're okay."

Marie turned her focus to Dr. Gill. She narrowed her eyes at him. "I don't like doctors much, ya know."

"I don't expect you do, given what you've been through, but I'll be quick, all right. Now, can you follow this light with your eyes? Good. I'm going to tap on each of your knees and check your reflexes. Great…" And so it went. Dr. Gill asked Marie a few questions she struggled with like what day it was and who the president of the United States was.

Marie had decided that Dr. Gill was okay. "I haven't kept up with current affairs, ya know? But I like to watch movies."

Dr. Gill took Tanner aside. "I think when the drugs clear, she's going to be quite cognizant. It might be best to get her clear of here before that happens."

"Yes, let's get the ball rolling here." Tanner knocked on the door to alert the director, Dr. Hart.

Tanner couldn't wait to let Carly know that Marie was

pretty much intact. So much better than they might have found her.

Tanner's phone buzzed. It was a text from Carly. *Carson is here and he's raising a ruckus about Marie. Says he's her legal guardian. Jake has taken him outside. Might want to find a back door. I'll try to figure out a way for the ambulance to meet you someplace else while we distract him.*

Carson. Of course it would be Carson. It wasn't like his involvement in this was a surprise. After all, when it came to Judge Keller, they were thick as the worst kind of thieves. And now this.

I'll try to figure a way to get Marie out a back door. Maybe the director will help us. She's loopy but not too bad off. Keep Carson distracted.

"We've got a problem, everyone." They all turned to look at Tanner. "Carson is at the front desk ranting about how no one is to see Marie because she's his ward."

Dr. Hart looked down at his phone and nodded. "I've just been informed. I believe you now after what my staff is telling me about Mr. Carmichael's behavior."

"Can you help us get her out of here?"

"Carson Carmichael? He's the snake who put me in here in the first place. I'm not goin' anywhere with him. He told me to keep my trap shut or I would disappear *forever*."

"He's her legal guardian, so I'm not at liberty to aid you, but you could take my key fob and I might not notice it was missing until you dropped it after you use it to swipe the back door that's to our left and down the corridor and right at the end of the hall. There's a ramp. Have the ambulance driver meet you out there along with some of the law enforcement in case there's an issue. I'll make certain our security stands down and lets you pass."

"Thanks so much. We owe you a lot for this, Dr. Hart."

Marie let out a *whoop*. "That bastard's not gettin' his paws on me. This is Independence Day, y'all!" Lisa laughed and quickly hugged her.

"Yes, it is. And we all believe you, so let's get the heck out of here as quickly and quietly as we can."

Tanner texted Carly and Jake. *One of you keep Carson distracted and the other tell the ambulance driver to meet us at the southwest corner of the building. There's an exit with a ramp.*

He didn't wait for a response in case they weren't able to type one in the moment. The building wasn't huge, so this might be fast and messy.

"Oh, Mr. Carmichael, might I suggest something?" Dr. Hart said. He laid out a plan in thirty seconds that was worthy of a great suspense novel. The plan involved a switcheroo and a wheelchair.

After only another minute or two, they were ready.

Good thing too.

Carly

"MARIE TRICHEL ISN'T leaving this hospital, do you hear me? I'll have you all arrested for endangerment." Carson's eyes were near to bulging out of his head. "Is Tanner back there? There are explicit instructions on her chart that she is not to be allowed visitors without my permission."

"Why on earth can't the poor woman have visitors?" Jake

demanded.

"Because I'm her legal guardian and I *forbid* it!" Carson was sounding more and more insane himself as he ranted. So far, he didn't know that anyone besides maybe Tanner had gone back to speak with her.

Just then, a woman with a headscarf on, being wheeled in a wheelchair by an attendant, with Tanner at her side came through the buzzing door. I thought Carson would pounce on the poor woman. The woman was slumped and appeared to be sleeping, but we couldn't see her face as the scarf was pulled forward.

Carson stepped forward toward Tanner. "How *dare* you try and slip this woman out without my permission."

"I've got a court order that she's to be remanded to my custody and that of her granddaughter temporarily. A psychiatrist has determined that we are *not* endangering her health."

"Granddaughter? She's got no family. The woman is demented, or didn't you take a moment to read her medical information?"

"She's not demented. She's been overmedicated to keep her from tearing the place down to get out of here, but she's not suffering from dementia. And she does have a biological granddaughter."

"That's bullshit. I've got a doctor who would say other-wise. And a judge who signed off on it. That makes a mental health panel. Legal in the state of Louisiana." Carson was smug.

"We've spoken to your doctor in Cypress Bayou. Miller, is it? Says you forced his hand in signing off on committing

Marie, and that she doesn't belong here. I've got it on record. The DA has listened to it. It's what convinced him to give us the court order."

Carson's face turned dark red then, as if he couldn't control his temper. He reached over to Marie and pulled on her headscarf. "Well, Marie here won't tell you anything because everybody knows she's crazy as a soup sandwich."

The woman who looked up at him didn't resemble a soup sandwich. In fact, when she raised her head, Carson pulled back as if he'd been shot. "Who the hell are you and where is Marie?" Lisa stared back at Carson with a satisfied expression.

"I'm Lisa Henry. You might have heard of me by now. I'm Marie's granddaughter, and the daughter of Justine Chaffin. Surely somebody's told you about me."

I'd never seen Carson at a loss for words, but he was now. He nearly staggered back. "It can't be. They said—"

"Something tells me there's something more here to learn, but if you'll excuse us, we've got to see to our ward." Tanner extended a hand to Lisa, who stood and shed the robe and slippers she'd donned for the excellent distraction they'd pulled off while Marie had made her getaway in the ambulance with the psychiatrist.

"Wh-what? She's gone? What have you done with her? You won't get away with this. I'll have you all arrested." Carson shook his fist.

"We've got all the proper paperwork. Oh, and tell Judge Keller he's in a world of trouble for participating in this farce and robbing Marie of her freedom. If I were you, I'd tread lightly. We've got enough evidence to send you both to prison."

"Nobody has the guts to testify. It's all circumstantial." Carson scoffed.

"I wouldn't be too sure about that. Oh, and if you're looking for Dr. Miller, he's gone. Even we don't know where." I couldn't help throwing that big dig in there to make him doubt himself.

"Nobody's going to believe a word Marie Trichel says. She's certifiable."

We turned our backs on him and walked out of Pine Hill while Carson continued to hurl threats and insults.

CHAPTER EIGHTEEN

Tanner

"Y'ALL GET AWAY, okay?" Tanner called Dr. Gill as soon as they were on the road, safely away from Carson. Tanner put the call on speaker so Lisa and Carly could hear the conversation.

"Yes. Marie seems to be handling the excitement pretty well, considering what she's been through."

They could hear her in the background laughing. "You tell my granddaughter I'm doing just fine. I haven't had any medicine since last night and when it wears off, I can finally think straight."

"She sounds good. Do you think we need to admit her to the hospital for observation?" Tanner asked the doctor.

"I think that's not a bad idea. She might be a little dehydrated from what I can tell. How about we meet you at Cypress General?" Dr. Gill spoke low into the phone as if he didn't want Marie to hear him.

"Got it."

"Any trouble getting out of there on your end?" Dr. Gill asked.

"I wouldn't call it trouble. More like an annoying complication. Ask the state trooper to hang out at the hospital with y'all for a few minutes until we arrive. We're about fifteen minutes behind you."

After Tanner disconnected the call, he spoke to Lisa. "Are you all right?"

"Yes. Thank you both. That was scary and weird back there, but I'm thrilled to see that Marie isn't nearly as bad off as I was afraid she might be." Tanner could hear the relief in her voice.

"You did a great job standing up for her in this. She owes you a lot for your part in making this happen."

"And I owe all of you for putting yourselves at risk on our behalf. I'm so grateful."

"We're all so excited that Marie's headed back to Cypress Bayou and that she seems pretty okay." Carly leaned toward the center of the console and turned around to face Lisa while she spoke.

Tanner glanced over at Carly, his adrenaline still high. She returned his gaze and lifted her lips into a small, satisfied smile that hit him right in the feels.

"I hope she doesn't freak when we ask her to spend another night in the hospital." Lisa sounded a little concerned. "Plus, where are we going to take her when she gets out? Should I book a hotel or B&B in town?"

"Yes, she might not receive that news about another night in the hospital very well. But while y'all were pulling off this caper, I called my nana and asked if her old friend Marie might stay with us until we figure out what Carson's done with her finances. We know she owned a house here in town at one point and then another in Leesfield. He's got control of her accounts as her guardian."

"What did Nana Elise say?" Tanner asked.

"She said Marie was more than welcome to stay with us until we figured out Marie's situation." Carly then turned back to Lisa. "Nana's house is quite large, and she's got plenty of room. She's also invited you to come and stay with Marie so the two of you can get acquainted."

"Oh, I couldn't intrude on your grandmother. She doesn't even know me."

"Believe me, if Nana invited you, she means it. She doesn't do things insincerely." Tanner backed up Carly on that.

"Yes, believe it. And Nana can't abide Carson and his kind. They've got a long-standing feud. You'll do better with her in your corner." Carly's tone was kind.

"Thanks so much, Carly. It's a shame my own family hasn't been in my corner the way yours is. That reminds me, I need to call my husband." She dug around in her purse for her phone.

Carly and Tanner shared a quick and meaningful glance. It was clear they'd been thinking the same thing by the slight alarm on Carly's face. "I hate to ask, but do you mind holding off for a little while before telling anyone else about what's gone on here? I want to report everything to Alan Litrell and get a sense of what Carson's next move might be before this all blows up." Tanner didn't know Lisa's husband or what his politics were, or whom he might talk to.

"So, I guess I shouldn't tell my parents anything yet either?"

"No. Not yet. I'm sorry to ask this of you." Tanner hoped he didn't come across as overbearing. "This is going to be sensitive for the next couple of days."

Tanner saw Lisa nod in his rearview mirror. "I understand completely. Marie's safety is my main concern. And finding out what she knows about my mother's disappearance. After everything we've done to get here, I wouldn't want to compromise our progress."

"Yes, Marie wasn't locked up for her own good. Carson went to a lot of trouble to keep her from talking," Carly said.

"At least he didn't get rid of her—like permanently—so there's that," Lisa replied.

"What was Carson doing there? How did he know what we were planning?" Carly said out loud what Tanner was thinking.

"That's something we're going to have to determine once we get back." Tanner had an idea about it but had refused to see the signs.

Carly

WE ARRIVED AT Cypress General around five p.m. Jake had followed in his truck, so he was there to help expedite things where Marie was concerned. She was first brought to the emergency room for triage, then taken back to a treatment room for fluids, as it was determined she was indeed dehydrated.

I called Nana to let her know what was happening. "Dr. Gill insisted on having Marie admitted for observation overnight to let the drugs from Pine Hill clear from her system. That way, he can do a psych evaluation and a physical to make sure she doesn't have any underlying conditions."

"Praise the Lord, they found her in good shape. It coulda been so much worse." Nana's relief matched theirs. "When I think of all the horrible things Carson's done, I swear this takes the cake."

"Tanner's meeting with the DA to fill him in now. It will be up to him as to whether to press charges. They'll have to question everyone involved to determine what laws have been broken and who broke them. It could take a while to figure it all out. Plus, there's got to be evidence, and we all know how well Carson covers his tracks."

"Well, let me know when you're coming home. And bring that sweet Lisa with you. No sense in her staying at the office another night. We've got plenty of room here."

"Yes, I'll tell her you said so. She's a little uncertain, but hopefully she'll be convinced."

"Well, I got some fresh blue crabs from the market brought in from the Gulf Coast this morning. I had them steam them for me, so I've been picking the meat all morning." Nana would spend an entire day picking crabs to make her "famous" stuffed crabs. They were a treat, and we only had them a couple times a season.

"My stomach's growling now. I can't wait."

"There's plenty, so y'all come home and eat when you can, and bring Lisa and Tanner with you. I'm assuming Lisa will come on over and stay with us now. We've got reason to celebrate. We'll save some for Marie for when she gets out of the hospital."

"I'll let them know."

I couldn't help but think about Tanner in his meeting with the DA I would have liked to be there with him. It felt strange not to be by his side. Yes, I was still having those crushy feelings, and it was happening more frequently lately.

Lisa and I were sitting in the general waiting area when I heard the clicking of heels on tile. Not just any heels though. When I looked up, I groaned. I thought about a quick getaway, but it was too late. Elizabeth Keller already had me in her sights.

Elizabeth was a cardiothoracic surgeon and Leah's nemesis, because Elizabeth had always had a crush on Jake. And she was a really nasty person, in my opinion. She was also Judge Keller's daughter, and my new sister, Allison's half-sister. So many reasons why I wanted to *not* deal with her.

"So, what's this I hear about y'all giving Daddy a hard time again?" Elizabeth didn't mind making a scene. Anywhere. And who knew what had gotten to the judge about all of this so far.

"I'm not discussing legal business, Elizabeth."

"And who's this?" Elizabeth nodded toward Lisa. Rudely.

"I'm Lisa Henry. You?" Lisa—I was finding out—could hold her own against the likes of the worst in this town.

Elizabeth's shoulders stiffened in great offense. "I'm *Doctor* Elizabeth Keller. Heart surgeon here at Cypress General."

"Remind me not to have my heart attack here. Excuse me, I've got to take this call." Lisa stood, and turned her back on Elizabeth, dismissing the woman completely.

"She's got good taste." Elizabeth stared at the back of Lisa. "Nice shoes." Elizabeth wore designer brands always.

So, I suppose, did Lisa. Elizabeth was a strange one. She could admire a good insult *and* a good pair of shoes.

"What do you want, Elizabeth?" I didn't have the patience for Elizabeth right now.

"I want to know what's going on with Daddy. Hasn't your family put him through enough?" Our family, meaning my momma's ratting him out for his fathering my sister thirty-five years ago. That secret had netted some stress for their family, I supposed.

"Whatever your daddy's done doesn't have anything to do with my family. If you want to know something, ask him. I'm not at liberty to discuss anything related to our cases. You should know that."

Elizabeth looked around, then unexpectedly sat down beside me. "Listen, I'm worried about him. He's being unusually secretive and he's very stressed. Momma says he's up all hours making phone calls. I don't doubt he's doing something that maybe he shouldn't, but I'm worried about his health. His heart isn't so great, you know?" It was the first time I'd seen her façade crack. Her perfect mouth with all the red lipstick wobbled a little. An unusual sign of vulnerability.

"Whatever he's got going on, Elizabeth, he needs to admit to. Trying to hide things will only make it worse for him in the long run. That's all I can say about it."

Elizabeth shrugged. "You know Daddy. He's proud. He won't go down without a fight."

I looked her directly in the eyes so there wasn't any confusion. "But he will go down this time. You can be sure of that, so if you're concerned for his stress and health, encourage him to come clean."

A gleam came back into Elizabeth's eyes. "You're trying to extort my emotions to get to Daddy. Very clever, little Bertrand. Too bad your big sister isn't as smart as you. Oh wait, your middle sister. I haven't figured out *our* big sister yet. That should be fun."

She stood and brushed off her lab coat as if my proximity had somehow contaminated her. "Lay off my daddy."

Her heels clicked back the same way they'd come.

Lisa returned from what I assumed was a nonexistent phone call. "Wow, she's a real piece of work. Nice shoes though."

Tanner

"I'M GOING TO place Carson under twenty-four-hour surveillance. It's time to find out all his dirty secrets. I've heard the whispers around town about how he's got nearly everyone in his pocket one way or another. I was elected with a promise to clean up corruption and this is my opportunity to do it. I'll need you to give me as much information on who *not* to trust when it comes to your father."

The district attorney was appalled at their account of what had gone down at Pine Hill. The fact that Carson had shown up a half hour behind them meant someone had tipped him off. Tanner now had a good idea of who that might be, and it disappointed him to think that his trust had been so misplaced.

"Yes, he's a nasty piece of work, I'm sorry to say. Mostly he keeps people loyal by finding their Achilles' heels, whether it be a dirty personal secret or that of a family member. It seems everybody has something they don't want found out. Carson is master at figuring out what makes people tick." Tanner felt like he had to explain his lack of affinity for his father. "I realize it's hard to understand our lack of family loyalty, but he was as terrible a father as he is a human."

"I know. We've known each other for a long time, re-member? I've paid attention." Alan nodded, his expression showing a depth of sympathy. "I'm sorry to say that he's even worse than I'd believed."

"Can we do a wiretap of his phone and office?"

Alan nodded. "I can get the cell phone intercept since we've already gotten compelling evidence regarding Marie Trichel and his collusion with Dr. Miller and Judge Keller. There are documents and witnesses to substantiate this. I'll need to figure out how to get someone in his office to place listening devices without his knowing."

"I've got an idea, but I'll need to have a conversation with someone first." Tanner now decided that Imogene might be his best solution to this situation, but he would need to find out exactly where her loyalties lay.

He didn't want to mention her name to anyone else until he was sure she was his mole. Giving her the benefit of the doubt felt like the right thing to do even though so far she appeared guilty as hell.

"Okay. But today, or we give Carson time to regroup and destroy evidence." Tanner understood the man's motiva-tion to keep his political promises, and finally they had an ally in the town's government who was willing to go boldly against Carson with a full-barreled offense. This had never happened before.

"I'll handle it when I leave your office."

"All right, I'll get warrants assigned quietly to Judge Watkins. It's fortunate he's the duty judge this rotation, so I don't have to explain bypassing Keller." The two district judges rotated taking cases depending on when they were scheduled to be the signing judge.

When he left the DA's office, it was around five thirty, so Tanner decided to stop by his office to see if he could catch Imogene before she left for the day. How he handled this situation would be important for their case against Carson and Judge Keller moving forward.

Imogene's car was in its parking space when he arrived. Tanner entered quietly through the back door, not wanting to alert Imogene to his presence until he got a feel for what she was up to.

He saw that she was sitting at her desk working at the computer. Nothing strange about that. "Hi, Imogene."

She startled and put a hand to her heart. "Oh, I didn't hear you arrive. How did everything go today? I've been worried sick."

"You've never been late, Imogene. Where did you go?" Best to ask her about this directly and see if she would come clean. "There's still no coffee, so I'm thinking you've got something to tell me."

Imogene's expression told the story. She was dead busted. "Well, I-I went to Carson's office. My behavior has been awful." She hung her head. "I'm so ashamed. I told him about Marie. About y'all going to Pine Hill. Fact is, Tanner, that I've been filling him in about your activities since I came to work here." She stared at him with tears in her eyes.

"I know. I figured it out a few days ago."

"I'm so sorry. He's been threatening me, and I haven't had the courage to stand up to him."

"Imogene, what you've done is inexcusable. We trusted you and you've let us down, but you know that. I'm going to give you an opportunity to redeem yourself."

"But how?"

"Carson is under investigation. We're gathering loads of evidence on him, which he doubtlessly knows. But he doesn't know that we are having this conversation, does he?"

"I haven't bugged the office if that's what you mean. I refused when he asked me to. I said I would let him know what was happening, but I wouldn't put bugs here."

"Okay, well, I want you to put bugs in his office and pretend you're still doing his bidding. You can feed him information about us still but you're going to work for the district attorney to bring him down. We'll have him arrested and he can't threaten you anymore."

"Y-you would trust me to do this?"

"If you give us your word that you're on our side. You'll need to testify against him in court once his case goes to trial. Can you do that?"

She nodded, anger and purpose in her eyes. "I'll do whatever I can to help bring him down. Even though my husband retired, Carson continued to threaten his reputation. In a town like this, it's all you've got, you know? Oh, how I despise that man."

Tanner nodded. He'd wondered why Imogene was still loyal to Carson. "Okay, we'll get on a call with Alan Litrell, and he can give you the particulars."

"I'm ready. And Tanner? Thank you for giving me a second chance. This was the worst thing I've ever done in my life. I've felt terrible about it."

"I know. And we forgive you."

CHAPTER NINETEEN

Carly

I STOPPED BY the office after leaving the hospital, and when I arrived, I noticed both Tanner and Imogene's cars there. It hit me then; Imogene was the informant to Carson. I'd not taken the time to think it through earlier. It explained why she'd been late to work yesterday since we were still low on coffee.

They were on a call together in the conference room when I got inside. Tanner waved me in. I lifted my eyebrows in question. Clearly, they'd made peace—and a deal with Alan Litrell.

"Imogene, I appreciate your willingness to work with us and I assure you we will have your back at all times during this process."

"You're welcome, Mr. Litrell. I'm honored you're putting your trust in me, and that—well—that Tanner is willing to give me another chance. I feel terrible about ratting them out to that awful man."

My earlier suspicion about Imogene was now confirmed. I looked over at Tanner and saw the disappointment in his grim expression. I guess he'd already figured it out and decided to try and capitalize on it. An offer she couldn't very well refuse.

"We all have the same goal here, so let's leave it in the past. What we'll need you to do is—" Alan went on to lay out a plan to plant bugs in Carson's office. She would meet with Carson at the end of the day as scheduled. Tomorrow they would supply her with the listening devices.

Once the call ended, we all kind of looked at each other, slightly awkwardly. "Carly—I want to apologize—" Imogene began.

I held up my hand to stop her from saying anything further. "I accept your apology. You've been in a tough spot. Carson has been manipulating people all over town for a long time. We're going to stop him and you're going to be a big part of that."

Imogene nodded. "I'll do everything I can to help bring him down."

"Good. It will solve a lot of problems, especially for Tanner."

Tanner looked up from writing notes on his legal pad. "I've still got a court date Monday to appear in front of Judge Keller, as ridiculous as that sounds." With everything else happening we hadn't really discussed his going to court to fight Carson's lawsuit against him.

"You've got to get Carson to drop the suit so you can get on with your life and get started with your business."

"They're both under investigation now. It's such a conflict of interest to have Keller involved at all. There's no way Carson will give an inch on this. It's his only play now to hurt me. He's like a rat backed into a corner ready to chew his way through anything or anyone in his path."

I nodded. "I'm not one to underestimate him, even backed into a corner." Carson was somebody that nobody should discount, not until he was locked in a cell with a long, long sentence. "What about the threats to bring him before the state bar for his behavior?"

"His only response to that was when he stormed over the night we had our fish fry. Otherwise, he's never responded to them. He's certainly not dropped his complaint with the court."

"Maybe Judge Watkins can have the case pushed to him instead of Keller since there's such a conflict of interest with all the recent stuff you've filed. I mean, there's no way Keller would find in your favor after you've brought evidence to the DA regarding his corruption."

"If everything plays out like it should, there won't be a case because Carson will be in jail," Tanner said.

"I hate to tell you this, but I've got to go to Carson's office now. I'm supposed to be there to give him an update on what y'all are doing," Imogene said. "So, what would you have me tell him?"

Tanner looked over at me. "What do you think would sound realistic?"

"Maybe she should tell him that we were discussing the court date and that we're concerned about Judge Keller's being on the bench for the hearing. It gives him information but nothing specific about *what* we're doing. Oh, and tell him Marie is in the hospital. It'll let him know that nobody can get near her."

Imogene nodded. "Yes. I know he doesn't want anything else provable tied to him. He underestimates me. Thinks I'm so frightened that I would never turn on him. The old buzzard."

"That should be enough to satisfy him for today. Tomorrow we'll get you set up with the listening devices."

After Imogene left, I remembered to invite Tanner over for stuffed crabs at Nana's house. "I know it's been a long day, but she wants to celebrate our springing Marie from Pine Hill. Plus, she's been cooking all day. Jake and Leah will be there and my parents, of course, though that's not a selling point, I know."

Tanner laughed. "I'd be delighted to join your family for dinner. I'll head over to the trailer and take a quick shower and meet you there. It *has* been quite a day, hasn't it?" He smiled at me then. *That* smile. The one that had my inner middle school girl crush waking up to full attention like latent antibodies when exposed to a known virus. Only not to fight it.

I wasn't one to back away from such a magnetic pull. I might've even stepped forward. But however it happened, Tanner Carmichael kissed me then. It was gentle and soft and warm. And it lit me on fire. My body came alive at his lips on mine, and I definitely stepped closer. And put my arms around his waist. I wanted more.

Tanner

KISSING CARLY HADN'T been part of his plan. In fact, he'd been careful up until now to keep a careful distance between them…besides holding her hand the other day. That had sparked something between them. And now, what now?

She tasted like honey and smelled like jasmine. He hadn't been with a woman in a very long time. His body responded instantly, yes, but it was more than that. She'd gotten under his skin from the first day she'd met him at Mother's Oyster Bar, her hair blowing in the wind as she stared out at the bayou. From the moment they'd discussed her coming to work for him.

They'd been together every day since. Working, talking, laughing. This had been building. A relationship of trust and friendship. This slow burn. They'd been slowly sparking this flint at every turn until it finally ignited and caught into a flame from the kindling they'd laid with their nearness. They'd passed in the hallway, almost making contact, caught each other's scent. So many near misses.

He'd known it would be like this between them, which was why he hadn't crossed that very thin line. Until now. Had *he* crossed it? Or had she been the one to make that first step? It didn't matter. Now that he'd tasted her lips, Tanner realized it was inevitable.

"I-uh." He stepped back. "Wow."

She laughed lightly. "Yeah. Wow."

"Should I apologize?" he asked.

Carly looked up at him, her hazel eyes that turned green sometimes. "Don't you dare."

"How about I see you in an hour at Nana's house?" His eyes crinkled as he grinned.

"It's a date." She winced. "You know what I mean."

Tanner wanted the awkwardness between them gone.

"Okay. Let's not be weird. We work together every day and we're grown adults. I like you, Carly, and I'm assuming that you like me too."

She nodded. "I do like you, Tanner, and I'll see you in an hour."

Carly

"I KISSED TANNER." I'd called Jo and added Sue to the call.

"Get out!" Jo yelled into the phone.

"Shut the front door!" Sue nearly blasted their eardrums simultaneously.

"I can't believe it finally happened, y'all. We've had so much going on and I kind of thought we were leading up to—something, but when it happened, I nearly ate his face."

"Pent-up demand, that's what it was. I'm not surprised. You don't date enough to satisfy those cravings. It isn't normal." Sue gave us her well-experienced opinion.

"Sue, you've never been pent up in your life." Jo's purpose in life was to put Sue in her place.

"I have *so*, smart-ass!"

I tried not to take it personally that my two besties had gone off on a sniping tangent when I'd called them to share my exciting, and certainly surprising news. "Um, don't y'all want to hear about it?"

"Yes, we want to hear about it. But it's not like you've been staying in touch much since you've been back home, ya know." Jo was always the one to remind me when I wasn't towing the friendship line.

"I'm sorry. I know, but there are some huge things going on that are going to rock this town if they get out. Things I'm in the middle of that I can't talk about to anyone but Tanner right now. It's been like a thriller movie in my real life lately. I can't wait until I can fill you in."

"Wait, you tell us this and then say you can't tell us what's going on. That sucks, girl." Sue didn't have a hard time expressing her feelings either.

"Just bear with me. I can't talk about work right now, but I was about to burst with the kissing Tanner thing, so I had to call and tell the two of you. Y'all are the only ones who could truly appreciate how crazy and awesome it was."

"Well, how awesome was it?" Jo asked.

"*So* awesome. It's like I've been dealing with boys my whole life and now I've met a *man*. That's what it felt like. Like anything beyond a kiss would teach me new things." And that's exactly what I wanted. To know what would be next. My imagination was running wild.

"Well, I don't care about men one bit, but I can appreciate the idea that you're in the big leagues with Tanner now. I'm happy for you. You've come a long way since making out with Tommy DuBois in his new truck, I'll give you that. If I wasn't gay, I'd go for a guy like Tanner."

"A *man* like Tanner." Sue giggled when she said it. "I'm so proud. Our girl's growing up. We should celebrate. Y'all up for drinks?"

"I wish I could. Nana's making stuffed crabs for the family tonight, and Tanner is invited. We've had a long day." And I wasn't sure how this evening would go or how it would end for that matter.

Sue moaned. "I'd give my engagement ring for one of Nana's stuffed crabs."

"I know. Now you see why I can't skip out. I've been thinking about them all day." I had been and I was currently starving.

"Tell Nana hi from me. It's been a minute or two since I've run into her in town." Jo and her paramedic colleague were often around town and ran into family members of mine.

"I'll tell her."

"Me too. It's been too long," Sue said. "And keep us posted as you round the bases with Tanner."

I pulled up at Nana's house to see that Momma and Daddy had already arrived. I would have to freshen up and change clothes quickly. Momma would want my attention immediately. I wondered how soon things might calm down. So much was happening, and I didn't see a resolution in the near future. But right now, it was all headed in the right direction. My stomach growled.

I could smell the broiled garlic butter and crabmeat stuffing the second before I opened the front door. My stomach growled.

"There you are. You moved home weeks ago and I've hardly seen you." Momma started the evening complaining instead of acting happy to see me. Wasn't that just the way?

I could feel the beginnings of exhaustion creeping up on me then. I decided not to respond to her bait. "Hi, everyone. I'm going to run upstairs and change into comfy clothes. I'll be right back."

"We'll be here, honey. Can't wait to hear what you and Tanner have been up to at work." Daddy spoke up then. I hadn't seen him but a couple times since I'd been back and I felt awful about it.

"Be right back, Daddy."

I quickly brushed my teeth and dressed. And did a quick spray of perfume. By the time I made it back downstairs, Tanner was walking in the door.

"Hi. Glad you made it." Our greeting was a little awkward. I'd left him not an hour ago at the office. I'd also kissed his face off not an hour ago at the office.

He grinned and moved slightly closer than he normally might have. "You smell good."

I was glad I'd taken a second for the perfume. "Thanks, so do you." I didn't overtly sniff him, but I could tell that he was fresh from the shower.

We walked into the kitchen together. Everyone looked at us. I felt particularly seen at that moment. Like they knew. Jake and Leah had arrived in the few minutes I'd been upstairs changing. Leah stared hard at me. She always knew.

Lisa, thankfully, arrived then. She'd gathered her things from the office after leaving the hospital where she'd been sitting with Marie this evening. She was going to stay here at the house with us—as would Marie once she was released from the hospital.

I made the introductions. "Thank you so much for welcoming me and my grandmother into your home. I so appreciate it." Lisa was gracious in her thanks to Nana.

"Of course, darling. Marie was a friend to me, and your momma was a friend to Karen." Nana nodded toward

Momma who stepped forward and took Lisa's hands in hers.

"Welcome, dear. You have your mother's eyes, no doubt about it. We have some photos here from when she was young, if you'd like to see them," Momma offered.

Lisa's eyes shone with unshed tears. "Yes, thank you. I would love to see them."

Why hadn't I thought of that? We'd been so distracted with everything, the pictures had slipped my mind. "Yes, I'll get them after dinner."

"All right, everyone. Grab a plate and have at 'em." Nana had set out platters of crabs stuffed with crabmeat brushed with garlic butter and broiled, sprinkled with paprika, and topped with a thin lemon slice. There were scalloped potatoes and a crisp green salad that Momma had brought. And a Jell-O salad. This one had watermelon in it and was made with oranges and yes, plenty of marshmallows. A weird variation on the green one.

"Look, Carly, Momma brought Jell-O salad." Leah bumped me on my side as she got next to me in line for crabs and potatoes.

"Knock it off, heifer, or I'll tell her you hate the color purple." This as a reference to the dresses for the vow renewal. We were calling the dresses what they were.

Leah snorted. "I do hate the color purple when it comes to bridesmaids' dresses."

"What's with you and my brother-in-law? Y'all are looking pretty cozy."

"Nothing. We work together." I tried to sound casual. Any unexpected moves and she would have me.

"Uh-huh. You can't fool me. I read the diary, remember?" Leah muttered under her breath as we moved closer toward our dinner.

"Shut *up*. There's nothing going on." I'm not sure why I bothered to lie to her. Probably because there wasn't any way to have this conversation right now. And what was happening between Tanner and I was so new that I hadn't even had any time to process it. Maybe it would turn out to be nothing. No matter what transpired, it was between us for now, and it was up to us to figure it out.

I served my plate with two crabs and a heaping serving of both potatoes and salad. I might want seconds as hungry as I was. Had we skipped lunch?

Tanner sat beside me to my right, and Lisa on my left. Momma insisted on her usual large prayer while we held hands. The Catholic eating grace. Then Nana added a quick prayer for Marie. "Dear Lord, we say a prayer of thanks for our friend, Marie, who's been returned safely to us through your mercy and grace. Amen."

And all the people said, "Amen."

"Thank you all so much for your kind welcome. This looks amazing." Lisa seemed a little overwhelmed. Of course, we were a bit overwhelming as a group.

"Don't think anything of it. How was Marie when you left her?" Nana asked.

"She was frustrated that they wouldn't let her out to come with me, but overall, I think she's in pretty good spirits considering what she's been through."

Nana nodded. "I'm so happy to hear it. When can we expect her, or do you know yet?"

"They said in a day or two."

"They've run some blood work and will know more tomorrow." Jake spoke up then, having gotten some information from his staffer who was treating Marie.

"Nana, you've outdone yourself with the crabs. They're fantastic!" Tanner hadn't spoken since he'd served his plate and sat down beside me. He had to be as hungry as I was since neither of us had eaten today since this morning."

"There's plenty more, so grab seconds if you want them. I've already set some aside for Marie for when she gets here."

"I know she'll appreciate it," Lisa said.

We were a much quieter bunch when our mouths were full, I had to say. We worked our way through dinner and dessert, which wasn't only Jell-O salad, as Nana had made a huge pan of bread pudding with praline sauce, which was one of my favorites.

We all pitched in to clear the table and clean up the mess as soon as the eating was done. "Carly, where did you put that box of pictures we were looking at the other day? The ones with Justine in them?" Momma reminded me on Lisa's behalf.

"Oh, yes. I'll get them."

"I put the box in the armoire on the middle shelf in the dining room." Nana had several armoires in this house. Some were in the bedrooms and called chifforobes because those had drawers in them. They were all antiques in keeping with the historic period of the house.

I headed into the dining room to retrieve the box.

I didn't hear Tanner follow, but when I turned around with the old box in my hands, I nearly ran him over. "Oh, hi."

CHAPTER TWENTY

"Hi. THOUGHT YOU might need some help." Tanner had followed me from the kitchen to the dining room. I hoped he'd been discreet about it. The last thing I needed was Leah's eagle eye noticing.

"Um, no, but I appreciate the thought." I felt a little flustered at having him so close. In a silly, kind of crushy way.

"Here, let me help anyway." He gently took the box from me, his hand brushing mine as he set it on the dining room table. This allowed him to be a little closer.

The dining room was enclosed, aside from the door, which was slightly ajar. This was a semi-private situation that could end at any moment, which made my heart pound faster.

He took my hands in his. "All I've been able to think about since I've been here is getting close to you again. Alone."

We were standing close and kind of staring at each other. "Really?" *Did I just say that?* Ugh. "I'll take that as a compliment."

"You should. You really should."

I laughed a little. "Okay."

"I'm not sure what to do about this. About us." Tanner's voice was low and deep, and kind of rumbly. I almost felt it rather than hearing it.

"Hmm. I'm not sure either."

"I guess this isn't the place for this conversation, but I'm glad we're here."

"Me too." We were standing there, kind of staring into each other's eyes, when I heard laughter in the other room. "I'm thinking they're about to come looking for me and those pictures." I tilted my head toward the box he'd sat on the table.

"Mmm. Probably."

"Meet me on the back porch after everybody leaves?" I suggested.

"It's a date."

When we re-entered the kitchen, Leah raised her eyebrows, but thankfully kept her opinion to herself. The very last thing I needed was for Momma to get wind of something going on between me and Tanner.

I opened the box of photos and spread them out across the table. I grabbed the magnifying glass so we'd be able to read some of the aged print on the backs of the pictures. I quickly found the ones of Momma and Justine, Lisa's birth mother, we'd identified the last time we'd looked through them. I passed those along to Lisa.

Momma was sitting next to Lisa and pointed to something in the photo. "You see here? We were sitting on the hood of Marie's old station wagon."

I passed the magnifying glass to Lisa. The photo was a little blurry from age, and because photos from years ago weren't as high resolution as they were nowadays. "Wow, I do see the resemblance. This is so awesome. I finally feel like there's some real connection between me and Justine. Well, besides Marie." Lisa sounded excited about finding a new part of her heritage.

"You're so welcome, dear. Oh, look, here's another one." Momma was handling this well—I had to give it to her.

We spent another hour looking through the photos before the party broke up. I could feel Tanner beside me, even without making eye contact. Leah and Jake left, with Momma and Daddy on their heels, which meant Lisa and Nana were still there at the house with us.

"Let's get you settled, then dear," Nana said to Lisa.

"Can I carry anything upstairs for you?" Tanner offered. He brought her things to her room, which was on the other side of the house from where my room was. Nana had put her in a bedroom in a guest area that had two bedrooms that shared a bath, and a sitting room. I couldn't remember the last time anyone had stayed in those rooms. But the setup was perfect for Lisa and Marie because it would afford them some privacy while they were taking time to get to know one another.

I helped to get Lisa settled with fresh towels and a few other items before returning downstairs.

"Good night, my dear." Nana was clearly tired, judging by the amount of work she'd put in today and the slight droop to her shoulders. "I trust you will see Tanner out."

"Good night, Nana. You outdid yourself on dinner. It was amazing."

"Yes. Thanks for including me." Tanner grinned at her.

Once Nana had ascended the stairs, we stepped outside onto the screened porch. There was a soft rain falling on the metal roof. I sat on the settee, leaving room for Tanner if he chose to sit beside me. He did.

"What a day, huh?" I might have sounded a tiny bit nervous.

"Yes, but we did it. We found Marie—and she's okay." I could hear the satisfaction in Tanner's voice.

"I'm so happy for Lisa, and for Marie." It was a simple statement, but so true. They'd followed the clues and solved at least part of the puzzle. There was so much more to be learned, but knowing Marie was alive and well was today's victory.

"Me too." The cicadas chirped and buzzed loudly, adding to the crickets and frogs. It was quite a background symphony. And then there was the falling rain on the roof.

The air was humid, but it was late enough that the heat had subsided. Since we were inside the porch, there weren't any mosquitos. I felt myself relaxing and thinking about Tanner sitting next to me. The fact that we'd moved into a new realm with one another was exciting.

"Wanna make out?" Tanner was right next to my ear.

I laughed out loud. "You bet I do."

So we did. Like a couple of teenagers in the back seat of his momma's car. Only we were full-grown adults who were on the back porch of my grandmother's house with her right inside. So, with that knowledge, things didn't get too out of hand. Second base, maybe. But, by the time we pulled ourselves apart and adjusted our clothes, we were both out of breath and still wanting more.

"Um, wow. I feel like I'm back in ninth grade." Tanner laughed but sounded a little frustrated.

"Sorry about that. Maybe we can go to your place next time," I said jokingly, but I wasn't joking. I'd never felt this kind of desire before. Not with anyone. And I could see it getting out of hand.

"Carly, I really like you. I like that you're stubborn and strong and have a soft heart."

He liked me for all the things the others never had. "I like that you like those things about me. I like you because you're a good man and you're a great kisser."

"I've been worried about ruining our professional relationship with a personal one, but you distract me enough that I think we need to figure this out." Tanner was frowning.

"We won't let it ruin our working together. Let's make a deal now."

He put his hands gently on both sides of my face. "Deal." Then, he kissed me so gently, barely pressing his lips to mine, making me want to restart our make-out session.

Tanner stood and pulled me to my feet and wrapped his arms around me, pulling me close. "Soon. Just as soon as we have time."

I could feel his heartbeat through his shirt. He was warm and solid and smelled so nice. I didn't know I'd been lonely before now. "Soon sounds wonderful."

Tanner

AS HE DROVE home, Tanner felt like he was back in high

school. Well, maybe college, during the early days of falling for someone. When he and Kerry-Ann had met in undergrad, it had seemed perfect. Nothing stood in their way while they'd studied and planned an entire future based on the idea that all would go according to that plan. But then, she had an opportunity offered to her after their first year in law school that she couldn't pass up.

On the one hand, he couldn't blame her because it was everything she'd dreamed of for her career. But she'd left him behind without the possibility of even trying to stay together. It told him everything. Tanner could see the same kind of ambition and drive in Carly, but Carly had come back here to Cypress Bayou because this was where she wanted to live. At least, she hadn't said anything to the contrary recently. And she was incredibly loyal to her family. But some of what he liked about her also made him a little nervous. What if she got a better offer someplace else? Would she pursue it? Would her independent spirit take her away just as Kerry-Ann's had?

Tanner decided he couldn't think like this. This was why he was still single—because he'd worked hard to protect his heart all these years. He'd spent so much time worried about getting hurt again, he'd not allowed anyone to pierce his tough shell. Somehow, Carly had gotten right past his defenses with no warning bells shouting at him. She'd completely flown under the radar because he hadn't seen her as a threat, until she was. Now, it was too late.

Some women believed that men were less inclined to be hurt than women. He figured that was all in the perception of where one sat. And Tanner Carmichael was now a sitting duck.

Carly

I SLEPT LIKE the dead and woke up at the crack of dawn. I'd been beyond exhausted last night and had no memory of laying my head on the pillow. I did remember everything up until I'd brushed my teeth and thrown on an oversized T-shirt. Nothing after that. But today was a new day and there was so much to be learned.

Nana was making bacon from the smell of things, and I was glad about it. Having Lisa here gave her somebody else to take care of and cook for. No matter how many times I tried to tell Nana that she didn't have to do all the cooking, she couldn't be convinced that good food wasn't the cure for pretty much anything and everything ill in the world. She often told me that it might not cure anything, but a good meal would put us in the best mind to handle whatever came our way.

It was an inarguable point.

I showered and dressed for the day, keeping in mind that almost anything could and might happen, based on recent events. I even took a few minutes with the curling iron. Tanner might not notice, but it was a tiny nod to my vanity. I normally just dried my hair and put a little product in it to combat the Louisiana humidity.

My fresh awareness of Tanner's opinion of my looks gave me a slightly nervy thrill. I'd had a few crushes through my high school and college years where I'd made an effort for guys to notice me. I never was any good at flirting because I'd been too impatient and too direct, which had not served me well when it came to subtle guy-and-girl romantic banter. In the South, the expectation remained for the guy to make the first move toward any kind of relationship.

Lisa emerged as I got downstairs and poured a mug of coffee. "Good morning. How did you sleep?" She appeared rested and well dressed, as usual, wearing a cute blue and white sleeveless printed dress paired with navy flats. She was comfort and elegance personified.

"I slept so well, thanks."

"Here, have some coffee." I moved away from the pot so she could help herself. Nana had set out fresh cream, sweeteners, and sugar beside the pot of coffee. There was bacon, eggs, and big cathead biscuits on the stove. But I didn't see Nana anywhere.

"Good morning, dears." Nana came through the back door off the kitchen as if we'd conjured her. "I do hope you both slept well. I picked a few blooms for you to take to Marie at the hospital." Nana indeed held a lovely bouquet of fresh-cut flowers from her garden. There were a couple lilies and a few roses, along with a few other varieties of greenery.

"That was such a kind thing to do. And thank you for breakfast. It smells heavenly."

"Well, dig in. Wouldn't want it to get cold." Nana rinsed off the flowers and began to arrange them into a bouquet as we served our plates. "There's some fresh orange juice in the fridge." She pointed.

"Your hair looks nice today." Lisa commented on my

lightly curled style.

"Thanks." I touched my hair in a mildly self-conscious motion. I was secretly afraid Lisa could see right through my somewhat pathetic attempts to lure a man. But women always noticed the small things like curled hair when one didn't normally curl hair.

CHAPTER TWENTY-ONE

L ISA AND I headed directly to Cypress General from Nana's house. We took separate cars because our schedules later in the day might diverge. Today was a potentially big day because we hoped to finally learn something about what really happened to Justine Chaffin, Lisa's birth mother and Marie's daughter.

Tanner was meeting us there. DA Litrell had sent confirmation that Lisa now had been granted emergency guardianship of Marie until it could be officially determined that Marie was fit mentally and medically to handle her own decisions. This should happen quickly now that she'd been evaluated by several medical personnel and the legal wheels were in motion.

There was a uniformed officer sitting in a chair right outside Marie's hospital room this morning, same as yesterday when I'd left. He nodded to us as we entered.

Marie was sitting in a chair beside her hospital bed when we entered her room. She was dressed in clothes Lisa had brought over to her at some point yesterday afternoon after I'd left to go back to the office. I reminded myself to share the name of Nana's hairdresser in town.

"Good morning, Marie." Lisa wasted no time getting to her grandmother's side and offering her the lovely flowers from Nana. "These are from Ms. Elise's garden. She hoped you would like them. How are you feeling today?"

"How nice of her. I'm a darn sight better now that I've had a good night's sleep with a guard outside. That guy's a real giant, isn't he?"

"He is impressive, for sure." I had to laugh at the confidence the officer's size instilled in Marie. I guess I couldn't blame her for feeling like his bigness would keep anyone from causing her harm.

Tanner arrived then, making the room feel much smaller upon entering. He smiled at us all, but I saw something in his eyes when he got to me. A spark of interest. Had it always been there, and I hadn't noticed?

"Good morning, all. I hope everyone had a good night." His well-fitting jeans were paired with a crisp blue button-down shirt and the boots he normally wore.

"Are we having a meeting now?" Marie asked. "Because I'm ready to tell you what I know. I've been kept quiet for a long time."

Tanner nodded. "We *are* having a meeting, Marie. Do you mind if I record our conversation?"

"Not at all. I have worries that somebody will try to come in and stop me before I have my say." Marie darted her eyes all around.

"We can relax. Our friend Clyde, who is watching the door, has been given instructions that nobody is to interrupt us, so let's get comfortable, shall we?" Tanner reassured us all.

There was a seat that ran alongside the window, so Lisa and I sat there. Marie moved back to the bed so Tanner could sit in the chair beside her and record her responses. He began by noting the date of interview, and prefacing notes regarding Marie's identity, et cetera.

"Marie, can you describe what you remember regarding your daughter Justine Chaffin's time after she left Cypress Bayou for college in New Orleans and enrolled at the University of New Orleans?"

"She was a sweet girl, you know? So excited to leave this small town and head off to college. She was majoring in graphic design because she was so artistic. She could draw anything. She was in her third year of college when I noticed she wasn't responding when I called her. She rarely came home as it was, and I asked her what was going on when we finally did speak."

"What did Justine tell you?" Tanner's voice was kind.

"It took her a minute, but she finally admitted she'd gotten pregnant by a young man she'd been seeing. And when I asked what she'd planned to do with the baby, she said she was keeping it. When I asked who the father was, she said she didn't want to share his name because it was someone I knew from our hometown, but he'd just started law school. You can imagine my worry…"

I tensed immediately and looked over at Tanner. "Did she ever say who it was?" Lisa asked then.

"Well, before that, when we'd speak, she'd mention a group of friends that included people I knew from Cypress Bayou. I'm sorry to say that group included your parents, Tanner, Arthur Keller, and a fellow, last name of Henry, and his wife from New Orleans. Back in those days, young people got married while they were still in school."

"Did you say a Henry couple?" Lisa's voice had a strangled sound to it.

"Yes, I don't remember their first names, but Justine seemed to really like them. They cooked out and spent a lot of time together if I remember correctly."

"Vivian and Hayes Henry?" Lisa asked Marie.

"Oh, yes, that's right. Justine called her Viv."

"Excuse me a moment." Lisa stood and exited the room.

"Is everything okay?" Marie asked. "Did I say something wrong?"

"Let's take a short break." Tanner was frowning and likely putting pieces of a puzzle together, like me.

I excused myself to go and check on Lisa. She was sitting on a small bench in the hallway. "Are you all right?"

She shook her head. "My parents knew Justine and Carson and Judge Keller back when Justine gave birth to me and when Justine disappeared."

I nodded. "Yes. That's more than a little suspicious." I only imagined the dark places her mind was going and wished there was something I could do to ease her pain and anxiety. "It sounds like you're going to need to have a conversation with them before all this hits the fan."

"Yes. I'm going to give Daddy a call, and I'm going to record our conversation. He's a lawyer and he's smart, but he won't expect me to do that. No wonder they've been fighting my finding Justine."

"Let's do it at the office so you won't be interrupted. I'm sorry about this." And I *was* sorry for her. All the lies and mystery were fresh for me with my own family. But at least nobody had died.

"No, I want the truth. I've had a feeling something wasn't right for years."

"Are you okay to go back in and hear what else Marie might have to say?"

Lisa nodded and stood, but she still seemed a bit shaky.

As we entered the room, Marie's eyes were wide with concern. "I knew this would cause some big trouble. I don't know who Justine was seeing, but I'd gotten the feeling it was Arthur Keller." Hearing Judge Keller's name again associated with another pregnancy of another young woman triggered something in me. A burning anger with men who used women and discarded them as if they were nothing once they became inconvenient.

"Can you think of anything else Justine told you? Did she say how the father reacted when she told him about her pregnancy?"

"She wouldn't talk any more about it. Said it wouldn't change anything. That it wasn't my business and that it was her life if I didn't have to pay for anything." Marie stopped talking for a second then and her eyes became sad. "It wasn't like Justine to tell me something wasn't any of my business. We were close…always."

"I'm so sorry, Marie. Just a few more questions. Did Justine say anything else about why she wouldn't need any help to pay for having a baby?"

"No, but I got the impression from the way she said it that someone had promised to help her that way."

"Okay. Why do you think people went to all this trouble to lock you away? Who threatened you?"

These were the questions we'd all been waiting to get the

answers to.

Marie frowned. "Why, Carson Carmichael and Judge Keller, of course. When I married Jay, Carson paid us a visit. Gave Jay money and told him bad things would happen if he didn't keep me quiet. And when Jay died, Carson warned me that if I kept carrying on about Justine and asking so many questions about what happened to her, he'd tell everyone I was crazy and have me locked up. Then nobody would believe a word I said ever again."

"Is that what happened? He warned you and you didn't do what he said?" Tanner asked.

"I was *done* listening to his threats. I wanted to find out what happened to my baby girl. I still do. But he really did do it. Carson got with that doctor—Dr. Miller, his name was. Made me say all kinds of things and then they declared me incompetent, and Judge Keller made Carson my legal guardian. The three of them ganged up on me and called themselves a panel. Took my cell phone away and threw me in that place."

"What do you think happened to Justine, Marie?" Tanner asked.

"I don't know exactly. I never talked to her again after she called to tell me she'd had the baby and it was a girl. Said it was healthy and that one day soon she would come home and introduce my grandbaby to me. Of course, I had a million questions, but she said she had to go and to be patient. You know, her daddy died right after that in the oil field and things went sideways for me. I lost everything all at once. I tried to find Justine, but when I went to New Orleans, there wasn't a record of anything. I filed a missing person's report, but nobody would call me back. I kept calling them and getting nothing."

I could feel Marie's pain and anxiety coming off her in waves as she relived the trauma of her past. "We're going to find out what happened to Justine, Marie."

"You know, I even contacted Carson and Arthur back then and they pretended to not know a thing about Justine or the baby."

I could feel my burning anger coming back with a vengeance. What they'd put Marie through was nothing short of a killing offense in my book.

"I'm here. I'll be here for you." Lisa moved over and took Marie's hand in hers. There were tears on Lisa's cheeks.

"I'm so happy you're alive and well, my dear. I didn't know if you'd come to a bad end too." Marie cried then. A sad, sobbing cry. "Nobody ever believed me or listened to me."

"We believe you and we're going to make sure that those who are responsible for what happened to Justine and to you are brought to justice." Tanner clicked off the recorder. "I'm saving a copy of this and sending one to the district attorney. It should be enough to get Carson and Judge Keller brought in for questioning."

Lisa cleared her throat. "Um, I want to speak with my parents first and document the conversation. We might find out more from them about Justine that way. You know, before they bring in their lawyers to defend them all. Now that I know they were somehow involved in all this, I don't see how they could pretend otherwise."

Tanner nodded. "Okay. Let's start there. I'll call Alan

Litrell and fill him in on our plans. He might need to do something procedural now that this has gone farther." Procedural, meaning filing charges or getting search warrants so we could further investigate what happened all those years ago.

Jake entered the hospital room then. "Hello, all. I thought you might want to know that Marie has been cleared to leave the hospital with Lisa." Jake looked down at his tablet where Marie's information was stored. He then turned his attention to Marie. "You're a little dehydrated still and we'll want you to continue with lots of fluids. Also, we noticed your blood pressure is slightly elevated. It might be all the excitement, or you could have a little hypertension going on that needs treating. We'll wait a week or so until things calm down and re-evaluate it."

"So, I can go? Just walk right out?" Marie seemed wary of Jake's permission to vacate.

"Yes, if Lisa signs off on it. Hopefully, that won't be for long. As far as the doctors are concerned, you are mentally fit to look after yourself. The courts will want to have a hearing before rescinding custody."

"I promise not to be too much of a drag." Lisa smiled at Marie.

"I'd rather be under your thumb than those awful men who call me crazy." Marie's expression was fierce.

Jake put a hand on Marie's shoulder. "Nobody's using the C word here."

"Let's get you over to Ms. Elise's house so you can settle in. Last night she served her famous stuffed crabs with the most delicious potatoes. She made a point to save you some."

"I haven't had a decent meal in years. And that's the God's truth." Marie declared this in such a solemn tone that I wanted to cry for her and with her.

"Well, I can assure you that's about to change. You'll be staying with one of the best cooks in Cypress Bayou. I don't think I've ever entered her house when there wasn't something bordering on amazing to eat." I said this with certainty and truth.

"I'm ready to go." Marie's tone was firm.

"I can attest to what Carly said about Nana's cooking. And I just got your discharge paperwork finalized. Someone will be here with a wheelchair any minute," Jake said.

"Marie, where are your things? Do you remember?" Tanner asked.

"Things? What things? Your daddy sold all my things, along with my house in Leesfield. And he laughed while he did it. He couldn't wait to tell me that all the money he'd gotten would go to pay his guardian fees and to pay the hospital for my care."

The rage emerged again. "That asshole! Somebody should punch him in the face." I couldn't control my anger or my words. I literally had the urge to punch Carson. Maybe I wasn't cut out to be an attorney.

"I get to go first." Lisa's expression showed a murderous intent. "How is this man still walking free?"

"We've asked ourselves that for years." Jake shook his head. "I hope you've gotten enough proof to finally bring him up on charges." Jake directed this statement toward Tanner.

"We are doing it right. Carson won't get off no matter

how connected he is. There's too much proof and too many people know what he's done. Once we get him behind bars, I'm hoping those he's wronged will have the courage to come forward and make statements for insurance to the case against him."

Tanner

TANNER LEFT THE hospital with a clear idea of what had to be done now. Alan Litrell was meeting him out of the office in case the moles around the courthouse were on high alert. They were both headed to Alan's fishing camp on Lake Breaux a few miles off the highway. Alan would bring his administrative assistant, Jeff, whom he trusted completely, and with whom they'd worked throughout this entire process.

When Tanner arrived at the small cabin, the DA and Jeff were already there.

"Thanks for meeting us out here. I realize it's unorthodox, but we're so close to nailing Carson for his crimes against the citizens of this town. I've called in the Louisiana Bureau of Investigation. They will be arriving shortly to set up a task force. I'm not taking any chances of this falling into some good old boy network and getting dropped due to straight-up political sleaze." Alan was more serious than Tanner had ever seen him.

"Thanks for taking this seriously. And for involving the LBI. If enough people know about it and it goes through official channels, even Carson won't be able to squeeze out of it."

"The fact that he essentially kidnapped Marie Trichel and that we have witnesses, and a paper trail allowed the LBI to become an investigative partner in our case. This isn't going away." The Louisiana Bureau of Investigation was the state branch of the FBI. They were virtually impervious to local corruption, as their agents were brought in and trained at a federal level. The agents answered to the FBI. DA Litrell worked under the umbrella of the Louisiana State District Attorney and there was a lot of information sharing at the state level between the two entities. As much power as Carson and Judge Keller might have within their own communities, it meant very little when the larger state and federal agencies got involved.

"Lisa is meeting me at the office to do a recorded call with her adoptive parents as soon as she gets Marie settled at Elise Porter's house. Marie will be staying there for a while until we can figure out what to do about her finances. Carson sold all her possessions and paid himself and Pine Hill. There's a money trail there, but that will take some time to unravel."

"We'll make it a priority by putting a forensic accountant on it. That's something I can do under the umbrella of investigation. The more evidence we have against Carson *and* Arthur Keller the better."

"We don't know exactly how involved the Henrys, Lisa's adoptive parents, were in what happened to Justine Chaffin, but Lisa believes they are our best opportunity to get some honest answers to all this before they lawyer up and refuse to cooperate."

"You say she's headed over to your office to call them? Make sure you get a clean recording. And have her ask as many questions about their relationship with Carson and Keller as possible. Hayes Henry is a prominent attorney in New Orleans, and he knows not to go down with the sinking ship. Throwing those two under the bus will be his only way out of this if he's involved."

Tanner nodded. "That's what I figured. I'll go over it all with Lisa before she calls them."

"In the meantime, I'll go over the recording of your interview with Marie Trichel and have Jeff transcribe the conversation so I can send it over to the LBI task force. Carson has holed up in his house, and so far hasn't made any calls that we know of. Unless he's got another cell phone that we're unaware of, which is likely because he knows we're watching him."

Tanner left the camp feeling a little better about the handling of things now that he knew the LBI had a task force involved. Before, he'd had a gnawing fear that this would end up going nowhere. When Carson was involved, one never knew.

Carly's and Lisa's vehicles, along with Imogene's, were parked in the lot when Tanner arrived. Just the sight of Carly's car gave Tanner a little kick in the gut. A nervous kind of thrill, even with all the other stuff happening.

CHAPTER TWENTY-TWO

Carly

W E'D JUST SET up the conference room for Lisa's FaceTime call with her parents when Tanner arrived. Lisa was pacing and was on her second cup of coffee. So, yeah, she was a little nervous at the idea of confronting her parents about what might be the most impactive thing they'd ever discussed.

"How did it go with the DA?" I asked him, unable to control my impatience at finding out what had gone down.

Tanner nodded. "Good. We met at his camp on Lake Breaux to make sure we had privacy. The LBI is creating a task force because of the kidnapping charges they plan to level at Carson. Marie's testimony, along with Dr. Miller's, should be a slam dunk. Having that extra entity will ensure this investigation moves forward."

My heart leapt in my chest. All my rage at the very idea that Carson might get away with his crimes against Marie, specifically, gave way to a fierce hope that he would be brought down in a hugely public and federal way.

Tanner motioned for everyone to sit. "Okay, let's get started. Imogene, were you able to place the listening devices in Carson's office?" Tanner had a list he was working from.

Imogene nodded. "He didn't suspect a thing. But I can tell you he's a basket case. I've never seen him like this before. He's obviously not sleeping and looks like he's lost twenty pounds in the last few days."

"Good. That means he's sweating it. It's a tough thing when all your chickens fly home to roost at the same time. This is a long time coming for him. He likely thought this day would never happen. Such a fool." Tanner made a face. One that showed only disgust for his father.

Tanner turned his attention to Lisa. "Lisa, this conversation with your parents is vital to finding out how involved Carson and Keller might have been in Justine's disappearance. So, let's come up with a ballpark list of questions that will lead your dad down the road without tipping him off immediately. It's likely he's already gotten word that we're on to Carson and the judge for various other offenses. I'm guessing he's politically connected in the state. *And* I'm guessing he's a little nervous about how all this investigating is going to affect him."

Lisa nodded. "Carly and I decided it might be best to do a video call so I can see his expressions, and if my mom's on the call, that will be even better."

They discussed the ins and outs of how the conversation should go to get the most information before Lisa's parents put the brakes on and clammed up.

We set up a voice recorder that would normally be used for recording depositions. Since Lisa was using her laptop, she chose the "record" option for the video conference call.

Lisa dialed her dad's number with the video link instead of a regular phone call. His face came on screen. He was a large, blond man with a surprising amount of hair for someone his age. "Hey there, Lisa. What's with the FaceTime? Haven't heard from you in a little while, darlin'."

"Hi, Daddy. I'm a little homesick and thought I'd call and talk to you and Momma."

"Well, she's around here someplace. I'm working from home right now, so you've caught us at a good time. Let me see if I can get your momma in here." He stood and called out the doorway. "Viv! Lisa's on the screen, here. Wants to talk to us, honey."

A woman's voice replied, "She is? Isn't that a surprise. I'm coming."

When Vivian Henry arrived on screen, I could see where Lisa got her sense of style. The woman was stunning for her age. "Hello, dear. Is everything all right? It's not like you to call us out of the blue like this, and on video no less." Viv smoothed her hair. Lisa had shared that her younger siblings FaceTimed their parents all the time, so it was something they were comfortable with.

"I wanted to let you know that I've found my grand-mother, Marie Trichel. She's my birth mother's mom."

Both of their faces registered an instant of shock. Viv more than Hayes. "Well, isn't that a surprise?" Vivian Henry worked to sound enthusiastic.

"Is she in good health?" Hayes asked, a pleasant expression on his face.

"She's okay. Only thing, is that we found her locked away in a mental facility against her will. *Someone* had gained her medical and financial power of attorney and stolen everything from her."

"How *awful*, darling. I'm so glad you found her. Is she...*all right?*" Vivian tapped her head to indicate mentally. "Who would do such a thing?"

I watched the shift in Hayes Henry's eyes as he listened and watched. I didn't get the impression he knew exactly what was happening. "Was Miz Trichel able to tell you why someone had her locked away? And who it was who'd done this to her? Maybe I can help." He was trying to get information when he should have been outraged and horrified.

"Yes, I know, Daddy. Marie had lots of information to share. She also said to tell you and Momma hello." Lisa dropped that like an H bomb right on their heads.

"*What?*" Viv inhaled sharply in shock, pulling back with a hand to her chest.

Hayes's eyes narrowed, but he didn't flinch. "Lisa, what in the Sam Hill is going on here?"

Lisa sat up a little straighter in her seat and began. "Marie told me in a recorded conversation that has already gone to the DA that my birth mother, Justine Chaffin, was dating Arthur Keller and was friends with the two of you and Carson Carmichael and his wife at the time I was born and during the time she went missing. And that Carson and Arthur lied about their relationships when my grandmother went down to find out what happened to her and to me. Be careful what you say now, Daddy." Lisa's breath whooshed out of her after that diatribe of info.

Viv and Hayes shared a long stare before turning back to the camera. "It wasn't like that, honey. Marie doesn't know what happened at all." Vivian appeared to lose her fight.

"We're going to tell you what happened as far as we

know because I realize that Carson and Arthur won't. They'll never admit to anything." Hayes took off his glasses and pinched the bridge of his nose. "I'm assuming you're recording this conversation, yes?"

Lisa nodded, her lip quivering a little.

"Marie Trichel deserves to know what happened to her daughter after all these years. And we're tired of carrying this secret around." Hayes grabbed Vivian's hand. "First let me say that we love you, Lisa. We have from the moment we laid eyes on you. What we did was to protect you, always. It's probably not what normal people would have done, but it was as a quick response to events that got out of control."

We all three in the room waited with bated breath. There was no other cliché that fit.

"You're not Arthur Keller's daughter, honey. You're Carson Carmichael's daughter, I'm sorry to say. Justine and Carson were having an affair. And his wife, Judy, had just given birth to their oldest son, Tanner." There was a collective gasp in the room. I looked over at Tanner, as did Lisa to gauge his reaction.

Shock.

Disbelief.

Lisa was also realizing what this meant. She and Tanner were siblings. And almost the exact same age. They shared a glance. Confusion. I remembered that feeling and all the emotions that went with finding out I had a new sister from a long-buried secret.

"I'm assuming you're there with his son, Tanner? Your attorney? If so, I'm very sorry to break this news to you all so unexpectedly. We were worried this might all come out at some point if you went to Cypress Bayou."

Tanner got in front of the screen. "Are you sure of this?"

Hayes nodded. "We all knew what was happening within our little circle during that time. Well, everybody but poor Judy. I know it's not what anyone wants to hear, but Carson and Justine, well, they simply didn't care to hide it, except from Judy. When Justine found out she was pregnant, Carson insisted she have an abortion, but Justine refused on account of her being Catholic. She demanded that he pay her expenses and medical care, or she would tell his wife and anybody else who would listen."

"How did Carson respond?" Tanner asked Hayes.

"Back in those days, something like this could get you thrown out of law school. Arthur Keller had a crush on Justine, and she'd blown him off, but he stepped up and offered to raise the baby as his own. But Carson couldn't be happy with Arthur solving his problem—no, Carson was obsessed with Justine. And still, he wanted it all. His wife, his son, and his mistress, minus the bastard child."

"So, *what happened* to Justine?" Lisa's tone was that of a woman who'd waited too long to find out.

Vivian took up the tale. "She got between two men who loved her. Literally. They came to blows on an upstairs landing in the old uptown home where Arthur lived. Justine knew Carson was there and she went over to force him to see you, Lisa. She had some hopeful notion that if he saw you that he would fall in love with you and leave Judy and Tanner. Instead, he became enraged, and Arthur stepped up to defend Justine. They came to blows and Justine tried to step between them. She was pushed aside and fell over the

247

railing to the marble floor below. She died instantly."

"How awful." Lisa covered her mouth as the truth pene-trated. Tanner put his hand on her shoulder in a protective gesture. I felt like I was watching the whole terrible movie unfold before my eyes.

Hayes continued, "They called me and Viv and asked us to take care of you while they figured out what to do. If they were to call the police, it would end their law careers before they began. Both swore it was an accident and so they proceeded to clean up the mess and bury Justine's body, but I never knew where that was."

"And me? How did you get the adoption to go through legally?" Lisa asked her parents.

Hayes answered. "We were law students and we figured it out. I was a couple years ahead of Carson and Arthur in school and they looked up to me for advice. We were mostly concerned about you, Lisa, and what might happen if everything got out. We didn't want you going into the foster system. So, we filed the paperwork for a private adoption and forged the signatures. Things weren't as hard to get away with back then."

"How could you both have gone along with this? Poor Marie never knew what happened to her daughter or her granddaughter." I finally spoke up, not in front of the camera, but from where I sat.

Viv answered, "We wrestled with it for years. We did a lot of praying for our souls, for Justine's soul. But we knew Lisa was in the right place and that we could provide well for her in the coming years, and we already loved her. From the very first moment."

"I don't even know where to begin. We need to find out where they buried Justine's body first, I guess." Tanner ran a hand through his hair. "And I think the next step will be getting one of the other men on the record admitting to what they did."

"I think we can make that happen. In their minds, we were all equally accountable for the cover-up, so if I bring it up, they won't suspect that I would rat myself out by recording a conversation. I could tell them that Lisa's been asking a lot of questions and that I need to come up with a good story about her birth mother and supply some facts now that Marie's out and talking. And maybe get the truth about where she's buried."

"Maybe you should come up here and have the conversation in Carson's office. Ask to meet with both he and Arthur there. They're still very close. We've planted listening devices in the office. Tell them you want to meet in person so nobody can hear you."

"I could do that. I guess it's the best way to find out where Justine is buried." Hayes sounded resigned. "If I could go back and change it all, I would. But I wouldn't change having you as my daughter, Lisa." He smiled into the camera at his daughter. "I'm very sorry, honey."

Viv joined the conversation. "We both are, Lisa. Daddy and I still discuss this all the time. The what ifs of how we handled things. I know we sounded like we didn't want you to find your birth parents, like we were unsupportive. We were trying to protect ourselves and you from all this."

Tanner's tone was stiff and businesslike. "I think we've got everything now. I'm certain the DA here in Cypress

Bayou will be in touch. Please don't share this information until you hear from him about moving forward with a conversation with Carson and Arthur. Thank you for your cooperation, Mr. and Mrs. Henry. We will be in touch." Tanner turned off the recorder and then he and I left the room so that Lisa could have a few private minutes with her parents.

We went into Tanner's office and Tanner shut the door. He sat down at his desk and whooshed out a breath. "Wow. Just wow."

"Are you okay?" I didn't know what else to say.

"I don't know how to process all this. Lisa is my sister. I've got to tell Jake we have a sister." He appeared dazed at the idea.

"If it helps, I actually do understand." I didn't know what else to say. But my heart was bleeding, and my mind was spinning. How could humans be so cruel to each other? So unconcerned with another's feelings? It made me think of how callous my attitude had been about the whole Allison fiasco. I had some making up to do on that front.

He focused on me then. "You do, don't you? How odd that we've both had this insane thing happen at this point in our lives. The secrets. The lies. My poor mother. I'm so glad she never knew."

"It's not the same scenario, I know, but the shock of everything you thought you knew about your family and your life suddenly changing in an instant, well, it stuns you."

"Yes. I'm stunned. This was completely unexpected. I guess if it had been Arthur who was Lisa's father, nobody would have been quite as surprised given that he's also

Allison's father."

"And sadly, Lisa has Carson as a father. But she also has two fantastic brothers she never knew about until now. That counts for a lot. And the two of you now have a sister, and you'll have to figure out how to work her into your tight twosome."

I reached across the desk, offering my hand to him.

"I'm having a hard time believing this. A sister." Tanner wrapped his fingers around mine.

CHAPTER TWENTY-THREE

Tanner

T HEY HAD A sister. Lisa was his and Jake's sister. This wasn't something he could do with a phone call. In fact, Tanner felt like it might take both he and Lisa to convince Jake of this news. Jake had been helpful with Marie and had a pretty good grasp as to what had gone on thus far, but this was going to be a real shocker.

After Lisa hung up with her parents, she emerged from the conference room looking almost as dumbstruck as he had. She kind of wandered down the hall and wound up standing at the open doorway to Tanner's office where he and Carly had been talking. "Is this for real?"

Carly and Tanner both stood and guided her upstairs where they all could sit comfortably and talk. "I never thought much about finding my birth father because I figured he'd either killed my mother or was some random dude. I had no idea he could be the worst human being I've ever encountered."

"Welcome to the family." Tanner meant it as a joke, but Lisa appeared horrified.

"That wasn't funny. Or maybe it was. I'm not sure right now. Maybe it was just too soon."

"Sorry. Jake and I have lived with the knowledge that our father is a terrible person and a likely felon for most of our lives. But we had each other, and until a few years ago, we had our mom and our grandad. So, we survived our childhoods. This is all new to you and it'll take some time for you to understand that he's merely a sperm donor. Don't expect anything from him emotionally because he's not capable of it."

"I have parents who care about me. I have a husband who is on the way here now. I just called him, and he's canceled his patients for the next few days to be with me. I never thought I'd see the day that happened."

"We'll all be glad to meet him. Let's take this a day at a time, okay? Jake and I aren't going anywhere. Speaking of Jake, I think we ought to pay him a visit and break this news to him. What do you think of that?"

Lisa nodded. "I guess now is as good a time as any. We've got a lot to tell Marie too. I hope learning about Justine's affair with Carson doesn't devastate her. She was proud of Justine, and I hate to cast ugliness onto her in Marie's memory."

"There's a way to tell the story that's truth but doesn't hurt Marie, I think." Carly said this at the right time and in the right way. "Justine was young and passionate, and she fell for the wrong guy. It happens to a lot of young women."

"Yes. I think it does. My husband is scheduled to arrive in town around dinnertime. That gives me a couple hours to see Jake and then spend a little time with Marie before he gets here."

"He is welcome at Nana's house, of course," Carly reassured Lisa.

"Thanks. You all have been so kind since I arrived in Cypress Bayou."

"Who knew we were welcoming family?" Tanner smiled at her.

Lisa shrugged her shoulders and smiled. "I'm proud to call you both my brothers."

"Speaking of our brother, we'd better get in touch with Jake and go break the news to him." Tanner texted Jake and asked if he had a few minutes to spare.

Tanner: *I've got some news you're going to want to hear in person*

Jake: *Sounds ominous. I've got a little time if you want to meet me in my office*

Tanner: *See you in ten*

"We're meeting him at his office in ten minutes."

Lisa stood and grabbed her purse from the conference room. "Might as well do it now."

"I'll meet y'all at Nana's house after you get back from the hospital."

Neither of them spoke on the way to the hospital. There were so many emotions rolling around in Tanner's mind. Mostly about Carson and his treatment of their mother, Judy. As far as she was concerned, Carson had mostly been decent to her, at least in the presence of others. Not always, but she knew how to handle him in a way that kept him in line to a point. Their mother hadn't been a fool when it came to Carson. She'd known what he was by the time they were kids and had given up believing he could change.

But to think he'd had a blatant affair that resulted in a child with Justine and then knowingly covered up Justine's death was next level hard to stomach. The depths of the man's disregard for human feeling were unfathomable.

Tanner and Lisa climbed out of the truck and Tanner apologized for his silence. "I'm sorry. I was thinking about Carson's lack of humanity in all of this."

"No worries. So far, I've seen nothing that makes me want to get to know him. Only deeds that motivate me to help take him down."

"We're all on the same page there. Jake will be equally livid when he finds out that Carson cheated on our mother in such an insulting way. Not at you. But he was especially close with our mom."

Lisa nodded. "I understand and I don't blame either of you for that."

They rode the elevator up to Jake's office.

Tanner knocked on the door, then opened it, not waiting for a reply.

Jake looked up from his paperwork. "Hey there. What's up? Oh, hi, Lisa. Is Marie okay?"

Tanner hated to do this to his little brother, Jake was a kind soul. He was a milder personality than him, and Tanner had always worked to protect Jake from the worst of people whenever he could. "I've got some news that couldn't wait."

Jake's eyebrows went up. "Okay. Shoot."

"You've met Lisa." They both smiled and nodded at each other. "Well, we spoke with Lisa's parents in New Orleans and found out that Carson is Lisa's biological father." Tanner waited a second to let that settle in on Jake.

"So, she's our—*sister*?" Jake's eyes widened. "Wow. I'd call that news. So, how—"

Lisa spoke then. "I'm sorry at having to barge in and surprise you like this. We just found out and figured we'd better tell you ourselves before word got out or maybe Carson decided to tell you for some reason."

Jake frowned. "No—it's okay. I-I mean, how is it possible that we have a sister somewhere in our own age group? I hate to ask how old you are—" Jake spoke to Lisa then.

"I'm the same age as Tanner. Thirty-two."

"Dad cheated on Mom in law school with Justine Chaffin at the same time I was conceived."

Jake's comprehension turned to anger. "That *bastard*! He's done so many rotten things over the years, but two kids by two different women at the same time? It's unconscionable."

"He's never had a conscience, so it's not out of the realm of believability where he's concerned."

"No. You're right about that. I'm so disgusted by him right now." Then Jake realized what he was saying and looked at Lisa like he was just seeing her. "No offense to you, Lisa." A ghost of a smile lifted Jake's lips. "A sister. Never had one of those, have we, Tanner?"

"No, little brother, we haven't."

"Um, I guess Leah doesn't know either yet, huh? She'll love this." Jake appeared to contemplate the idea further. "Well, welcome to the family, Lisa. Just remember, we are nothing like Carson, and neither are you."

Lisa nodded, tears in her eyes. "Thank you, Jake."

"I hate to do this, but we have to go and see Marie. There are some other things we learned that she needs to know right away. The good news is that Carson shouldn't be a free man for long."

"Finally? He's going to pay for the evil he's done in this world to others? I find it hard to believe." Jake appeared stunned.

"I know. Me too. But it's all about to go down, so be ready for it. There'll be gossip and a big hubbub. Most people here in town will probably cheer, but being Carson's sons has never been easy, so this might not be either."

Jake gave a humorless smile. "I'm willing to take the social consequences as long as he finally pays for his crimes, whatever they are. Especially his treatment of our mother. Even if it wasn't an actual crime by law. Hopefully he'll get what's coming to him.

"I'll see you soon, Jake. And again, I'm sorry to show up with this announcement out of the blue like this." Lisa smiled at Jake and Tanner could already see the beginnings of a big sister–little brother relationship budding between the two, which eased his heart a little.

Carly

I GOT TO Nana's in time to overhear Momma telling Nana that Allison was flying in in two weeks just prior to hers and Daddy's vow renewal. I was glad to hear it. Something about this emotional discovery of Lisa being Tanner and Jake's sister made me want to see Allison and make a better effort to get to know her.

I realized during this manic journey to find Marie that I

hadn't let myself soften toward Allison. I'd held her apart from everything else. Like she was some unknown brand that I'd yet to pass judgment on. Whether she was good enough. But it didn't matter what I thought. Allison was my sister. Everyone else seemed to accept her without any real questions. Maybe I'd worried too much about how her entrance into our lives might change things within our family.

"Where's Marie? I wanted to check in on her while Lisa is tied up with something else." I needed to see how she was doing today so I could take the temperature for Lisa's and Tanner's coming discussion about Justine and the past. We now had almost all the answers, but presentation would be everything.

"So, have y'all found out anything new about Justine?" Momma asked the question as benignly as if she were inquiring about the weather. She had no idea the answer was about to come out.

"This is a delicate subject, Karen, and Carly has to be careful what she discusses." Nana stepped in between us quite literally. "Marie is resting upstairs, but she should be down any minute, I'm guessing. She ate lunch and retired for a short nap." Nana answered my question I'd asked before Momma interrupted.

"I must say, she looks pretty chipper considering what happened to her." Momma continued with her own thoughts.

"She's doing amazingly well, I'd say." Nana was protective of Marie, as were we all.

I really didn't want Momma there when we spoke with Marie about Justine, and I wondered how to get her to leave.

"So, what's happening today?" I tried to be subtle.

"We're firming up some of the details for the ceremony. The flowers, the photographer, and the tent rental are all confirmed. I've got a picture of my dress. Here, look." She pulled up her phone and showed me what looked like a wedding gown, except it didn't reach quite to the floor.

"White?" I couldn't help myself.

Mom scoffed. "It's a baby pink. You can't tell by the lighting."

I stated the obvious. "It looks like a wedding gown."

"Well, of course it does. I couldn't wear any old *dress*. Isn't it gorgeous?"

"Yes, it's lovely, Momma." I wouldn't argue over that.

I glanced over at Nana, who pretended to be busy tidying up a stack of wedding magazines. It's funny how I could almost read her thoughts. They were the same as mine. My mother was going way overboard and throwing herself a second wedding because she adored attention. But it wasn't my event and if Momma wanted to throw a wedding, who was I to judge? I honestly let it go then. What had I been so rigid about anyway? She loved Daddy and he loved her.

"What's on your agenda today, Carly?" Nana asked.

"Lisa and Tanner are coming over in a bit to talk with Marie about some details. They'll need privacy for their conversation." I had to say it, and I knew Nana wouldn't take it personally.

"Well, I guess we all know who's going to have to clear outta here when they arrive." Momma made everything sound like it was a personal affront.

I didn't respond to her passive aggression.

"Can I make y'all some lunch?" Nana asked.

"No. I'll make a pitcher of iced tea and cut up some lemon slices. That should do it."

"There's some turkey, ham, lettuce, and tomatoes in the fridge if anybody's hungry while they're here. Oh, and I've got some fresh cheese straws in a container on the counter you can serve with the iced tea." Nana had a plan, of course.

"Well, I'll get out of the way. Tell Marie I'll see her again soon." Momma air-kissed my cheek. "You might want to make sure your dress fits so we don't end up having to get it altered at the last minute."

The oddly lavender dress hung in my closet waiting for the big day. "It fits. I'll try it on again just to be sure."

"I can't wait to see the three of you together all dressed up." Momma sounded giddy at the thought. And she was happy, which loosened my heart a little toward her.

"We'll look like bridesmaids all dressed in purple." I couldn't help but speak the truth.

"You'll look gorgeous. You all will. And it's not purple, it's lavender."

Once Momma had gone, Nana asked, "So can you tell me what's going on?"

I sighed loudly. "So much has happened since yesterday." I glanced upward toward where Marie was. I didn't want her to overhear me.

"I'll put the tea on, and we can talk on the porch while it brews."

"Good idea."

We got settled on the sunporch and I filled Nana in with what I felt was okay to share. Of course, I knew she'd never betray my confidence to anyone, so I shared more than I would with anyone else at this point.

"You mean to tell me that Carson is Lisa's father?"

I nodded. "Yes, according to Lisa's parents."

"That sorry old coot. He's done some nasty things in his day, hasn't he?" Nana's question was clearly rhetorical and required no answer.

I got a call then. A New Orleans number I didn't recognize. "Excuse me, Nana."

When I answered, a woman's voice asked, "Hi, is this Carly?"

"Yes, this is she."

"Hi, Carly, I'm glad I caught you. This is Samantha Bonner from Jackson and Jackson on Canal Street. We've been looking over your résumé and the partners are very interested in having you come in for a meeting to discuss employment."

I sucked in my breath. *The* Jackson and Jackson wanted to interview me. It was every young lawyer's dream to get a gig at such a prestigious firm right out of school. "Oh, hi. Sure, I'd love to meet with the partners." I said it before I really thought about it. I had to go, *right?* We arranged a time and a date, and I ended the call.

"I'll only ask about that if you want me to." Nana eyed me speculatively.

"Thank you." I wasn't ready to put words to my emotions right now.

We heard the doorbell ring, which signaled that Tanner and Lisa had arrived. Marie must have heard it too because she was descending the stairs by the time I got to the front door to open it. "Hey there. How are you feeling today?" Lisa asked Marie as soon as she saw her.

"I'm feeling pretty good. I had those dynamite crabs for lunch and then a nap. Wait, why is everyone here in the middle of the day?" Marie suddenly stiffened. I couldn't blame her after what she'd experienced.

"We found out some new information about Justine. We'd like to share that with you if you're ready to hear it." Tanner's voice was comforting and strong and I had a strong urge to be beside him during this difficult conversation. Breaking hard news was tough for anyone. Tanner had a tough exterior, but I'd seen firsthand how hard he'd fought to save Marie. The last thing he would want was to hurt her as the messenger.

"I-I'm not sure." Marie's hand shook as she reached for Lisa's.

"Why don't we all go out on the porch? Nana's made some sweet tea." I suggested this because the porch was a soft, comfortable setting. It's where bad news was often broken around here. How hard would it be to leave here now if I got this job? To leave Tanner, my family, and my home?

"I'll do the tea." Nana nodded and went into the kitchen to prepare the tray while I escorted the others out on to the porch.

Once they were seated—Lisa next to Marie—Lisa took Marie's hand gently and began, "Marie, I spoke with my parents today and they finally told me the whole truth as they know it. Justine and my parents were friends during the time she became pregnant and when she gave birth to me, as I'm sure you figured out by my questions the other day."

Nana came in quietly with the tray bearing a pitcher of tea and glasses with lemon wedges attached to the sides of them. Everyone except Tanner took one.

Lisa continued speaking. "Justine was at a carefree time in her life, one where she wasn't thinking so much about consequences, as young people often do. Apparently, she fell for a married man."

Marie inhaled sharply. "What? She was sleeping with a married man? How awful."

"I know this is a bit shocking, but nobody is judging her. She was your daughter and you loved her—and she loved you and her dad."

"Yes, she was a sweet girl, but she always had a bit of a streak for the bad boys, even in high school. It worried her father and me."

"Well, we've learned that my biological father is Carson Carmichael." Everyone braced for Marie's reaction.

Marie's eyes went immediately to Tanner when she heard this. "Oh, my. I'm so sorry, Tanner. That must've meant Carson was cheating on your momma."

"Yes, it was quite a blow to know he'd done that to my mother."

"Are you okay?" Lisa asked Marie.

She nodded and sighed. "I can't change any of it. I knew something was off back then. My daughter had changed somehow, and I felt as if I was losing her."

Lisa darted a glance to Tanner and then to me. "We also found out that Arthur Keller offered to raise me as his own, but Carson was angry that Justine hadn't aborted the pregnancy. They fought one day when Justine was with them both and Justine got between them."

Marie's hands covered her eyes. "Is that how she died?"

Lisa nodded. "She fell over a railing and was killed instantly. There was no pain."

Marie fought to control her tears. "My poor girl. I'm so glad she had the baby though—you." Marie looked at Lisa. "You're so beautiful, and I'm lucky you found me."

Tanner spoke then. "Marie, we're trying to find out where Carson and Arthur buried Justine. They didn't report her death to anyone, just covered it up. It was an accident, as far as we can tell, but they obviously wanted to avoid any scrutiny."

Marie seemed to relax then, but there was a determination in her eyes. "I want to get her back. I need to see that she has a proper Catholic burial."

Lisa continued, "My dad is planning to meet with Carson and Arthur to try and get the information. They never told him where they buried Justine."

Marie looked around the room at us all. "You all have saved me. Now that I understand what happened to Justine, and Lisa has found me, I can live out my life in peace. But I don't have anything left. No money and no home. I don't know how to take the first steps."

"We are going to get your money back from Carson, if it's the last thing we do." I said this with all the intensity I'd been feeling since I found out about the injustices done to Marie at the hands of Carson and Judge Keller.

"And I've got money, Marie. It's the one thing I've got plenty of, so don't worry about that. I will make certain you are cared for." Lisa smiled.

"Thank you, dear. I'm truly blessed. I suppose I'll have to trust that things will work out for me."

Lisa's voice was solemn and determined. "They will work out. You're not alone anymore."

I wanted to tell them both that neither of them was alone nor without family. Nobody would abandon Marie now that we'd found her. And finding out that Lisa was Tanner and Jake's sister guaranteed that she would have lifelong additional family whether she liked it or not. And if she was a part of Jake's life, that meant she was a part of all our lives. Such as it was with our crew.

CHAPTER TWENTY-FOUR

Tanner

HAYES HENRY ARRIVED in town to meet with Judge Keller and Carson the next day. Carson really had been keeping a low profile, which was unusual for him, considering his contempt for anyone who dared question him in any way, and that included investigating his actions.

But with all the things he'd done to all the people through the years, most of which Tanner didn't even know about, Carson must be feeling the squeeze. Carson knew for sure that Marie had told them about his part in keeping her isolated against her will, and that Dr. Miller had given Carson up to save his own skin for a lighter sentence, should he be indicted. All of this originated from the cover-up of Justine's fateful death and disappearance.

Today, the three men involved in that disappearance were meeting at Carson's office at Hayes's request. Hayes hadn't given Carson an option to refuse. Judge Keller was under surveillance now, as was Carson. Surely they understood how tenuous their position must be. It was hard to hide the fact that agents were following them around, dogging their every move. For all their idiocy, they weren't stupid men.

Tanner, Carly, and Alan Litrell sat at the conference table ready to listen to the conversation through the devices that Imogene planted when she'd met with Carson a few days ago. The purpose of this was to get as much solid admission from the men to support what Hayes had told Lisa about Justine's death. And it was to add to the mounting evidence against both Carson and Arthur Keller in colluding to take away Marie's civil rights as a citizen, which was a federal crime. Hence, the LBI and FBI's involvement. There were a host of charges that could be filed against them, but right now, they were going after the ones that were inescapable. The others could be tacked on later.

There was shuffling and what sounded like a scooting of chairs. They heard Judge Keller speak. "Hayes, it's good to see you, though I'd prefer the circumstances be different."

"Yes, well, this meeting is far overdue in my book. The two of you don't have a daughter who's dogging you constantly and asking questions about her birth mother," Hayes said.

"Why the interest all of a sudden?" Carson's voice cut in.

"Who knows? She got a bug one day to find her birth mother and nothing Viv or I could say would dissuade her. I wasn't going to admit we knew her, of course."

"Of course." Arthur said this. "I've had a bad feeling about this ever since it happened. Poor Justine. If she'd only taken me up on my offer."

"Ha! *Poor Justine.* Listen to yourself, Arthur. What a sop you were when it came to her. You were willing to take her and that brat—no offense, Hayes—when she wanted nothing to do with you. She was a party girl. A user. She wanted to break up my marriage and family because she got pregnant."

"Women don't just *get* pregnant, Carson. It takes two for a baby to happen. And you were the other half of that. The father to the infant Viv and I adopted. Our daughter. I think you've forgotten."

"I haven't forgotten. What do want from us? Why are you here, Hayes?"

"I want to know where Justine is buried. I must give my daughter some closure and for her mother, Marie."

"No way am I going to disclose that. And neither are you, Arthur." Carson's tone was ominous.

A chair scooted back as if shoved hard. "You will. And you'll do it now. Today. I've kept quiet all this time to save us from trouble. But what we did was wrong. What the two of you did was wrong. You don't let a young woman die and not tell anyone."

"*That* was an accident. She fell because she got in the way. Stupid girl. I wasn't going to let her ruin my life. I wasn't willing to put my fate in the hands of some asshole DA who wanted to make a name for himself and take us down for murder."

"Yes, but if y'all were innocent, it would've been proven out. As it happened, a woman's life ended, and her parents never knew what became of her or her newborn daughter. I'm not saying that what Viv and I did was right either, but I'm trying to fix that now. All I'm asking is for you to tell me where the poor girl is buried so we can give her family some peace and feel better about what happened."

"How do I know you're not going to turn this against us?

You know we're already in a tight spot here." Carson's voice rose.

"Why would I do that? Viv and I faked an adoption and helped you cover up a woman's death after the fact. We essentially stole her baby and never told the grandmother." When Hayes said it like that, it sounded like he and Vivian should be indicted. Maybe they would be. It all depended on how the prosecutors moved forward with the case once things were sorted out.

There was a moment of silence. Maybe Carson was deliberating whether to reveal what he was asked.

Before Carson could respond, Arthur Keller blurted, "She's in the Creole cemetery outside of town. There's a pile of stones next to a grave marked CLAIBORNE."

"Arthur! You son-of-a—" There was a shuffle and it sounded like a chair was knocked over.

Another chair went down, as if Arthur might have also leapt to his feet. "No! For too long you've called the shots, Carson. I'm not doing this anymore. My career is in jeopardy because of you. I kept silent about Justine all this time because you threatened me. I helped put Marie Trichel away in an institution because of you. I caused Karen Bertrand to give her baby up for adoption on your insistence because you said *we* had a plan, and her baby would ruin it. Well, Carson, that was my child too. And Justine—"

"That woman was a nuisance—"

Keller continued, "*That woman* is dead because of us. Not because we killed her, but because of the way you treated her."

"That's nonsense, and nobody can prove a thing."

"But what about all the other things, Carson? You insisted we file a suit to keep Tanner from practicing law with no probable cause because your ego couldn't handle the fact that he wants to go out on his own. I'm tired of you manipulating me because I'm a judge. I've got the power, Carson, not *you*. I refuse to do your bidding any longer."

"You're a fool Arthur. Always have been. Nobody's going to believe a word you say. You'll go down for all of it and I'll skate away like always. There isn't anybody in this town who would dare go against me in court."

"HAVE YOU SEEN the front page of the newspaper?" Tanner held up the *Cypress Times* to show Carly and Imogene.

The look on Carson's face was captured perfectly on the front page of the local newspaper by an excellent courtroom artist who was present at the hearing. The indignation, disbelief, and sheer outrage that he was well and truly caught doing the awful things he'd been getting away with for years in Cypress Bayou was a source of great satisfaction for so many folks in town when the judge read the indictments. There were so many: racketeering, jury tampering, witness intimidation, conspiracy (several counts), kidnapping, blackmail, fraud... The list went on.

The citizens gathered outside the courthouse waiting to hear Carson's fate. Not his eventual fate, but that of his initial hearing. They came together in solidarity for all the wrongs he'd done to them and those they loved. They gathered to protest the threats and intimidations. The manipulation. The sheer audacity of one human to treat others and abuse them the way Carson Carmichael had with his perceived power in the community.

A cheer went up when it was announced that he wouldn't be eligible for bail because he was determined to be a flight risk. When one has done so much wrong to so many, the sweet victory in watching him get his deserved justice, or even the beginnings of it, could, and did, bring an entire town together on that day.

And nobody was more satisfied with the beginnings of this justice than his own sons and daughter.

Judge Arthur Keller's hearing was scheduled for next week. His would be more involved because a separate investigation was being done by the state's Judiciary Committee, due to his being a judge. If Keller turned on Carson like they figured he would, it might take a few years off his sentence, but the man had enough crimes to answer for on his own.

CHAPTER TWENTY-FIVE

Carly

One Week Later

T ANNER AND I were in the office and my appointment in New Orleans was looming. I'd not had the courage to bring it up. And I wasn't even sure I wanted to go. "I'm headed down to New Orleans for a job interview with Jackson and Jackson." There, I'd said it.

Tanner's eyes widened. "Jackson and Jackson is the biggest firm in the state, Carly. That's…awesome." But I could see that he wasn't excited.

"I…don't know what to do. I feel like we're building something here, Tanner. Together." Professionally yes, but emotionally together too. We hadn't really discussed our feelings for each other since that night on Nana's sunporch. I'd been at Nana's since Carson's hearing, helping her out with Momma's big event whenever I could, so Tanner and I hadn't really had much chance to spend time together. And Tanner had been extremely busy working with the DA on all the filings.

"I can't tell you not to follow your dreams, Carly. This is a huge opportunity." He smiled but didn't quite pull it off.

I wanted him to tell me not to go. To tell me he couldn't run this place without me. And I'd hoped for something more...

But he didn't say any of that, so I left at the end of the day. Tomorrow would be my interview. If I left around eight o'clock in the morning, I'd have plenty of time to make the drive and get there in time for my three-p.m. interview.

Tanner

TANNER LEFT THE office unsure of what to do. He was crazy about Carly, but just like with Kerry-Ann back in law school, he couldn't get in the way of her future, if Jackson and Jackson was what she wanted.

Tanner hesitated going straight to his trailer after work, so he stopped by Jake and Leah's place. "Hey there. Anything new with Carson's trial?" Jake still wore a pair of blue scrubs from the hospital.

Tanner shook his head, not wanting to talk much about anything right now.

"Everything okay, man?"

Tanner couldn't really answer without going into it. "Sure."

Leah entered the room then. "Who stole your thunder?"

"I guess you heard that Carly's going to New Orleans for a job interview tomorrow." Tanner wasn't sure why he'd said that.

Leah nodded. "I get the feeling you're not thrilled about

that."

Tanner pressed his lips together hard and shook his head.

"I guess she'll be hard to replace, huh?" Jake said the obvious.

"Have you told her how you feel?" Leah asked, her face softening with understanding.

Again, Tanner shook his head. It was all he could do not to tear up, and that wasn't manly. But he didn't feel strong or manly right now.

Jake caught on. "Ooh. I thought y'all were getting a little cozy, but I had no idea how you felt about her."

Tanner managed to speak then. "I can't tell her not to go if it's what she wants. This is big-dream stuff."

Leah sat down at the kitchen table and motioned for him to do the same. He did. "I know my sister, Tanner. And she's had a mad crush on you since middle school. I've got a feeling if you told her you wanted her to stay and why, she might change her mind about going."

"She had a crush on me in *middle school*? I had no idea." Tanner was perking up a little.

"I didn't either until I saw her diary with all the entwined hearts with your name on them." Leah laughed at the memory. "The fact that I didn't know just goes to show you how private Carly is and how tightly she guards her emotions."

"Like somebody else in this room." Jake motioned toward Tanner. "Man, sometimes you've got to take a chance on love."

"Wouldn't that be selfish of me? To stand in her way?"

"It depends if she's sitting at home wishing you would

ask her not to go."

In that moment, his decision was made. He couldn't let her go without telling her how he felt.

He abruptly stood and pushed his chair back. "Wish me luck."

AS HE DROVE toward Nana's house, he was a hot mess of fear and excitement. They'd shared some moments, to be sure. But had the feelings been more serious on his part than hers?

As he rang the doorbell, his heart was beating out of his chest. "Hi. I didn't expect to see you here tonight." She was there. Right in front of him and had been for these past couple of months.

"Carly, I—" But words failed him. Instead, he gently put his hands on either side of her face. "I don't want you to go. I love you."

Her eyes welled up. "I was only going because you said I should."

"Really?"

She nodded and smiled then. "Couldn't you tell I wanted you to protest?"

"No. I didn't want to stop you from following your dreams." Was he crying too?

"Tanner Carmichael, I've been in some form of love with you since I was twelve. I know that sounds crazy, but it's true. And somewhere out there is a diary with lots of hearts and your name in it that proves it."

Carly

Two Weeks Later

"I CAN'T BELIEVE we're just lying here, not doing anything." The hammock swung slowly with our weight. It was tied to two very substantial trees with a view of the bayou. We were shaded and the temperature was cooler than usual, given the dead of summer was here. I was lying halfway on Tanner, our legs tangled together.

"Hmm-mm." He might have been half asleep, his arms stretched over his head. "I'm never moving from this spot." He spoke but didn't open his eyes. There was a day's growth of stubble on his jaw. He was so sexy.

This, right now, was perfect. "So, what's next?" I wasn't one to sit still for long.

"Next?" Tanner opened an eye.

I elbowed him in the ribs.

"Ow!" He put his arms around me and kissed my head.

"I mean, with everything. We worked so hard to bring your shady dad to justice and he's finally sitting in jail. And now we can move forward—with everything." The suit against Tanner filed by Carson was obviously dropped since both the plaintiff and the judge in the case were being arraigned and charged with numerous crimes.

"That sounds like you answered your own question."

"I mean with us. I kind of like it here with you." I'd spent the last couple weeks mostly with Tanner. We finally found our stride together and now had time to explore our pent-up feelings for one another.

"Well, as you know, I'm crazy about you, Carly Bertrand. And I can't ask you to live with me in this trailer forever." His grin was mesmerizing.

"Yes, that shower is far too small to wash all this hair." I wiggled against him as I pulled my long, thick hair out of its clip and plopped it on his chest.

"I want to build a house on this property. And I want you to live in it with me. It might take a while, but that's what I hope is next—for us."

I sat up, causing the hammock to swing. "You do?" I knew Tanner wasn't one to say things he didn't mean.

"I do. Oh, and speaking of that, I've got something for you." He rolled us to the side and I squealed, but Tanner's big legs caught the ground and stabilized the hammock. "I'll be right back."

My heart thudded in my chest. Was he really doing what I thought he was? When I went to work for Tanner, I'd not expected such an adventure. And I'd definitely not expected to fall headlong, crazy in love with my former childhood crush. He was a good man. The best, as Leah had said. He was so much more than that, but *the best* kind of summed it up for me.

When Tanner returned, he still wore the same old gym shorts, faded T-shirt, and he was still barefoot. But he clutched something in his hand. And before I could process it all, he sat down cross-legged at my feet where I perched on the edge of the hammock.

"Oh, hi." I smiled at his gorgeous face.

He took a deep breath before he spoke. Was he nervous? "Carly Bertrand, I had no idea what was missing from my life until you showed up and started managing it."

I laughed. "Me? Managing?"

"I needed managing. I needed your ideas, passion, and your huge heart. You came into my life like an infusion of sparkling light. I never want to be without you. I love you, Carly. Will you marry me?" He held out a gorgeous diamond ring. It looked like an heirloom.

My eyes widened at the magnificence. As far as proposals went, that was fantastic. "Oh, Tanner. You've been a part of my life since I can remember. I've loved you from childhood. You'll never be without me. And, yes, I'll marry you."

He pulled me gently down onto his lap from the hammock and I slid into his arms like I'd lived there my whole life. His voice was husky. "How could I get so lucky? And how could I be so blind? You've been here all the time and I've missed it."

"Well, it's not like we've had much time to bond until recently. And to be fair, my feelings for you are well documented in my hormonal middle school diary, so there wasn't any confusion on my part."

His chest rumbled as he laughed. "I'll need to see proof of that."

"Never. In fact, as soon as I find it, I'm going to burn the evidence."

"Just as long as you make me the happiest man in Louisiana, I won't require written proof." Then, he kissed me so gently, and so lovingly, I might've melted into a puddle.

I sighed. "I will make you so happy."

EPILOGUE

T HE SHEER AMOUNT of purple, sorry, *lavender*, everywhere made the wisteria growing in the trees throughout Nana's backyard seem paltry in comparison to the amount of lavender at the ceremony. And there was plenty wisteria. Enough that it was cut back every year so as not to destroy the healthy flora and trees.

Daddy managed to appear happy to be there as he and Momma renewed their vows. As promised, nearly half the town was in attendance. I suspected more for the latest gossip about Carson and Judge Keller than a burning desire to see Momma and Daddy repledge their love to one another, no matter how delightful the chocolate fountain might be. No, this Carson thing was big news and affected a *lot* of people in town.

Allison, Leah, and I shared plenty of eye rolls during the days leading up to the blessed event. Momma figured out how to become a true bridezilla, even at her age. Allison found it all very amusing, while Leah and I threatened mutiny.

Tanner had caught my gaze and held it as the hired string quartet played the wedding march. Yes, it *was* a wedding. I flushed because every time I saw Tanner I behaved like a woman in love. Like I'd seen all the others behave. Now I understood. We'd announced our engagement the day after he'd proposed. Momma accused me of trying to upstage her event. Then she realized it gave her another wedding to plan and she simmered down. Maybe we would run away to exchange vows.

Allison was delightful. She was slowly getting her energy back after the bone marrow transplant, and her hair had just started to grow back. It would take a while yet before she was back to her old self, but she appeared happy to be back in Cypress Bayou with us all. I wasn't sure what her plans were, but I hoped we'd have some time during her visit to discuss that.

Lisa, her husband, Doug, the Henrys, and Marie were in attendance. Doug turned out to be rather a surprise. He was funny and so nice once he figured out that Lisa was among people who cared about her. Her earlier comments had puzzled me. But we realized that he'd been very concerned about her getting crushed if she didn't find her family. And he really seemed to hit it off with his new brothers-in-law.

After the "wedding" and the party that followed, another celebration would be planned. That of Justine Chaffin's life. She deserved to be remembered and celebrated. After getting Carson and Judge Keller's admission about what happened to her, and where they'd buried her, there was no taking it back. It was the nail in their own proverbial coffins, though I felt that Carson would receive the lion's share of indictments.

"Wanna dance?" I looked up from the punchbowl at the sound of Tanner's voice. He was dashing in a dark suit. A "church suit," he called it.

"I might have room on my dance card." I allowed myself

to be led to the dance floor. He took my hand and twirled me around.

"You look so beautiful." I loved how he looked at me.

But just now, in this getup, I wasn't exactly feeling beautiful. "You're kidding, right? Is this a joke about the purple dress?"

He pulled me into his arms, close enough that I could smell his clean scent. "I would never joke about how lovely you are."

I followed his gaze. The vows were done, photos taken, and people were busy visiting, gossiping, drinking, and dancing. "Follow me." He pulled me by the hand out to the porch and sat me down on one of the cushioned chairs, then gently pulled off my shoes. "Better?"

"So much better." I put both hands on either side of Tanner's face. "And my life is so much better with you in it."

The End

Want more? Check out Leah and Jake's story in
Home to Cypress Bayou!

Join Tule Publishing's newsletter for more great reads and weekly deals!

If you enjoyed *Secrets in Cypress Bayou,*
you'll love the next book in the…

Louisiana series

Book 1: *Home to Cypress Bayou*

Book 2: *Secrets in Cypress Bayou*

Book 3: *A Bayou Christmas*
Coming in November 2022

Available now at your favorite online retailer!

More books by Susan Sands

The Alabama series

Book 1: *Again, Alabama*

Book 2: *Love, Alabama*

Book 3: *Forever, Alabama*

Book 4: *Christmas, Alabama*

Book 5: *Noel, Alabama*

Available now at your favorite online retailer!

About the Author

Susan Sands grew up in a real life Southern Footloose town, complete with her senior class hosting the first ever prom in the history of their tiny public school. Is it any wonder she writes Southern small town stories full of porch swings, fun and romance?

Susan lives in suburban Atlanta surrounded by her husband, three young adult kiddos and lots of material for her next book.

Thank you for reading

Secrets in Cypress Bayou

If you enjoyed this book, you can find more from all our great authors at TulePublishing.com, or from your favorite online retailer.

TULE
PUBLISHING